Malia Rose

Born September 23, 1995
at 2:32 a.m.

Weight—6 lb. 7 oz.
Length—19 in.

Riverview Hospital
Heron Point, Oregon

Mommy & Baby doing fine!

Dear Reader,

I can't imagine anything that generates more excitement in a family than the anticipation of the arrival of a new baby. It was certainly true at our house. Only, our "babies" arrived aged ten, eight and four, courtesy of the State of Oregon, with two bicycles and a guinea pig named Gertie.

But they were beautiful, healthy and bright, and we felt every bit as though a doctor had run out of the delivery room, shouting, "It's a boy! And another boy! And a girl!"

Since that day, thanks to our sons, new baby excitement has been generated by grandchildren. And as I write this, our daughter expects her first baby.

When the idea was "born" for romances involving the mothers of three babies born in the same hospital on the same day, I was nervous. Could I do this? Book research can take one only so far.

But fate intervened. My new editor was just back to work after *maternity leave*, and every book is a joint effort between author and editor. She promised to keep a sharp eye out for inconsistencies.

So we offer you, *Mommy on Board,* the first in my three-book series, Mommy and Me, a celebration of babies born without a father in the picture, and the mothers determined to change that.

Muriel

Muriel Jensen

MOMMY ON BOARD

Harlequin Books

TORONTO • NEW YORK • LONDON
AMSTERDAM • PARIS • SYDNEY • HAMBURG
STOCKHOLM • ATHENS • TOKYO • MILAN
MADRID • WARSAW • BUDAPEST • AUCKLAND

To Wanda Wetherill, partner in crime
and aggressive turnstiles

ISBN 0-373-16603-6

MOMMY ON BOARD

Copyright © 1995 by Muriel Jensen.

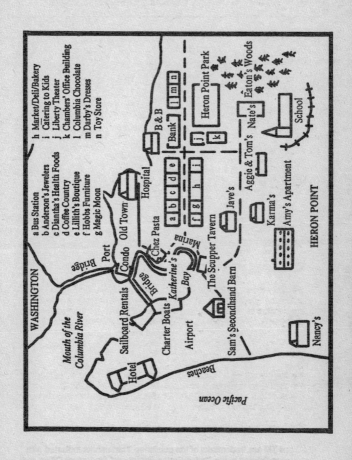

WASHINGTON

*Mouth of the
Columbia River*

a Bus Station
b Anderson's Jewelers
c Diantha's Health Foods
d Coffee Country
e Lillith's Boutique
f Hobbs Furniture
g Magic Moon

h Market/Deli/Bakery
i Catering to Kids
j Liberty Theater
k Chambers' Office Building
l Columbia Chocolate
m Darby's Dresses
n Toy Store

B & B

Heron Point Park

Eaton's Woods

Nate's

School

Bank

Old Town

Hospital

Port

Bridge

Condo

Chez Pasta

Marina

Katherine's
Bay

The Scupper Tavern

Aggie & Tom's

Jave's

Karma's

Amy's Apartment

Sailboard Rentals

Charter Boats

Bridge

Airport

Sam's Secondhand Barn

Beaches

Hotel

Nancy's

HERON POINT

Pacific Ocean

Prologue

There are ninety-one more days until I am born—at least, I hope so. Mom's been out since early this morning shopping for a desk chair, and that was after eating mocha macadamia cake for breakfast. Her indigestion sounds as bad as mine. If she isn't careful, I'm going to be born right now with my eyelids half-open and still wearing this tacky lanugo mink coat that I was promised would be gone if I make it full term.

But, you gotta love her. She's explained to me about my father. He's been out of the picture for three months, and though she insists it isn't going to matter, I have my own thoughts about that. But if she's willing to give it a shot, so am I. I mean, he wanted me out of the picture, and in order to keep me, she gave up everything—including him, her job in New York, her rent-controlled apartment—that place on Forty-second Street with the cheese and onion bagels. It's like I owe her.

Whoa. What was that? Ouch! Oh, no. I knew this would happen.

Hey, not yet! No! Mom? Mom, I'm not going anywhere 'til I have toenails! Mom!

Chapter One

"Something wrong, ma'am?"

Nancy Malone concentrated for one more moment on the vibrating echo of the pain in her abdomen that had made her gasp. The fisting sensation was gone now, but it had left an unsettling discomfort in its place. She rubbed the spot worriedly, then returned her attention to the burly, bearded man in coveralls, who was loading the old upholstered desk chair onto the back of her truck.

"I'm fine, thanks." She smiled reassuringly at him and raised the tailgate into place.

He did not appear convinced. He frowned at the mild but definite swell of her stomach. "You sure? Pregnant ladies shouldn't be hefting furniture. You got someone to help you unload this at home?"

No, she thought defensively. *And I don't want to talk about it.* But aloud she said, "I'll manage. Thanks," and offered her hand. "Good doing business with you, Sam. If you come across an old-fashioned wide-top desk, you'll call me?"

He delved into the bib pocket of his coveralls and produced the note with her telephone number, which Nancy had handed him just before the pain hit. "Right away. Want me to keep an eye out for baby furniture, too?"

No. She wanted to buy one of those pristine oak-and-white sets with five matching pieces and fluffy bunny decals all over them. But she'd priced one at Hobbs Furniture, and unless she won the lottery, it was far beyond her means.

She nodded and hauled herself into the truck, pleased that at almost six months pregnant, she still had a measure of grace. "I'd appreciate that."

Sam tipped his dusty baseball cap and walked back to the old hipped-roof barn that sat in the midst of a sea of appliances, automobile parts, and old furniture in various stages of stripping and restaining.

Nancy waved and turned the key in the ignition. At the same instant—as though it, too, had been controlled by the turn of the key—her abdomen cramped and tightened.

She fought momentary panic. "No," she told herself firmly as the sound of the tubercular truck engine filled the cloudy, early summer morning silence. "This is not going to happen. I have overdone it a little, but I've felt so *well*. It'll go away when I get home and put my feet up."

The knot of pain in her abdomen loosened and she drew a deep breath. She put the truck in gear and moved to the exit of Sam's Super Seconds parking lot. Traffic was light on the road that connected the small Columbia River town of Heron Point with coastal Highway 101 and Nancy let the truck idle for a moment, considering her options—north to town and Riverview Hospital, where her obstetrician had an office, or south to her beachfront cottage and the blissful solitude she so enjoyed.

With the rationale developed over a lifetime of depending on herself, she turned south. The little pains were a reaction to the tiring move across country; to bringing

her small cottage into order; to feeling generally so well
that she'd forgotten she had a problem.

Nothing was wrong. All she had to do was go home,
leave the chair on the truck until later, settle down with
Dashiell Hammett and a cup of herbal tea, and put her
feet up. Or she could watch Oprah. It was always comforting to know how many people there were in the world
in more bizarre situations than her own.

She cranked her window down, turned up the volume
on Michael Bolton, and headed down the beautiful, me-
andering, tree-lined highway that bordered the turbulent
ocean.

The next pain brought a small scream from her and
made her yank the wheel instinctively toward the grassy
shoulder. She came to an abrupt stop. She panted, waiting for it to abate. It didn't.

She suddenly experienced a profound revelation. She
may have needed only herself in the past, but she was
carrying a new life now. She was dealing with Mother
Nature at her most forceful, and when the lady flexed her
muscles, she was a most powerful opponent.

"All right!" Nancy conceded aloud, her voice breathless with the pain in her abdomen. "I'm going. But don't
try to get tough with me. I've done almost everything else
in my life alone. I can do this, too! And I'm uninsured,
remember? Pick on someone with total coverage!"

THE PAIN WAS GONE. Nancy tried to relax as she waited in
the darkened room for the radiologist. She'd taken in so
much water in preparation for the test that lying still was
difficult. But she'd done this once before in New York.
She knew the drill; a stomach filled with water provided
an acoustical window for sound vibrations.

The emergency-room doctor had called her obstetrician, who had prescribed a drug whose name she couldn't remember at the moment. All she knew was that it had stopped her premature labor. She said a silent prayer of thanks and promised God that she would turn over a new leaf, make a point of putting her feet up and eating better. And even if she needed no one else, she would reach for Him more often.

Meanwhile, she'd been admitted for several tests and a night of observation.

The door opened and a tall man in a lab coat walked into the small room. He kicked a rolling stool aside and came to stand over the gurney. His features were in shadow, but his form was tall and broad. A fresh-air fragrance wafted toward her.

"Good morning," he said, glancing up from her file to smile at her. She saw white teeth in the dim light. "Contractions stopped?"

"Yes." She heard the relief reflected in her own voice. "Scared myself there for a few minutes."

He nodded. "Bet you did. Okay, let's have a look at this baby and see how he's doing."

"He's a girl," she said, removing her hands from atop the blanket as he tugged her gown up and out from under it, folding it back above the small bulge of her stomach. He folded the blanket out of the way just below it.

He looked into her gaze, his eyebrow raised in question. "Just a guess, or do you know for a fact?"

Nancy opened her mouth to reply as he moved closer. That placed his face and upper body in the feeble glow of the room's only light—a goosenecked lamp placed over his equipment. Her reply stopped in her throat as she stared. He looked just like Harry Boeneke, Portland, Oregon police lieutenant. Considering Boeneke was entirely a figment of her imagination, the resemblance was doubly remarkable.

His hair was that same golden brown, his eyes a level, steady hazel. His nose and chin were angular and well-defined, his mouth nicely shaped. He even had a small scar on his chin, along with that same air of competence allied with danger that provided alternating states of fantasy and ecstasy for Geneva Frisco, Private Eye—the fictional heroine in Nancy's mystery novel in progress.

"Ah...no." Nancy forced herself to concentrate on his question. "I mean, yes. I did have an ultrasound at four months in New York, but I didn't want them to tell me the sex. I just know."

His eyebrow rose in surprise, arched in curiosity. The name tag on his lapel, she noted, read J. V. Nicholas, M.D.

"Then, if you *know*," he asked, "why don't you want it confirmed?"

She laughed softly. "I want being right to be a surprise."

And that was about as much sense as pregnant women made sometimes, Jave thought as he powered up to perform the test. He guessed this woman was single. After ten years in radiology, he prided himself on being able to see inside his patients almost as well as his equipment did.

He could tell single mothers by their eyes. It wasn't that the excitement wasn't there; many of them were more thrilled about their pregnancies than married women were. But beneath it all, he could see the fear—particularly with first-timers. They were worried about the delivery—worried about having to do it alone.

And he'd be the last one to fault them. By the nature of his work, and because one of his sons had been a preemie, he knew a lot could go wrong.

And this one, Malone, Nancy R., had that look in her eyes. And with good cause after the morning she'd endured.

"You told the ER nurse," he said as he squeezed out a few inches of gel, "that your mother took DES when she was pregnant with you." Diethylstilbestrol was a drug taken by many women several decades ago to prevent miscarriage. Jave knew that studies of the female children born to those women revealed a tendency to disfiguration of the reproductive system, which sometimes resulted in problems ranging from an inability to conceive to difficulty carrying a baby full term.

"Yes," she replied, her head turning toward him in the darkness. Her voice was calm. "My mother called me when she first heard about the effects of DES. I saw my doctor right away. He said my problem was relatively minor. I had a slightly weakened cervix, and he warned me that I might have to deal with preterm labor."

He nodded. "I'm going to put coupling gel on your abdomen. If you've had an ultrasound before, you'll remember that it's cold. Here it comes."

She lay absolutely still as he rubbed the icy solution over her rounded stomach.

"So, you've been taking it easy, remembering to nap every day, to stop before you're tired?"

"Well... I did before the move."

He wiped the gel off his hands. "The move?"

"From New York," she replied. "I bought a cottage on the beach a couple of miles out of town. I've been working a little too hard trying to get things in order. I guess it's a nesting frenzy or something."

Her obstetrician was McNamara. That was good. He'd take good care of her. Probably already chewed her out for overdoing it.

"I bought a desk chair today," she said in a jovial tone that sounded false despite the smile that accompanied it. "I'm going to write a bestselling mystery novel and win the Edgar."

He couldn't tell if her chattering meant she was relaxing or growing more nervous. "Is that anything like the Nobel?"

"Not *quite* as prestigious. It's like the Oscar of mystery novels." She heaved a deep sigh and closed her eyes. "That way I can work from home after she's born."

Jave placed the convex probe on her abdomen and fine-tuned the picture on the screen. He saw the baby—a black-and-white form about a foot long in the windshield-wiperlike swath of the echoes' image. At the center, the tiny heart beat steadily. He felt a sense of relief.

"Okay," Jave said, concentrating. "Here it is."

"Where?" She propped herself up on an elbow to look, holding on to the gurney's rail, her eyes alight with excitement and trepidation. Jave and the machine were slightly behind her and to her right.

Jave moved back to the gurney to reposition her. "This generally goes better if my patients don't try to climb into the machines." Her eyes, wide and whiskey brown, locked with his. Her small-fingered hands clasped his forearms as he eased her back to the pillow. She clung to him for one protracted heartbeat, then dropped her hands and relaxed.

"Sorry," she said, turning just her head to look this time. "I got a little excited. Do you see her?"

"I do." He pointed to a movement in the image. "Has its back to us," he said, grinning as he traced the image with the tip of his pen. "Probably upset with you for all you've put it through today."

Nancy laughed. "Oh, dear. Mother-daughter disharmony already. Does she look all right? Can you tell if this morning hurt her?"

"Dr. McNamara will explain everything to you," he said, studying the image. "But the heartbeat's good, movement's normal. Looks like everything's developing all right." A tiny hand, digits clear and visible, moved on the screen. "Whoa. There's a wave. Let's get a Polaroid of that for the baby book." He pushed the button that would give him a photograph. "We can label that one, 'Hi, Mom.'"

Mom? Hi! It's me! Didn't know this thing lets me see you, too, did ya?

We got lucky today, didn't we? Whew. Had me worried there.

I like the man on the machine. Nice eyes. Nice touch, too. Ask him if he's married.

NANCY WAS GIDDY with relief. "Thank God," she whispered. "I was so afraid she was having a problem."

Jave changed her position slightly and fine-tuned the machine again. "*She* doesn't seem to be having a problem," he said, obviously concentrating on the image, watching for the details he knew her doctor would want to see. "But you'll have to remember that *you* do. The baby's counting on you to keep it safe."

Nancy felt a stab of irritation at the suggestion that she was being careless with her baby's life. It quelled the euphoria of a moment ago. "I've been feeling so well that I overdid it. I wasn't deliberately behaving irresponsibly."

"You moved," he said evenly, ignoring her indignation as he repositioned her. "We'll have to reshoot that one. Lie still."

Irritation deepening, Nancy cooperated.

When he'd taken the shot, he explained quietly, "I wasn't impugning your sense of responsibility. I was just reminding you that what seemed like a normal range of activities to you before your pregnancy has to be curtailed now, or you'll get both of you in trouble."

Nancy propped herself up on an elbow, not caring if she ruined his shot. For the past few months she'd had everyone telling her what *they* thought she should do, and no one listening to what *she* wanted for herself and this baby.

"Look," she said firmly. "I am not being careless with this baby, so don't lecture me. You're not my doctor."

Jave turned on the stool to face her, resisting the urge to smile. It was good that she was pugnacious. It was a quality she'd need.

She was right. He wasn't her doctor. But he couldn't help himself. Single mothers made him feel protective.

"No, I'm not," he said gravely. "When Dr. McNamara explains the results of the pictures to you, I'm sure *he'll* lecture you. I just don't want to see you back in here with pictures that might not look so good next time." She drew in a breath to fling a heated reply when the telephone interrupted her. Jave stood and reached across the machine for it. "Nicholas," he answered.

Nancy looked away from his neat form in gray slacks. The fabric molded itself to his slim hips as he leaned forward to accommodate the short telephone cord. Men had a way of looking wonderful, she thought, and being far less than that when you needed them.

And this one had some kind of a messianic complex. Well, she wasn't going to be her mother's rehabilitative project, and she certainly wasn't going to be his.

Not that that would ever even be within the realm of possibility. She just had a bad habit of considering every man she met in terms of his husband potential even though she never wanted another one. It was a quality she'd inherited from her mother, who was currently planning wedding number four.

He turned to look at her, the telephone still to his ear. "Almost finished. Five minutes. All right, I'll ask her." He grinned. "Yeah. You can use my office if you promise not to disturb my careful filing system." He listened a moment. "Right. Bye."

He leaned forward to hang up the phone, and this time Nancy let herself look. She sighed, grateful she wasn't having her blood pressure taken. He had long legs, a wonderful backside and a long-armed reach. She closed her eyes. Not for her. Never again.

Her eyes flew open when his hands settled gently on her shoulders and guided her onto her side. "One more shot and we'll have it," he said. He went back to his machine. "Take a breath and hold it. One more. Hold it. Okay. All finished." He made adjustments on the machine and shut it down. Then he came to the gurney to pull up her blanket. "That telephone call was for you," he said, crossing the room to turn on the light.

Nancy blinked against the sudden brightness as she sat up, holding the blanket to her. "For me?"

"Amaryllis Brown from public relations wondered if you'd mind talking to her in my office for a few minutes before I take you back to your room."

Nancy blinked, waiting for the message to make sense. "Public relations? Wants to see me? Why?"

He grinned. "I didn't ask. But Amy's an experience. I'm sure you'll enjoy the interview." He went to the corner where the nurse who'd brought her down had stashed the requisite wheelchair.

"She must have me confused with another patient," Nancy insisted as she slid into the wheelchair.

"She had your name and your due date," he said as he began wheeling her down the corridor.

"My due date?"

J. V. Nicholas turned into a tiny, narrow office that reminded Nancy of her crowded galley kitchen in Manhattan. He pushed the chair farther into the room, blocking in the tall blond woman who stood at his cluttered desk.

Nancy took in the confined space, most of its room taken up by file cabinets and a desk, all of which were covered with papers and storage boxes. She decided that his remark on the phone about disturbing his filing system had been a joke.

Then her attention was redirected to the woman who turned a nuclear-powered smile on her. "Nancy Malone?"

Nancy nodded.

"Amaryllis Brown, public relations coordinator for Riverview Hospital. Everybody calls me Amy." She offered her hand, then smiled at the man standing behind Nancy's chair. "Thanks for the use of your office, Jave. I brought a pot of tea. You don't mind, do you?"

"Not as long as you leave some. Don't keep her too long."

"Ten minutes tops."

Jave closed the door behind them. Despite the flicker of antagonism that had grown between her and the radiologist, Nancy almost hated to see him leave. The woman now seating herself in the desk chair had a friendly but curiously predatory air about her, which filled Nancy with foreboding. She couldn't imagine why, but she had a feeling she was going to regret agreeing to this meeting.

Amy Brown began to talk about how Riverview was a small hospital, always seeking to solidify its patient base by trying to provide as many of the refinements to quality care as big city hospitals offered. Unable to see how that related to her, Nancy allowed herself to be distracted by Amy Brown's appearance—a fashion nightmare.

Her dress was pale pink with full, puffy sleeves, a nipped-in waist too high for her long body and a flared hem that hung to midcalf. There were bows down the front and on the sleeves. She wore patterned white stockings and pink flats. Her hair was silvery blond, but was caught back in a lank ponytail. Clear-framed glasses sat on the bridge of a pretty, straight nose in the middle of a pleasant face completely devoid of makeup.

"...anyway, we're all very proud of the project. The Riverview Foundation picked out the wallpaper, our designer made everything look as much like home as possible while still keeping everything required for a safe, conventional delivery at the doctor's fingertips. Wait until you see it. It's like a bedroom out of *Town and Country.*"

"Oh?" Nancy brought herself back to the conversation, confused that she still couldn't figure out how all this related to her—or even to the hospital. A beautiful bedroom in *Town and Country* magazine? She wished she'd been paying closer attention.

Amy went on, frowning over Nancy's tepid response. "Birthing rooms!" she said with a sweep of her hand. "Here in little old Heron Point. Now you don't have to go to Portland for the amenities of a home-style delivery. We'll have it right here. No more hard labor in a dingy little room. No more having to separate the mother-to-be

from her husband or any other family member who wants
to be part of the birth.''

Nancy smiled, delighted and relieved to finally grasp the
issue. Birthing rooms. Of course. She'd read about them
in women's magazines, and several of her New York ac-
quaintances had talked about having used them.

She nodded enthusiastically, compelled by Amy's passion. ''That's wonderful. I've read about them. They
seem like an intelligent and sensitive innovation.''

That remark seemed to please Amy. She beamed. ''I'm
so glad you think so. Because . . . guess what!''

''What?'' Nancy asked warily.

''Ours are under construction even as we speak, and
they'll be ready . . . guess when!''

There was a trap here somewhere and Nancy thought
she could see it yawning, waiting to spring. ''When?''

Amy spread both hands, palms up, in a sort of ta-da
gesture. ''Two days before your due date!''

''Oh.'' Nancy proceeded cautiously. ''So . . . I'll get to
use one?''

Amy placed both hands on the arms of the wheelchair,
her smile widening even farther. ''Not only that, but I've
picked *you* out!''

Uh-oh. ''Me? For . . . what?''

''To be the very *first* to use one! We're planning a big
extravaganza—'' she made a wide, exploding movement
with her hands to underline the word ''—for the opening
of the rooms, and our auxiliary has gotten the entire
community involved! There'll be newspaper and radio
coverage, saturation advertising, merchant parti—''

''Wait. Wait.'' Nancy spoke gently, almost reluctant to
stop the woman's excited spate of information, but this
was beginning to sound like the kind of thing she hated.
She was basically shy and always resisted anything that

attracted attention to herself. And since Jerry's defection, she found herself even more reclusive. All she wanted to do was hide out in her little beachfront cottage, help this baby grow big and strong, and raise her quietly amid the serenity of one of the most beautiful spots on earth. She did not want to be part of Amy's extravaganza. "Thank you," she said politely, "but I'm really kind of a... a private person. I—"

"But the timing's perfect." Amy looked stricken. "You'll have your picture in the paper. You'll be famous."

"Thank you but I..." Nancy searched her mind for something to say besides the truth. Then she was suddenly inspired. "Don't you think it would be safer to wait for a mother whose due date is more reliable than mine? I mean, I have this cranky cervix that could—"

"That doesn't matter. One of the smaller rooms is within a couple of weeks of being ready. We'd like you to use the biggest room, but if you did deliver early, we could still put you in the smaller one." She leaned an elbow on the desk and heaved a sigh. "To be honest, I knew you'd be perfect the moment I saw you. You're attractive, probably photogenic, it's your first baby, and..." She patted Nancy's hand and said softly, "And I'll bet you'll be able to put the gifts to good use."

Nancy was sure the woman meant well, but she wasn't anxious to be patronized or pitied. She tried to smile but look firm at the same time. "Thank you, but I don't need gifts. I—"

"Most of the gifts are for the baby," Amy interrupted.

Nancy stopped in the act of searching for the wheelchair's brake. She let a heartbeat pass while she reconsidered. "Gifts for the baby?"

"Yes." Amy picked up a typed sheet from the cluttered desk and read from it. "Silver cup and spoon from Anderson's Jewelry Company, chocolate cigars to announce the birth from Columbia Chocolates, a two-hundred-dollar gift certificate from Falmouth Toys, new shoes for you and the baby from Isaac's Bootery, linens for the baby's room from Lillith's Boutique, free passes to the movies for you and your husband from the Liberty Theatre." Amy made a show of gasping for breath. "An outfit from Lolly's, a dress from Dine and Dance, lingerie from Magic Moon, an outfit a month for the baby's first year from Catering to Kids, and..." She glanced up from the sheet to assure herself of Nancy's attention. She needn't have bothered. Nancy was now hanging on her every word. "Are you ready for this?"

Nancy couldn't speak. Clothes for the baby's first year? Shoes for the baby? Toys? It would be like winning the lottery. She nodded and whispered, "I'm ready."

Amy cleared her throat, then announced, like Bob Barker at his best, "A complete set of top-of-the-line furniture for your baby's room, complete with crib, chest, dressing table, three-way teddy-bear lamp and night-light, windup musical mobile and bumper pads for the crib and dressing table." She dropped the sheet of paper to her lap and finished with a flourish, "And a glider rocker with ottoman for you to rock the baby to sleep. All from Hobbs Furniture."

MOM! CHOCOLATE CIGARS! A teddy-bear lamp. Say yes! Please, say yes!

NANCY STARED AT HER, eyes glazed with avarice. Her baby would have everything she'd despaired of being able to provide. Everything! More than she'd imagined in her wildest dreams. All she had to do was agree to be part of Amy's extravaganza. Deep down, she shuddered at the thought. But closer to the surface, right under her heart where her baby lived, she knew that she had to do it.

"All right," she said, smiling brightly and trying to inject sincere excitement into her voice. "I'll do it."

Amy looked stunned by her own success. "You will?"

"I will."

"All *right!*" Amy whooped excitedly, then poured tea from a hot pot into two institutional white cups on the desk. "Let's toast the deal. You're going to love this, Nancy. I know you are. I appreciate your shyness, but having a baby tends to kill that in the average woman anyway." She rolled her eyes expressively, then added seriously, "But I promise to keep anything you consider too personal out of it, and just make you, the mother-to-be, the symbol for all mothers in the county who now have a comfortable, cheerful place to have their babies with their families close at hand."

She handed Nancy a half-filled cup of the aromatic tea, then tapped her cup against it. "To babies!"

"To babies!" Nancy toasted, refusing to acknowledge the little niggles of doubt and conscience that prodded at her.

Amy's extravaganza was a gift to her and her baby from the heavens. She wouldn't question it, wouldn't doubt it. When Jerry had walked away, she had vowed she wouldn't infect her baby with bitterness. She would be serene and hopeful and a firm believer in the glass-half-full, silver-lining theories.

"Okay." Amy put her cup down and lifted another sheet of paper off the desk. From Nancy's vantage point, it appeared to be a form of some kind. "I just need a few more details from you that weren't in your file."

Nancy, too, put her cup down, prepared to provide them. "Right. What do you want to know?"

Amy poised her pen expectantly and glanced at her. "Husband's name?"

Chapter Two

Nancy blinked. Husband? So the extravaganza *was* too good to be true. She didn't have a husband, and she understood with sudden clarity that the hospital wouldn't want her to represent "all mothers in the county" without one.

"I really wasn't snooping in your files," Amy explained quickly. "But I happened to be in Dr. McNamara's office talking to him about this project when he put the ultrasound order on your chart."

Nancy nodded, buying time by letting Amy talk.

"Dr. Mac had sent to New York for your files when you had your first appointment with him. They were sitting on his desk. I glanced at it to get your name so we could talk, and I noticed your husband's name, but I can't remember it." She leaned over the form, ready to fill in the name, and confided intimately, "It wouldn't matter to us if you were single, but I think the foundation and many of the old-guard contributing merchants will be pleased that you aren't. And it's appropriate for what we're trying to do. Birthing rooms are for everyone, but particularly for loving couples who want to share the experience of giving birth to the child they've created together, the child they intend to nurture together."

"Jerry," Nancy heard herself say with detached fascination. "Gerald W."

GOOD WORK, MOM. Stay calm. We can do this.

NANCY WAITED FOR the next question in a kind of panic, her cheeks warming, her hands fidgeting nervously.

"His occupation?"

This was going to be tricky, Nancy foresaw. Next, she'd be expected to produce him. Then inspiration unexpectedly struck again, and she wondered if the drug that stopped her labor had somehow managed to multiply her gray matter.

"He's in the Coast Guard," she said with convincing ease. "Aboard the *Courageous*."

Amy looked up, apparently thrilled by the news. "Heron Point's own *Courageous*? Oh, this is getting better and better."

Nancy blessed the fact that the ad for Sam's Super Seconds in last night's paper had been placed directly beside the story about the *Courageous* leaving on a three-month patrol. She'd perused the article, thinking about the wives of the men aboard the vessel being separated from their husbands that long—never imagining that she'd be fictionalizing herself among their number.

"It just left, didn't it?" Amy asked as she hurriedly made notes.

Nancy nodded, then imparted further information in a convincingly knowledgeable tone. "They're heading south on a standard law-enforcement patrol. You know, watching for drugs, enforcing fishing regulations. That sort of stuff."

Amy's eyes widened. Nancy guessed she was hoping the father of her birthing room's first occupant would somehow distinguish himself and return home a hero. She let herself smile. Amy didn't know Jerry.

"He'll be home in time to be with you for the birth, won't he?"

It would be safer to say that she doubted that and eliminate the need to produce him. But she felt a very real fear that Amy would withdraw the offer if it didn't look as though she'd have every member of the family available for her extravaganza.

"He's due in the week before," she said with a broad smile. She was *not* giving up the baby furniture—or the chocolate.

"What's his rank?" a male voice asked from the doorway.

Amy looked up with a smile. Nancy, her back to the door, didn't like the tone of the question. It sounded suspicious. She looked over her shoulder to see that the radiologist with the messianic complex had been eavesdropping.

What was worse, she didn't know a private from an admiral. She smiled at Amy hoping to distract her with other details. "He's been in since right after college. About ten years."

"Really?" The PR coordinator made hasty notes. "And what does he do aboard the *Courageous?*"

"Well..." Making him the captain would have been overplaying, but that was the only title Nancy could come up with. She prayed that her newfound extra gray matter wouldn't fail her now. "He...ah...oh, you know. He keeps everything running. Motors...all that stuff."

"And what is that called?" Amy insisted.

Nancy was about to either pretend renewed contractions or tell all and abandon this hospital and this scheme while she was able, when the male voice behind her spoke up. "He must be the engineering officer."

Nancy gave him a drop-dead smile over her shoulder. "That's it. He's the engineering officer."

WHEW! HE SAVED OUR SKINS, Mom. Not that mine's much to look at right now. Let's take him home.

JAVE DIDN'T KNOW WHETHER to trust Malone, Nancy R.'s, word, or his own usually reliable instincts. He'd have sworn she was single. But he'd been about to step into his office when he heard her reply to Amy's request for her husband's name. He had two young boys. He knew lies when he heard them.

But he also knew the innocent could sometimes *look* guilty.

Yet, a woman should know her husband's rank. And she should be ready to boast about his duties with his formal title. But then the world—and male-female relationships in particular—weren't always what he thought they should be.

So the pretty dark-eyed woman, who pretended courage but appeared lost and frightened, was married. Or wanted them to believe she was.

He decided to reserve judgment. That array of gifts, along with Amy Brown's intimidating enthusiasm for her first solo PR project, were enough to encourage a single woman to produce a husband.

"Time's up," Jave said, reaching over the back of the wheelchair to disengage the brake. His cheek brushed her cool, silky hair for a moment, and he inhaled the fragrance of a floral shampoo.

Nancy looked up with a frown at his abrupt interruption...and found her eyes looking directly into his. She felt two things simultaneously—sexual awareness and the suspicion that he could see right through her. Both alarmed her.

"Sorry," he said to Amy, pulling the chair backward toward the door. "McNamara wants her to rest tonight. If all's well and she goes home tomorrow, the two of you can talk before she leaves."

"Of course." Amy stood to follow them to the door. "You just sleep well, Nancy, and dream about all the wonderful things you and your husband and baby are going to get."

"I will," Nancy promised, then added for effect, "I can't wait to tell Jerry when he calls."

She glanced up at J. V. Nicholas, giving him an innocent look, daring him to question her. His expression was neither accepting nor challenging, but simply steady and deliberately neutral. She felt her wide-eyed sincerity wilt just a little.

With a wave, Amy turned left down a side corridor. Jave pushed Nancy past a plate-glass window against which rain slashed at a deep angle.

"Rain!" Nancy exclaimed, suddenly faced with a new dilemma. She pushed upward in her chair with every intention of getting out of it.

"No, you don't." A firm hand pushed down on her shoulder. "What are you doing?"

She pointed to the window. "Rain!"

"Yes," Jave said, continuing to push the chair down the hall. "I recognized it right away."

"Ohh," she groaned. "How long has it been raining? My chair will be ruined."

"What chair?" He stopped the wheelchair and came around in front of it to push open the double doors that separated the obstetrics wing from the rest of the hospital.

Nancy leaned back in the chair, looking grim. "The desk chair I bought for my home office. It's sitting in the open bed of my truck. It's secondhand, but it was high backed and upholstered. It'll be drenched!"

"You're supposed to keep a tarp in the back of your truck," Jave said, turning into room 221. "It's an Oregon rule. Otherwise, everything you try to transport will get soaked or moldy, or blow away."

Nancy sighed as he stopped the wheelchair beside her narrow hospital bed and leaned over her again to set the brake. He didn't touch her, but she absorbed his nearness. There was something . . . solid in it. She pushed herself up, reaching for the back of her gown, annoyed with herself for being so aware of him.

"Well, I haven't been here long enough to know the *rules.*" She climbed into the bed and frowned at him as he pulled the covers up for her. "What kind of a state is this anyway? It's like living in Atlantis. The sun hasn't shone since I've been here."

"Oregon's rainfall is notorious all over the country," he pointed out. "Why'd you come if you don't like rain?"

She sighed again and gazed grimly out the window. "It was a long way from New York."

"That's interesting," he said. "I'd have thought you came because your husband was transferred here."

HE'S ON TO US, MOM. But don't panic. I'm already doing that. Just think of something!

NANCY SWORE SILENTLY, but had her expression composed by the time she turned away from the window to look into J. V. Nicholas's eyes. "We were. But Jerry had a choice of several places. We decided on Heron Point because it's a long way from New York.''

"What didn't you like there?"

"The snow," she replied with an icy tone that defined the word and discouraged more questions.

But he'd never been easily discouraged. He smiled. "Are you a hothouse flower, Mrs. Malone?"

"No." She pulled the blankets up to her chin. "But I could do with a little less rain—and a lot less interrogation."

He acknowledged her complaint with a grin and turned the chair around. "Describe your truck."

She was puzzled by the non sequitur. "What? Why?"

"Maybe there's something I can do about your chair."

She was quiet for a moment, completely surprised by his reply. "It's an early seventies blue pickup with a dented right front fender," she said finally, then added in a dry tone, "You can't miss it among the Mercedeses and the Blazers in the parking lot."

"All right." He pushed the chair toward the door, then turned to offer her a quick smile. "Rest well," he said before pulling the door open.

Nancy fell back among the pillows with a mighty yawn. This day had not gone at all the way she'd planned. She'd expected to have her office chair in place by now, to have her curtains up in the kitchen and dinner in the oven.

Instead, her office chair was probably underwater, her curtains were still folded over the sewing machine, waiting to be hemmed, and there was nothing for dinner but a container of strawberries and a plastic tub of nondairy topping in the refrigerator.

And she'd made an enemy—or a friend. It was difficult to gauge at this point the status of her relationship with Dr. J. V. Nicholas. She had a feeling he didn't approve of her, didn't believe her story about Jerry, and yet he said he'd do something about her desk chair. He probably had the requisite tarp in *his* truck and would toss it over her chair.

She watched the rain drive against the windows and wondered if anything would help her chair stand up against this monsoon.

She settled into her pillows, thinking he'd simply reinforced her theory that men were the complex gender, while women were the ones falsely accused of being so—by men.

The door opened and a candy striper walked in with a tray of food. It smelled wonderful.

"Hi!" the girl said cheerfully. She was all of sixteen, with curly masses of bright red hair and gleaming braces. "Chicken pot pie, salad and ice cream. I brought this by twice, but you weren't here. I was hoping they'd sent you home and I'd get to eat this."

The girl, whose badge said April, balanced the tray on one hand, expertly positioned the bed table, then placed the tray on it. Everything looked as good as it smelled.

"I was having an ultrasound," Nancy said, realizing for the first time in hours that she was hungry. "I'll tell you what, April. You can have the salad."

April laughed. "Gee, thanks, but can we do a deal on the ice cream?"

NO! KEEP THE ICE CREAM. It's the salad, or nothing.

NANCY SHOOK HER HEAD. "Not a chance. Vanilla's my favorite."

April pretended disappointment. Then she smiled with genuine warmth. "I'm glad your baby's okay. I was taking coffee to the ER staff when you came in."

Nancy forgot the food for a moment and enjoyed sharing her good fortune with someone. She felt truly lucky that all was well. "Thank you. It was pretty exciting to see a strong heartbeat on the ultrasound."

The quality of April's smile changed, became unmistakably female. "Did Jave do it?"

Nancy nodded, recalling how Amy Brown had also used that name—Jave for J.V.

April rolled her eyes and sighed. "Isn't he just too cool?"

Nancy presumed that was a compliment and wasn't sure she felt inclined to give him one. Of course, all the remark required, really, was a clinical assessment. And that was easy.

"He's gorgeous, yes," she admitted, turning her attention to the pot pie. She savored the crisp crust and succulent chicken and vegetables in expertly seasoned sauce. It was five-star quality.

"Oh, it's more than that," April corrected earnestly. "Don't you think? I mean, some guys are hunks, but they're like so—" she considered the word, her turned down mouth saying what she couldn't seem to describe "—and I mean, like you'd die before you ever let them touch you. But Jave..." Her bright green eyes glazed over. She joined her hands together and drew a gusty breath. "I keep hoping I'll get a gallstone or something and he'll have to do an ultrasound on me."

Nancy was appalled. "I understand gallstones are very painful."

"It'd be worth it."

Nancy shook her head at the girl's unfocused gaze. "He's probably not the marrying kind."

April came out of her dreamy spell. "He was once. He has two little boys."

That surprised Nancy into stopping a forkful of chicken pie halfway to her mouth. "He does?"

"Yeah. And a dog."

In the girl's eyes, that apparently made him a family man. "Well, you have to beware of men other women have divorced. There's usually a good reason."

April nodded. "There was. She ran off with Dr. Templar, the orthopedist. A year ago. I wasn't here then, but my mom volunteers afternoons. Everyone was talking about it. Specially 'cause she left the boys."

Nancy put her fork down, feeling sympathy—even empathy—for Jave Nicholas *and* his children. Her husband had also walked away. And when she'd been a child, her mother, too, had left her and her father and struck out on her own.

Nancy rubbed the gently moving mound of her stomach and wondered at the wisdom of bringing a new life into a world filled with such undependable people. Her only comfort was that she had enough love for this baby to make up for any shortfall in their tiny family of two.

April glanced at her watch, then excused herself. "Gotta go. I'm supposed to help with stories in pediatrics. But tomorrow's Saturday. I'll be here bright and early with your breakfast."

WHEN HER TRAY had been taken away and a watery dusk began to settle in beyond the louvered blinds at her windows, Nancy closed her eyes and concentrated on relaxing. It wasn't difficult with her stomach full and with the knowledge that her baby was healthy and strong.

But what must the evening be like for Jave Nicholas? she wondered. Was he lonely and bitter, or grateful to be single again? And how were his children dealing with their mother's abandonment? She had always pretended that she'd adjusted, and she guessed in some ways she had, but there'd always been an emptiness, a curious feeling of inadequacy. And there'd always been that question in the back of her mind. If she'd been different, would her mother have stayed?

Well, she could empathize all she wanted, but ultimately it wouldn't matter. If she remembered to curtail her activities and follow Dr. McNamara's directives to the letter, she need never see Jave Nicholas again. She curled into her pillow, the baby moving lazily inside her, and drifted off to sleep.

"WHY DO WE WANT to save this chair?" Pete asked, holding the roaring blow dryer to the blue-and-gray-tweed contoured seat. He was seven, and it was very important to him that the colors of things matched or coordinated. It was an inheritance from his mother. "It's old. It's even kind of ugly."

Eddy, three years older, took after his father. He chose things for comfort, not for style. "It isn't ours," he explained with an impatient lack of grace as he dried off the legs with a rag. "It belongs to some pregnant lady at the hospital. It was outside in the rain all day."

Jave and his boys were sitting on a carpet remnant in the middle of their garage, doing their best to salvage the chair after its amphibious experience. Jave had unscrewed the back of the chair and now propped it up a safe distance from a space heater. He would turn the heater off before going to bed, but hoped the few hours of heat would begin to dry the thick wadding inside.

Pete transferred the blow dryer from hand to hand as he pushed up the sleeves of his *Lion King* sweatshirt. "How come *we* have to do this? She's not *our* mom."

Jave's head came up at that, and he focused on the disgruntled expression on his younger one's face. He felt the stab of worry that had plagued him since Bonnie had walked away. Pete had cried for two days, then had emerged from his room on the third day and simply pretended that it didn't matter.

Yet under it all was something that worried Jave more than the tears—a curiously insidious dislike for other people's happiness, a selfish unwillingness to give or share or otherwise participate in anyone else's life. Jave thought he understood the reaction; it wasn't that different from his own feelings for the first month or so. However, having to cope with important work, two little children and a mother and a brother who simply refused to let him be lonely, he'd snapped out of it and found a way to cope.

But he didn't know how to make that happen for a seven-year-old. He'd explained clearly and honestly to both boys that their mother was gone, but that didn't mean she didn't love them. It just meant she couldn't find a way to be with them at this point in time. And he'd done his best to make them believe that he'd stretch himself as far as possible in any direction to see that they had everything she would have provided.

That was impossible, of course, but they didn't know that. And he'd done his best.

Eddy had understood, and though he, too, had been devastated when his mother left, he was coming out of it and functioning well. He had all the aggressions and sweetness of a normal ten-year-old.

But Pete was another story—he showed all the signs of becoming a problem.

Jave opened his mouth to offer a reply, but Eddy beat him to it. "Because she doesn't have any kids, stupid. Didn't you hear me say she was pregnant? That means she hasn't had kids yet." Eddy stopped rubbing the chair legs and sat back on his heels to fix Jave with a look of complete disgust. "I thought when he turned seven, he'd start getting smarter. But he's just getting worse."

"*You're* stupid!" Pete turned the blow dryer toward Eddy's face, sending his longish, already dusty and play-tossed blond hair flying every which way. "A lady can have kids and still be pregnant for another baby. Darren Bolger's mother is."

With a cry of rage, Eddy leaped at his brother, intent on doing him bodily harm.

"All right, that's enough," Jave said quietly. He always tried that calm, authoritative tone first. It had yet to work. "Enough!" he shouted, injecting an undefined threat into the single word.

The boys sprang apart, glared at each other with utter loathing, then went back to their tasks.

"This particular pregnant lady," Jave said, getting to his feet to check his shelf of paint and stain cans, "just moved here from New York. And she doesn't have any other kids but the one she's carrying."

Pete shouted over the blow dryer, "She has to have a husband, doesn't she? A lady can't have a baby unless she has sex. And she has to have a husband for that."

"No, she doesn't." Eddy's tone changed from scornful to instructive. He turned the rag over and lay on his back under the chair, rubbing at the wood that braced the seat. "She can have sex with any guy and get pregnant. It doesn't have to be her husband. Right, Dad?"

"Right." Jave pulled a can of gold oak stain off the shelf and went to join the boys on the floor. "But most women don't do that because having a baby's too important. It all works better if she does it with someone she loves. Like a husband."

"Well, doesn't this lady have one?" Pete asked.

Jave nodded, running his fingertips over the wood Eddy had wiped off. "She does," he said. There was no point in sharing his doubts with the boys. "But he's in the Coast Guard and his boat's gone for a couple of months. She needs help, and because she's new here, she doesn't know anybody yet."

Pete made a face. "This is a dorky chair."

"It's an old-fashioned desk chair," Jave corrected. "She's making an office in her house because she wants to write books."

Pete's interest was piqued. He had an extensive, eclectic library of children's books, and he loved every one. "You mean like *Cat in the Hat* or *Goodnight Moon?*"

"Sort of. Only she wants to write books for adults. Mystery books."

Now Eddy looked interested. "Like the Hardy Boys grown up, or something?"

Jave smiled at him and decided to give the chair a few more hours to dry before sanding and restaining the battered legs. "Close. You guys know what Grandma's fixing for dinner?"

"Something with noodles," Eddy replied. "And you'd better be careful, 'cause her arthritis is kicking up again and she's grumpy."

"I am *not* grumpy." A formidable presence in a gray sweat suit appeared in the doorway from the kitchen. A wonderful aroma wafted past her into the garage. With it came a very large, long-haired black-and-brown dog of indeterminate heritage. It ran straight for Eddy, barking excitedly, and wagging its tail. "But when two boys and a dog run through the house, collide with me, and dump an entire bowl of chocolate cake batter onto the floor, it tends to diminish my sense of humor."

Jave looked from one boy to the other. Both were suddenly very interested in the dog.

"Pete had my ball glove," Eddy explained simply. "I wanted it back. Mo was helping me get it."

Pete made a scornful sound that suggested his brother overdramatized. "I just borrowed it."

Jave focused on Eddy, then on Pete. "There is no running in the house, and no borrowing what doesn't belong to you. Now, go get washed up for dinner."

Their grandmother stepped aside as the boys hurried past her, shoving each other, the dog behind them. She fixed her son with a grin as she came toward him. "You know, I could stay home and watch my soaps, visit the senior center and paint greenware with Hazel and Betsy, or I could find political causes to picket for in front of the post office. But, no. I come here every afternoon at two-thirty—not to mention all day, every day, during the summer—so I can be here when your boys come home from school and put your dinner on, and what does it get me?"

"Your lawn mowed every Saturday and your groceries picked up on Wednesday evenings." Jave got to his feet and kissed his mother's cheek as he passed her to check on the chair back drying in front of the space heater.

"Besides that."

"I offered to pay you, but you refused."

Agnes shook her head, impatient with his faulty replies. "Aggie Nicholas gets knocked on her keister, that's what. At sixty-seven years old, that's not a pleasant experience."

Jake hooked an arm around her shoulders and led her toward the door. "What I want to know is, did the dessert survive?"

Aggie elbowed him in the gut. "I managed to put together an alternative. So, what's with the chair?"

"I explained when I carried it in, Mom," he said, flipping the garage light off as they stepped up into the kitchen.

"You said an emergency patient had bought it this morning and left it in her truck out in the rain all day. But you didn't say how it became your responsibility."

He went to the kitchen sink to wash his hands. He could hear the boys laughing and splashing in the utility room down the hall. "Her husband is at sea. She's young and alone and six months pregnant," he said, making every effort to sound casual. His mother read him like an X ray. "She was worried about the chair. I was just trying to be a Good Samaritan." He glanced at her over his shoulder as he rinsed his hands. "You're the one who taught me that we have to care about each other."

"Single men," she said, lifting the lid on a pot and giving the contents a stir, "should let someone else care about married women."

He dried his hands on a dish towel and crossed the room to look over his mother's shoulder and into the pot. "Come on. Someone has to provide healthy scandal to this staid and proper community."

Aggie snickered. "This family's already done that once."

Jave laughed mirthlessly and crossed back to the sink to hang up the towel. "True enough, but that time was no fun for me. I was the victim."

"You get involved with a married woman," she warned, "and you'll be the victim again."

"Mom." Jave opened the refrigerator and pulled out a beer and a carton of milk. He frowned at her as he bumped the door closed with his elbow. "I'm not involved. I saw her all of half an hour. She was worried about the chair, her husband's on the *Courageous* on his way south, and she's only been here a couple of weeks. She doesn't know anybody. So I thought I'd help.''

Aggie carried the pot of chicken noodles to the table. "That's probably what Lancelot told *his* mother when he got involved with Guinevere. 'Mama, she's new here from Cameliard, her husband's always at the office, and I'm just gonna show her around because she doesn't know anybody at the castle.''' She straightened and placed both hands on her hips. "And look at the tragedy that resulted."

Jave put a hand over his eyes and summoned patience. It was futile to fight her logic, so he fought her facts. "Guinevere was at Came*lot* some time before Lancelot arrived."

She swatted his arm with a pot holder. "That's not the point!"

Jave opened his mouth to counter his mother's portent of doom when the back door opened and his brother walked in, a grocery bag in his arm. He looked from Jave to his mother and grinned.

"She's got you on the ropes again, huh?" he assessed. "What is it this time? Your diet? Your poker night? Your celibacy?"

Aggie went to take the grocery bag from her younger son. "He's in love with a married woman," she said.

Tom raised an eyebrow at Jave. "You are? Does she have a sister who could fall in love with a master carpenter with no money but great prowess in the bedroom?"

Jave placed the beer and the milk on the table, then went back to the refrigerator, asking over his shoulder, "Prowess at *wallpapering* the bedroom, you mean?"

"Ha-ha," Tom replied without the smile to accompany the words. He pulled out a chair at the table and sat down. "Now, what's this about a married woman?"

Jave returned with a second beer and handed it to him. He briefly related the story of the young woman and the chair. "That's it. I am not in love with her. I hardly know her. I was trying to be a good guy."

"Well, stop it," Tom said. "You'll hurt yourself."

"Ha-ha," Jave mimicked him in return. "I thought you were finishing that roof tonight and wouldn't make it for dinner."

"So did I. But I found dry rot when I put a leg through it. I have to back up and rebuild before I can go on. Hey, guys. How's it going?"

Eddy and Pete ran into the room and converged on their uncle, delighted to see him, and Tom quickly shifted his attention to his nephews.

"Don't try to tell me you don't feel something for this woman," Aggie said under her breath as Jave reached into the cupboard over her head for the bowl beyond her grasp.

Jave slapped the bowl into her hand. "Mom," he said, also under his breath, "if you mention Nancy Malone or the chair one more time, I'll hire a *real* nanny for the boys."

She dismissed the threat with a wave of her hand. "Right. Like anyone other than the CIA could deal with them." She put the bowl aside and grasped his elbows— that was as high up as she could reach. Her dark eyes were earnest and concerned. "I can see it in your face," she said. "You care. Oh, I know you're not in love—at least not yet—but I know you. You did this before. You loved a woman who wasn't good enough for you, and you thought your love could cover everything. It can't. You have to get love back or it doesn't work. I know you're lonely, but I don't want you to get hurt again, Jave."

Jave held her shoulders and leaned over her until they were eye-to-eye. "Now, listen carefully," he said in a voice just louder than a whisper. At the table, the boys were busy putting a head on their uncle's beer. "I am not lonely. I do not want another wife. I have no interest in this woman other than to fix her chair. And the last thing on earth I will do is allow myself to be hurt again. I learned a lot from the divorce. Trust me. Now can we have dinner?"

Aggie sighed. "Certainly. If you want to take my concerns so lightly. Who warned you that Clinton had no skill in foreign policy, that Wynonna Judd *could* make it on her own, and that the queen should have been tougher on her children? Who, huh? Who?"

Chapter Three

"Hi, Mickey." Jave stirred the oak stain with a thin stick while cradling the cordless phone on his shoulder.

"Hi, Dr. Nicholas," the bright voice of the switchboard operator on night shift replied. "Nothing for you. Bingham's on call tonight."

"I know. I'm checking on an O.B. patient in 221. Can you connect me to—"

"Hold on."

Jave dropped the stick into the can. "*Not* the room, Mickey, the nurses'—"

"Hello?"

Jave closed his eyes as he heard Nancy Malone's voice. He had intended simply to ask the night nurse for a progress report. He put on a brisk, professional voice. "Mrs. Malone. It's Dr. Nicholas."

There was a moment's surprised silence. "Hello, Dr. Nicholas," she said finally. Then her voice took on a panicky edge. "Did you find something wrong after all? Is the baby...?"

"No," he assured her quickly, firmly, regretting the impulse to call. He should have left well enough alone. "Everything's fine. I just...wanted to make sure you were comfortable."

"I'm fine," she replied, sounding vaguely confused. There was another small silence, then she added, "I'm watching 'Mystery' on public television."

He heard sinister music in the background and smiled to himself. "Research for an Edgar-winning book?"

"Simple entertainment," she said on a yawn. "Sorry. It's been a long day."

"Well, sleep's what you need right now, so I'll leave you to it." He found himself suddenly anxious to get off the line. Her voice was soft and drowsy and did curious things to his ability to concentrate. "Good night, Mrs. Malone. I'll see you tomorrow."

"You will?" Nancy asked. But the line was already dead. She looked at the receiver in her hand and wondered why the radiologist had called to check on her progress, and not her obstetrician.

She smiled wryly to herself. Probably because the radiologist didn't trust her. It was too bad, she thought as she yawned again. Hearing his voice made her feel less lonely.

She chided herself for the thought. It was nighttime, she was vulnerable, and the whole thing was too complicated for her sleepy state. She cradled the receiver, turned off the television, and closed her eyes.

It occurred to her as she dozed off that she should have asked him if he'd found her chair.

JAVE PUT THE PHONE ASIDE and recognized Tom's paint-and putty-spattered shoes directly in front of him.

He frowned up at him, then dipped his brush in the can of stain. "What are you doing back? You took Mom home three hours ago."

"She's crocheting and watching Letterman." Tom came to crouch beside him. "I thought you might have something to tell me that you don't want to tell her."

Jave groaned and concentrated on staining the chair leg. "Don't start with me, Bro. Mom manufactured the whole thing. You know her policy—if there's no news, make some."

Tom nodded and sat on the floor beside the chair, one knee drawn up, his elbow resting on it. "But you deal with dozens of women, young and old, every week of your life. And you've never repaired a chair for one of them before. Who was that on the phone?"

"A patient," he replied without looking at him. The nearest leg finished, Jave lay on his stomach and propelled himself on his elbows to the one on the far side. "I felt sorry for her, and that's the sum total of my feelings in the matter."

"So, she goes home tomorrow?" Tom absently rubbed at his knee.

"Right."

"And you're going to put the chair in the back of her truck and that's it?"

There was a moment's silence. Jave had been thinking about this for the past few hours. And the sound of her voice had decided him. "Not exactly."

Tom leaned back on an elbow. "What, then?"

Jave answered with another question. "What are *you* doing in the morning?"

Tom appeared to consider what the question could mean, then asked hopefully, "She *does* have a sister?"

Jave gave him an impatient glance then leaned around the back of the chair to reach the inside of the leg. "I thought I'd drive her home. She doesn't have anyone to pick her up, and if she goes home on her own, she'll never

get the chair out of the truck by herself. The wet upholstery weighs a ton, and it'll probably take days to dry. I'll
drive her, and you can follow in my truck. We'll unload
the chair for her and place it where she wants it. Then
she's out of my life.''

The chair leg finished, Jave straightened from under it,
capped the can of stain and gave the lid one solid whack
with the side of his fist. He looked up to find Tom watching him.

''What?'' he demanded.

Tom sat up. ''I just wondered if it's really going to be
that easy.''

''Yes,'' Jave said, wiping his hands on a rag. ''It will.''

''Then I'll be available to help you. What time?''

''Nine. I think she'll be released right after breakfast.''

''All right.'' Tom stood and pulled something out of his
hip pocket. He handed it to Jave as he, too, stood and
tossed the rag into a metal can in the corner of the room.
''*Oregonian*'s classifieds. I've circled the boat that could
change our luck. No more buying burgers on the way
home from fishing.''

''Really.'' Smiling, Jave unfolded the page Tom had
torn out of the newspaper's classifieds. ''I've kind of
gotten used to the supermarket folks laughing at us.''

Tom started for the door and Jave looked up in time to
note his limp. He put the paper aside and caught his arm.

''What's the matter?'' he asked. ''Leg acting up
again?''

Tom flexed his knee and winced. ''It's been pretty
good, but that episode on Wilkins's roof this afternoon
set me back a little. It'll be all right.''

Jave noted the carefully concealed pain in his brother's eyes, but was careful not to comment on it. ''Maybe
you should consider a Jacuzzi instead of half a boat.''

Tom made a face. "A Jacuzzi is for old guys."

Jave laughed. "Yeah. And pro athletes, and play-boys."

"You just want to buy the boat by yourself so you don't have to share it with me."

Jave walked with him through the house to the back door he always used. "I wouldn't know what to do with something I didn't have to share with you," he grumbled good-naturedly. "It's been the story of my life since I was five and you were eighteen months old and took my favorite fire truck."

Jave hadn't thought out the remark before he'd said it. He'd thought he'd simply been reminiscing, then the word "fire truck" came out before he could stop it.

There was a moment's silence, a deepening of the pain in Tom's eyes. Then Tom smiled and pulled the back door open. "If you'd given it to me," Tom said reasonably, "I wouldn't have screamed and Mom wouldn't have punished you. Live and learn."

Jave gave him a fraternal shove into the driveway. "I'll read the ad and tell you what I think. I'll meet you in the hospital parking lot at nine."

"Why not in your office?"

"Because it's my weekend off, and if I show up, someone will find something for me to do. See you tomorrow."

"Right."

Jave waved his brother off, then turned back into the house, wanting to kick himself for the fire-truck remark. It wasn't that Tom required they walk on eggshells around him, but the road back from the fire that had killed Tom's best friend and put him in the hospital for three months had been long and slow.

In the intervening year, he'd started his own business and learned to cope with constant pain. He'd made major strides forward. Tom had been a rock for him when Bonnie left. He hated to be the one to set him back, even in a small way.

Jave locked the back door then walked back into the garage for a last look around before going to bed. Satisfied that all combustibles were put away, he flipped the light off and locked the garage door. He went through the house, turning lights off as he went, creating shadows in his wake as he climbed the stairs.

This vague disquiet in his gut had nothing to do with Nancy Malone. It had to do with...loneliness. It had to do with a longing for some nameless something that was always just beyond his reach.

He'd seen that same longing in her eyes—that's what was forming this strange connection he felt toward her.

Well, he didn't need it, he told himself firmly as he pushed soundlessly at Eddy's half-open door. What would be the point of developing a relationship with a woman who also lacked what he lacked? The man/woman covenant was about *providing* what each other needed, wasn't it?

He suddenly found his foot entangled in a pile of clothes. He shook his head over Eddy's slovenly habits and reached down to scoop up what felt like jeans and tossed them at the laundry basket near the door.

He approached the bed and found his elder son lying on his back, arms spread wide, Mo lying beside him, his big head resting on the boy's chest. The dog's thick tail slapped against the bedclothes as Jave rubbed between his ears.

Jave gently folded the boy's arms in and pulled the blankets up. Mo lifted his head to allow the adjustment, then settled back down again, tail still thumping. Jave leaned down to kiss the boy's cheek, patted the dog, then left the room, leaving the door partially open.

Pete's door was closed. The floor of his room was clear of debris, and his war-worn sneakers were lined up neatly in front of the nightstand. The boy was curled up in the middle of the twin bed, the covers pulled over his head and tightly gathered in.

Jave frowned at the picture he made. It was so indicative of what was happening inside him, as well. He was hiding, closing himself off, making neatness an obsession at seven years old. Jave fought an impulse to rip the blankets off him and throw on the light. To make Pete share all the tumultuous feelings he shouldn't have to deal with alone.

But the situation was delicate; he knew that. He just didn't know what to do about it. His pediatrician had seen him and told Jave to try to relax about it—to keep the lines of communications open, to simply be there. This was just a normal reaction to his mother's departure, and when he was over being angry, he would find a way to cope.

Jave patted the roundest part of the bump under the blankets and left the room, pulling the door closed. Then he walked into his own bedroom and left the door slightly ajar.

Jave deliberately turned away from the skillful contrast and coordination of green and berry fabric patterns that composed the curtains, bedspread, pillow shams and dust ruffle, and went into the bathroom.

He peeled off his old jeans and sweatshirt, wondering if there was a psychological connection to his abiding hatred of his bedroom. Bonnie had redecorated it several months before she left. He'd come home from a three-day radiology convention in Seattle and walked into this bower of saccharine country charm.

There were layers of plump coverlets, deep lace trims and enough pillows for a harem. And his desk was gone. In its place was a small round table covered with a cloth that matched the curtains. It held two small carefully placed books and a candle.

Bonnie's cheeks had been flushed and she'd greeted him with a fervor that had surprised and flattered him after months of lukewarm response.

Then he'd come home several months later while the boys were at summer camp, to find her side of the closet empty and a note propped up against the philodendron on the dining-room table.

"We no longer want the same things," it had read. "You could move to a metropolitan hospital and make a fortune, but you have no ambition. Well, I want more out of life. I'm moving to Houston with John Templar to help him open a clinic." She'd gone on to explain that the boys related to him better than they did to her, so she thought it best to leave them with him. "I know it's cowardly to do this while they're away, but tears and recriminations wouldn't help anyone." She'd finished with "I made over our bedroom, but I couldn't make over our lives."

He'd been dumbfounded that a relationship that had been founded on a genuine passion, and that had developed so comfortably, was simply over.

Then he'd overheard a conversation between a young woman from payroll and one of the ER nurses that suggested something had been going on between Bonnie and Templar for some time. "She wasn't even discreet," the payroll clerk had said. "Bringing lunch to Dr. Templar's office, picking him up at the hospital when Dr. Nicholas was at the convention. *Everyone* knew."

"Except Dr. Nicholas," the nurse had replied with a pitying tone in her voice.

Then he'd become angry. He hated being stupid. And he hated missing important details. His work required meticulous attention to everything visible to him, and constructive understanding of everything that wasn't. How could he have failed to notice an affair between his wife and his colleague being conducted right under his nose?

Standing under the spray of a hot shower, he let the anger wash over him anew, then drain away like the water. It was over. It didn't matter how it had happened, or how he had missed it. The important thing was that he had two boys to raise who required his complete attention. He had a job that demanded his dedication. And if that left nothing for the man inside him who longed for something he couldn't name, that was life. God didn't make any promises. Even the constitution only promised an individual's right to the "pursuit" of happiness. It never said you'd catch it.

He climbed into bed, telling himself that in the morning, he'd rip everything off the bed and scour the boxes in the garage for the old blue quilted bedspread. Who cared if it didn't match the curtains? And he'd move the round table into the garage and put his sander on it, then find his desk and put it back in front of the window.

Those decisions made, he closed his eyes and tried to relax. The image of Nancy Malone's face floated across his mind's eye. He could hear her sleepy voice. He tried to dismiss them. She was married.

Then his brain re-created the picture of her as he'd first seen her, lying on the gurney, waiting for him to conduct the test. Her eyes had been dark and defiantly nervous, as though she was impatient with herself for being unable to control her early contractions.

Then he saw her as she'd looked when she'd told him she knew she carried a girl. He had to smile at that, remembering when the image on the screen had turned.

Jave turned onto his side and let himself remember the confusion on her face when he'd taken her back to her room and asked her to describe her truck so that he could save her chair from the rain. She'd looked confused. He'd enjoyed that.

So, he'd take her home tomorrow, carry her chair in for her so she could write her mystery novels and make enough money to stay home with her baby, and he'd feel as though he'd done his good deed.

Then, unbidden, the moment when she'd strained to see the ultrasound image flashed in his mind. He'd caught her arms, and she'd clutched his. He'd felt a desperate need in that grip.

He felt something prod at his heart and somehow change him from clinical radiologist to interested male. And once he admitted that, he felt a twinge in his groin that was a clearly sexual reaction.

He groaned aloud, and pushed his face into his pillow. Come on, man, he told himself. She's six months pregnant and she claims to be married. What's wrong with you?

The answers were too numerous to contemplate, and probably too alarming. He thought about the description of the boat Tom had clipped for him from the newspaper, and tried to imagine the two of them, alone on Willapa Bay in some sleek motor boat with salmon nibbling at their lines.

He drifted off to sleep.

Chapter Four

"Nancy!" April rapped on the bathroom door. "Telephone for you!"

Nancy pulled her blue sweatshirt on over her stretched-out black sweatpants and determined she would never leave the house again in her grubbies, even to go to the secondhand barn. She pulled the door open, her expression clearly surprised. "I don't know anybody here. Is it Dr. McNamara?"

April shook her head, her eyes wide. "Not unless he's moved to Greece," she whispered, and pointed to the telephone she'd left off the cradle on the table beside the bed. "The call's from Athens."

"Oh, no," Nancy whined. She hated herself for it, but couldn't help it. Only her mother could reduce her to whining. She sat on the edge of the bed and picked up the receiver.

"Hello," she said, as though she were answering the switchboard for General Motors. There was more business than warmth in her tone. "What is it, Mother?"

"Thank *God!*" The exclamation on the other end of the line was delivered in a deep, throaty voice. Nancy could imagine the roll of large, velvety brown eyes that accompanied it. "Are you all right? What happened? I can be there in twenty-four hours!"

Oh, God. Anything but that. "I'm fine, Mother," Nancy replied, trying to inject her voice with brightness and conviction. "I just overdid it a little. I had an ultrasound and half a dozen other tests and I'm fine."

"But Dr. McFarland said you went into labor!"

"Dr. McNamara," Nancy corrected. Then as April pushed her gently back against the pillows and pulled her feet up onto the bed, she asked, "How did you know to call him? How did you know I was here?"

"I called you at home all afternoon yesterday," her mother replied, "and when I couldn't reach you last night, I began to panic. I *knew* you'd get into trouble with that move. I wanted you to meet me in Laguna and let me take care of you, but nooo, you had to go to some pine-tree, flannel-shirt, salmon-stew outpost in the middle of the northwest wilderness to have your baby. Honestly, I—"

"Mom," Nancy interrupted, rolling her eyes at April, who was obviously straining to listen.

"Well, I called Dr. Carmody in New York, and he told me that an obstetrician in Seagull Point—"

"Heron Point."

"Heron Point, had called for your records. Well, I called *him,* sure you were in trouble and, well, there you are *in* trouble!"

"I'm not in trouble, Mom," Nancy insisted, rubbing her forehead where a small pain was beginning to grow into a major one. "I'm fine. I was given medication to stop the contractions. It worked, and all I have to do is continue to take it easy until delivery time. And everything will be fine."

"I'm coming out there."

"No!" Nancy shrieked the word so loudly that April jumped. There was a profound silence on the other end of the line.

MOM, YOU'RE SHOUTING! Don't do that. Water carries sound, you know.

"MOM." NANCY DREW a deep breath and tried to collect herself. She spoke in a reasonable tone now, though she still felt the panic that had prompted her desperate negative. "You're vacationing. There's no need for you to leave Athens to come here. I'm fine. April, tell my mother I'm fine." Nancy raised the receiver to April, who backed away, then took it reluctantly when Nancy scowled at her.

"She's fine, Mrs.... um ... ?"

Nancy couldn't hear the exchange, but guessed by the expression on April's face what had happened. The Denise DiBenedetto magic had reached halfway across the world.

April swallowed. Her eyes, large as lily pads, went to Nancy. Nancy reached up impatiently for the phone. April took a step back with it, and turned protectively away from her.

"*You're* Denise DiBenedetto?" she asked in an awed tone into the receiver. "Nancy's mother is the Country and Western star!"

There was more conversation Nancy couldn't hear. She crossed her ankles and closed her eyes, thinking this was the story of her life. Upstaged by her mother when the woman was thousands of miles away.

"She's really doing very well," April was saying. "Dr. McNamara was in this morning and told her he wants to see her every two weeks, and she's to call him if she feels the least little twinge." Then April giggled. "I *loved* your

'Denise in Devon' video. You looked excellent in that silver, off-the-shoulder thing, and Willy Brock is *so* cool."

There was a moment of silence while April listened, then her eyes grew even wider still and her tin-tracked mouth flew open.

"You *are?* You're *marrying* Willy Brock?"

April placed a hand over the receiver and whispered loudly to Nancy as though certain she didn't know, "Your mom is Denise DiBenedetto and she's *marrying* Willy Brock!"

Then she put the phone back to her ear, and nodded. Nancy could hear her mother's voice giving directions.

"Ah, no," April said. "Jave Nicholas is going to take her home. He's our radiologist."

"What?" Nancy pushed herself carefully off the bed, torn between concern about the threat her mother posed from thousands of miles away, and that posed by Jave Nicholas, very close by. She pulled the phone from April and held her hand over the mouthpiece. "What are you talking about?" she demanded.

"Jave..." April said, obviously perplexed by her dismay. "He's going to drive you home. I saw him and his brother in the..." She pointed vaguely in the direction of the parking lot.

Nancy didn't want to hear any more. "Mother," she said firmly, "I am fine. There is not a thing wrong with me or the baby that rest and the medication won't take care of. Now, do *not* come to Oregon. Do you hear me? That would upset me, and you don't want to do that, do you?"

"Nancy—"

"Mother, I mean it. I was fine by myself for all those years, and I will be fine..." Nancy suddenly remembered that she'd created an elaborate charade about a husband and that April was listening intently. She placed her hand over the mouthpiece again and turned calmly to the very interested aid. "April, would you go ask the nurse if I can have another pair of those footie things to take home with me?"

April began looking around on the floor for the little socklike slipper the hospital provided. "But I put them right . . ."

Nancy kicked the visible one out of sight under the bed. "I know, but I misplaced them somehow, and I'd love to take a pair home. Would you mind?"

"No. Of course not." April headed for the door, then turned back to grin with delight. "Say bye to your mom for me," she whispered.

The moment April was out the door, Nancy returned her attention to her mother. "I will be fine alone!" she said, trying to imbue her voice with the sincerity she felt over her solitary stand.

"No one should be alone," Denise observed quietly.

"Really." Nancy's voice became flat. "Curious that *you* forgot that when I was eight."

Another silence. Nancy closed her eyes, hating herself for sinking to petty barbs and old grievances.

"I've explained that many times," Denise said, her tone husky but controlled.

"Yes, you have," Nancy replied, "but it doesn't excuse it. So let's just forget that, and let me say for the last time that I feel wonderful this morning, and I know I'll be fine as long as I'm careful."

"Who is Jave . . . ?"

The man walked in the door pushing a wheelchair, as Denise posed the question. Nancy decided to rid herself of both problems immediately.

"Have to go, Mother," she said. "Thanks for calling. I'll be in touch." She hung up the phone and turned to Jave as she grabbed her purse from the chair. "Hi," she said. "I ... ah ..." The dismissal on the tip of her tongue was stalled by a weird little warmth that formed in her chest and stole up her throat into her face. She remembered his call the night before and how the sound of his voice had dispelled her loneliness.

J. V. Nicholas was truly gorgeous in "civilian" clothes. He wore a mossy green cotton sweater this morning instead of his lab coat, and an old pair of jeans faded to the contour of his long thighs and spare hips. The color of the sweater darkened his hazel eyes, and his casual appearance destroyed whatever distance his professionalism had placed between them.

She felt suddenly very vulnerable. And very interested. And then she remembered she was supposed to be married.

"No need for the wheelchair," she said, offering her hand. "Thank you for your help. I'll just be—"

He took her hand and pulled her gently down into the chair. "Hospital rules. You have to leave the grounds in a wheelchair."

April reappeared with a pair of Footies in a plastic bag. Behind her was Amy Brown, hugging her clipboard to her chest.

"Did you know that her *mother* is—" April began in wide-eyed excitement, eager to share her news with Amy and Jave. Nancy shook her head discreetly but quickly. She didn't want her mother to intrude on her new life in Oregon, and the way Amy ferreted out information, her mother could be on her doorstep by morning.

April stopped, looking confused.

"My mother called from Athens," Nancy said to Jave and Amy, who waited for April to go on. "She's traveling with a friend. April got excited about getting such an exotic phone call."

Amy nodded heartily. "I can relate. Athens conjures up images of whitewashed buildings, beautiful ruins, blue sky and bluer water...." She sighed longingly.

"Greek men," April breathed.

"Mmm," Amy purred.

Jave made a scornful sound and turned the wheelchair in a tight circle. "What is it about foreign men that's so appealing to women anyway?"

"Their foreignness." A short, square nurse with a cap perched on a bun of dark hair planted herself firmly in the doorway. "They're over there and not over here, so they can't bother us." She placed both hands on her hips. "Where are you going with my patient?"

Nancy had been visited by Nurse Beacham several times in the past eighteen hours, and had quaked in her "footies" every time. The woman had an Attila-like bedside manner.

"She's Dr. Mac's patient," Jave said, returning her authoritative glare, "and he's released her. I'm taking her home."

"But I don't need..." Nancy began.

Beacham folded her arms. "He didn't tell me."

"That's because you never listen to anyone, Beachie," Jave said amiably, and headed for her with the wheelchair. April and Amy leaped out of his path. "Now get out of my way before I mow you down."

Beacham stood her ground. Nancy thought she saw amusement invade her glare. "Do that and you'll find yourself on the fracture table, Dr. Nicholas." Then she stepped aside. He pinched her chin as he passed and Nancy watched in shock as the woman fought a blush.

Nancy tried to protest again that she didn't need the wheelchair and was capable of driving herself home, but no one was listening to her.

Amy and April walked them to the double glass doors. "Remember," April said, holding one of the doors open for them, "when the baby comes, I'm an excellent sitter."

Nancy waved as Jave pushed the wheelchair across the parking lot in the direction of her battered blue pickup.

"Bye," Amy called after them. "I'll keep in touch, Nancy!"

The day was gray and windy, late June feeling more like a blustery March. Nancy rubbed her arms against the chill.

"My chair!" she groaned as they approached her vehicle. The bed of the pickup was empty. "Where's my chair?"

"Relax, Mrs. Malone," Jave said quietly, pointing to the elegant red-and-silver GMC parked beside her truck. A man about Jave's age smiled and waved at her from behind the wheel. Something was covered by a tarp in the back. "I told you I'd take care of it for you."

Jave helped her out of the wheelchair, then gave it a roll toward April, who waited and waved.

He turned back to Nancy, holding a hand out, palm up. "Keys?" he asked.

Nancy squared her shoulders. This was going no farther. "Thank you," she said again. "But you're not driving me home. I feel fine. If you'll just put the chair in my—"

"Tom's going to drive it home for you."

"Tom?"

"My brother."

She looked up toward the cab of the fancy truck again and returned the driver's warm smile with a polite wave.

"That's kind of you, but unnecessary," she insisted. "If you'll put it in my truck—"

"You'll be faced," he cautioned reasonably, "with unloading the chair by yourself when you get home. Or leaving it in the truck until someone comes along to help you. And it's going to rain again. Even the tarp won't keep it dry forever. Now, will you give me your keys?"

Nancy knew it was critical that she make this stand and hold it. She didn't know why, she just knew.

"No," she said with quiet firmness. She walked around the truck to the driver's-side door, then took hold of the mirror when she got there. Her knees were wobbly. She wasn't quite as strong as she'd thought. But she was strong inside. She always had been. She looked into Jave Nicholas's steady hazel gaze and lied. "I have a neighbor who can help me with the chair."

Jave saw that touching toughness in her. Something about that desperately brave look reminded him poignantly of Pete. "I know your box number," he said candidly. "You're two miles from your nearest neighbor. Now, it's my weekend off, but my brother has a business to run, and he came to help me this morning out of the goodness of his heart. Are you going to give me your keys, or am I going to keep your chair?"

Nancy opened her mouth to suggest that that would be theft, but he probably had a point about his brother. And she couldn't wait to get back to her comfortable little cottage and put her feet up. She reached into her brown pouch bag and took out her keys. "All right," she relented. "You can unload my chair for me, but *I'll* drive."

He considered a moment, then accepted the compromise. "Fine. But let me help you climb into the seat."

Before she could agree, he literally lifted her up into it, then locked and closed her door. As he loped around to the passenger side, she sat immobile, completely flustered.

As he leaped in beside her, she turned the key in the ignition. The engine coughed asthmatically.

"Doesn't sound very healthy," he said, buckling his seat belt as she put the truck into gear and headed across the parking lot toward the road.

Nancy patted the dash affectionately. "Well, it climbed so many mountains coming here. I think it gave me its all." She pulled jerkily into the light traffic and headed for the coast highway.

"I'm surprised your husband left you alone for three months in your condition, living that far out of town, with a truck that's on death row." Jave responded to her quick glance with an innocent expression, hoping to catch her in a look that would reveal the truth about her husband.

But she quickly turned her attention back to the road. "He knows I'm competent. He doesn't worry about me."

There was a moment's silence in the cab of the truck.

"Does he love you?" Jave wasn't sure why he asked that, unless it was that he wanted very much to catch her off guard. She'd placed a barrier between them, and he didn't like that. It made no sense, considering that he intended to drop off the chair at her place and drive away with Tom. But he'd found that much of life didn't make sense. So he followed his instincts.

Nancy gasped indignantly. The exclamation was completely false, but she thought it sounded good. "What a question! Of course he loves me. He loves me enough to know I can handle myself in an emergency."

As the road widened, Nancy turned into the right lane. A glance at the rearview mirror showed Jave's brother falling in behind her.

"When a man loves a woman," Jave said, remembering the early days with Bonnie, "he never considers her completely capable without him. It isn't that he doesn't trust her competence, but he feels so necessary to her every breath that if he can't be there with her, he usually makes certain he's cleared all the obstacles from her path."

Nancy entertained that philosophy for a moment and even emitted a dreamy little sigh over it. She'd never known a relationship like that. She was content to be responsible for herself, but it would be nice to be so cherished.

"He has to keep the boat running," she said, straightening in her seat and dismissing futile longings. "He forgets about the truck."

Jave wasn't sure he believed in the husband, but if he did exist, he was a jerk.

HER COTTAGE WAS WHITE where the paint remained, and square and solid looking despite its cosmetic disrepair. It had a deep front porch, a picket fence that closed it in on three sides and a grassy hillside that hemmed it in from the road. Along the front of the property, bright pink tea roses cascaded in full bloom all along the fence, making the cottage look like a plain woman in a beautiful dress.

Nancy opened her door to leap down before Jave was out of the truck. He turned to caution her to wait, then saw that Tom was there to help her.

"Hi." Nancy smiled into the warm brown eyes of the man who held both her hands until she eased herself to the sandy ground.

"Hello," Tom said with a courteous dip of his head. He was darker than his brother, Nancy saw, and possibly an inch taller. His smile hid something, she thought, but when she looked more closely, he looked away toward the cottage. "I'm Tom Nicholas," he said, freeing her hands. He angled his chin at the house. "Pretty cottage. Needs some work."

She nodded. "I'm trying to make the inside livable before the baby comes. Then I can have the roof repaired, along with a few other things."

Tom looked up at the roof with a critical eye. "Then it'll be fall. The time to fix a roof is *before* the cold *winter* rain."

"She's not from here," Jave said with a grin, coming around the truck to lower the tailgate. "She doesn't understand about the rain. She doesn't even keep a tarp in the bed of her truck."

Tom shook his head. "Bad, Nancy. Gotta be prepared."

Even as they spoke, rain began to fall. It was thin but strong, and Nancy hunched her shoulders against it as she watched the men pull the chair to the edge of the gate.

"I know," she conceded. "Your brother gave me the lecture yesterday. I just didn't expect there to be this much rain. I feel as though I'm living an episode of 'sea-Quest.'"

Tom laughed and pulled the chair toward him to lift it off the truck. Jave stopped him with a hand on the tarp. "The upholstery's still a little wet, it weighs a ton, and you're favoring that knee." He added reasonably but authoritatively, "Let's do it together."

Tom looked heavenward in supplication. "I'm not helpless, all right?"

"Neither am I," Jave retorted. "I asked you along to help me, not to do it for..."

He stopped as Tom ignored him, lifted the chair, and headed for the house with it. Jave took Nancy's hand and pulled her out of the way.

"*You* can explain to Mom why the limp's worse," he shouted after Tom.

"Oh, stow it!" Tom shouted back at him.

"House key's the round one next to the car key," Nancy said, pushing Jave toward the house. "Go ahead. I'll be right behind you."

Nancy pulled her hand from Jave's and watched him lope past his brother and up the few porch steps to the door. He opened it and stepped inside to hold it out of the way.

Nancy went up the walk, trying to recover from having her hand held. That was such a simple gesture, one of the more innocent steps of courtship, yet it had always been one of the most appealing to her.

It represented a sense of security, of belonging, that she'd never experienced—except for those first few months with Jerry. And Jave Nicholas had a good grip, a strong hand that was hard and gentle and felt rather wonderful wrapped around her much smaller fingers. She flexed them, trying to dismiss the impression. He'd meant nothing by it. She was alone, she reminded herself. She wanted it that way.

When Nancy reached the living room, the men had the still-wrapped chair between them and were placing it in front of the table she'd put near the window to serve as a desk. Her computer and printer sat on it, and a neat row of reference books stood up between two simple metal bookends

Tom untied the rope that held the tarp in place and pulled it off. Nancy's gaze narrowed on the chair as she approached it. She ran a hand over it, thinking it appeared considerably better than it had yesterday morning when she'd bought it. And cleaner. And the legs looked less rough, almost as though they'd been . . .

She turned to Jave with suspicion in her eye. "What did you do? It looks fifty years younger than it did yesterday morning."

Jave shrugged. "My boys and I shampooed it since it was drenched anyway, but it's still pretty wet. We put a little stain on the legs. It could use a few more coats, but there wasn't time."

My boys and I . . . That was the first time he'd mentioned his children to her. Warmth tugged at her unexpectedly. She could imagine him with children. He had the kind of quiet, autocratic demeanor that made young children feel secure.

"That was very thoughtful," she said, feeling suddenly indebted—and just a little awkward. She laughed softly. "I thought you were just going to throw a tarp over it."

He studied her with frank masculine interest for a moment, and she found herself desperately wanting to make a friend of him. To tell him that she had no husband. That she was competent but just a little afraid. That she needed someone.

But for the sake of her baby, he had to believe she was married. And what appeal could she have for him anyway? She was beginning to look like she'd swallowed the moon.

She lowered her eyes. No. She had to do this alone. Thousands of women did. She could, too.

Jave saw the small step toward him that had taken place in her eyes—then the two steps back. He had to admit to feeling disappointment. And more than that, he felt a fascination he couldn't simply turn off. Not until he understood what was going on. Not until he understood her.

"Well," he said, thinking she was beginning to look pale. "You can't win an Edgar in a moldy old chair. Anything else we can do before we go?"

"No," she said, both relieved and upset that he was leaving. "But, thank you. And thank you, Tom."

Nancy turned to Jave's brother, who stood in the middle of the kitchen, looking up at the ceiling. Each room on the bottom floor meandered into the other so that living and dining rooms and kitchen were all connected, separated only by artfully placed screens and tall plants.

"You're welcome," Tom called back, still looking up. "This ceiling tile's going to fall on your head from the leak in the roof."

"I know," she replied. "It's on my list of things to take care of."

Tom wandered into the living room and handed her his business card. "Call me when you're ready. I'm pretty good. And my rates are reasonable."

Nancy read the card aloud. "Nicholas Carpentry and Repair. Roofing, Siding, Painting, Papering." She smiled up at him. "Do you have an easy payment plan?"

"You bet."

Nancy accompanied the brothers to the front porch steps, then leaned against the pillar and watched them walk away, two tall, impressive physiques, one limping slightly.

Jave took the tarp Tom carried and tossed it into the back of her truck. He turned and shouted over his shoulder, "Now you're an Oregonian!"

She laughed and waved. They climbed into the red-and-silver truck and drove away. Her world fell suddenly silent, except for the sound of the surf in the background.

She put her hand to a flutter of feeling in her upper abdomen. Almost as though she'd been patted.

DON'T FEEL SAD, MOM. I'm here. And we're going to have baby furniture and chocolate and movie passes. We're gonna be okay.

NANCY WENT BACK into the house and locked the door.

Chapter Five

Boenecke caught a glimpse of her across the fog-shrouded bridge. He ducked behind the limo, afraid of what she'd do if she knew he'd followed her. Temper would overtake good sense, he was sure, and she'd probably blow her cover. He hunkered down and waited.

Nancy reread the paragraph, considered it passable for the moment, and reached for her glass mug. She put it to her mouth, trying to decide whether to let Geneva notice Boeneke or not, then was completely distracted from her plot plans by the disappointing taste of lukewarm tea.

BLECH! Nuke that stuff, Mom.

SHE PUSHED HER NEW CHAIR away from the computer and went into the kitchen to brew another cup. The room was shadowy this morning, despite the daylight, and she turned the small old-fashioned light on over the sink. She filled the kettle and put a fresh tea bag in her glass mug and the spoon that tradition insisted absorbed the heat from the boiling water and prevented the glass from cracking. Tea in a glass was an eccentric indulgence, but she liked it. And of all her cravings, it was one of the more harmless and easiest to satisfy.

Outside, the sky was pewter again and threatening more rain. The grassy slope behind her cottage rippled beautifully in the wind and Nancy watched it, rubbing her stomach absently as she waited for the water to boil.

THANKS, MOM. That makes up for the cold tea.

THEN SHE SAW THE CAT. He was black with eyes so light they were almost silver. He'd been coming to the back door every day since she'd moved in, but he wouldn't let her near him. She guessed he'd been wild for some time. He'd plumped up a little in the weeks she'd been feeding him, but he still ran away every time she opened the door. He would stop halfway up the slope, then turn and watch her put out the food. He never came down until she'd gone back inside.

She called him Shaman because he was like a mystical, mysterious shadow with connections to another world.

She took a plastic butter tub full of dry food, filled a glass with water, and carried both outside to the corner of the porch. Shaman ran halfway up the slope and turned to watch her. She poured the water into the other bowl she always left out, then placed the dry food beside it.

She turned to look at the cat before going inside. She was patient with him, understanding his suspicion. But she felt the need to make contact with another life today, and for some reason her fictional characters simply weren't doing it for her.

"You know I won't hurt you," she called to him.

He sat unmoving, an eerie stillness in the waving grass, his eyes intense.

Nancy thought she could read them. "I'm not worried about physical pain," they said. "I'm worried that I'll trust you and you'll move away and I'll be hungry again."

With a last wry look at him, she went inside and closed the door. No matter how much she would have liked contact, he preferred not to have it, and she could relate to that. She went to the whistling kettle, accepting that she and the cat would coexist along parallel lines.

That had more or less been the story of her life anyway. She hadn't connected with anyone in a long time, except Jerry, of course, and he didn't count because he was gone.

Nancy dunked the bag up and down in her mug, watching the rich redwood color darken. She rubbed her stomach with her other hand. A small kick met her palm and she felt suddenly less lonely.

She carried her mug to the table-cum-desk in the dining room, patting where she'd felt the kick. "Hi, Malia Rose," she said. "I was wondering if you were up. We're writing pretty well today. Listen to what Boeneke discovered about Geneva."

"HI, MOM. I'm glad the work's going well. Could you send something down? Not that lumpy white stuff with the raisins and the milk, but something cold and creamy, maybe with chocolate in it? Oh, good. I'm glad we're sitting down. I felt like I was swimming against the current."

NANCY HEARD THEM before she saw them. She was so engrossed in Boeneke's pursuit of Geneva, who was in pursuit of the killer ambassador, that she thought the sound of the engine came from Boeneke's Cherokee. Then she heard children's voices and the bark of a dog, and knew she'd written neither into *Death on the Danbury Bridge*.

She looked over the top of the computer screen and saw what almost constituted a crowd, coming through her gate and up the walk. There were three adults, two children and a dog. And one of the adults, an older woman, stopped to lean over and admire the profusion of roses on the fence.

Nancy felt a little jolt of... alarm?... excitement?... when she recognized Jave Nicholas. His brother Tom followed.

WHOA. There's foaming adrenaline in here.

EVERYONE WAS CARRYING something. The boys had grocery bags, the woman, a box she balanced carefully on both hands. The men carried a ladder between them, and Tom had a toolbox.

Nancy pushed open the front door and stepped out onto the porch, a confused smile on her face.

"We invited ourselves over to fix the roof," Jave said from the bottom of the steps. He held the ladder upright now, one hand leaning over a rung to support it. She saw his eyes go over her with one quick assessing glance before settling on her face. "How do you feel today?"

There was something intimate in the question, something that isolated them in the little crowd.

"I'm fine," she said, ensnared by his gaze. He wore a blue shirt this morning that complicated the color of his eyes. She finally pulled hers away in self-defense.

The two boys stood on his other side, the taller blond one studying her with interest, the smaller dark one looking as though he'd been torn away from his favorite cartoons. "This is Eddy..." He touched the head of the taller boy. "And Pete."

"Hello," Nancy said, coming down the steps. Eddy came toward her, holding out the bag. Pete shrank against his father and kept a firm grip on his sack.

"This is from the Farmers' Market," Eddy said. "Dad and Grandma went shopping and got too much stuff."

Nancy peered into the bag. It was filled with half a dozen tasseled ears of corn, several enormous golden onions and a pint box each of strawberries and raspberries.

"Well . . . thank you!" Nancy looked from the boy to his father, touched by the kindness.

"You're welcome." Jave indicated the woman. "And this is my mother, Agnes Nicholas."

"Aggie," she corrected. She gave Nancy a polite smile that didn't quite conceal suspicion and disapproval. She held out the box she was carrying. "Chicken enchilada casserole," she said. "We've also invited ourselves for lunch." The implication was that she didn't think that was such a good idea, but had been forced into compliance. "Can we put this in the refrigerator? Do you have a microwave?"

The dog stayed out with Jave and Tom while Nancy led the way inside. She placed the bag of produce on the counter, then placed the casserole in the refrigerator. Pete continued to clutch his grocery bag.

Aggie wandered slowly around, studying Nancy's eclectic collection of furniture odds and ends and framed advertising prints from early in the century. Eddy followed Nancy from the refrigerator to the stove.

"Do you have hot chocolate?" he asked.

She picked up the kettle and carried it to the sink. He followed her again.

"No, I don't," she said, "but I have Russian tea."

He frowned as they retraced their steps to the stove with a full kettle. "What's that?"

"It's tea made with orange juice and lemonade. It's sweet. I think you'll like it."

"Tea?" he asked doubtfully. "That's kind of for old ladies, isn't it?"

He had deep blue eyes, Nancy noted, and the spark in them of a bright and well-loved child. She prayed her baby would have that look in her eyes.

Nancy laughed. "I drink it, and I'm not old. Well, not *too* old."

Eddy considered. "Okay," he said finally. "As long as there aren't any girls or dolls or anything. Usually when there's tea, there's a bunch of old ladies or girls dressed up all fancy with their dolls."

"That's a tea *party*," Nancy said, pulling mugs down from the cupboard, deliberately searching out those without teddy bears and cutesy patterns. "This is just tea—without the party."

"It is too a party," Pete said, joining them at the counter with his bag. "There's cake in here. And ice cream." He handed it over. "That makes a party."

Nancy accepted it. Both boys followed her to the freezer. "I guess you're right, Pete," she said, putting the half gallon of strawberry ice cream away. "This does look like a party. Would you like to try some tea?"

"Yes, please," he answered politely.

Nancy turned toward Aggie. The woman's smiling but remote good manners filled the space between them with tension.

"Can I make you some coffee?" she asked.

Aggie studied her a moment. Nancy refused to let herself squirm. "I'll try the Russian tea," Aggie said finally.

Nancy put on the television in the living room for the boys, and blessed her foresight in contracting for the Disney Channel with her cable hookup. A cartoon feature was in full swing and immediately absorbed the boys.

She made the tea, adding cold water to the boys' mugs. It met with their approval.

Aggie, sitting at the kitchen table, sipped it and nodded. "A tad sweet, but good."

Nancy explained that it was made with ingredients for instant juice drinks and instant tea. "An old neighbor of mine in New York used to make it and got me hooked."

"I've never been to New York," Aggie said. Her tone suggested that was something she didn't intend to rectify.

"It's a wonderful place," Nancy said charmingly, smilingly defensive. "I grew up in a neighborhood in Queens that was just like any small town in the Midwest. Then I lived in the Village when I was trying to be a playwright, and that was very exciting—full of actors and artists and dancers. I loved it."

"Is that where you met your husband?" The question was asked conversationally, but as Nancy looked into Aggie's eyes, she understood what the hostility was all about. Aggie thought she was married. And she probably didn't approve of her son showing such care and concern over a married woman.

Well, Nancy didn't, either—though for different reasons.

"Yes," she replied. It was the truth. "He was an actor, and we were working together on a small, low-budget play a friend of ours was producing."

Aggie's gray eyebrows came together. "I thought your husband was in the Coast Guard."

Nancy didn't even blink. "He was. He is. But he's always involved in community theater in his free time." She had to remember, she told herself sharply, that the honest elements of her story only stretched so far.

"How long have you been married?"

That was safe. "Four years." Divorced for four months, but who's counting?

The sound of ripping and prying apart came from overhead. Several roofing tiles went sailing past the kitchen window to land on the ground.

"Jave was married for ten years," Aggie said, glancing toward the boys, then lowering her voice. Eddy and Pete were completely entranced by the television and unaware of their conversation as they sipped at their tea. "She ran off with an orthopedist a year ago."

Nancy nodded. "I heard about that. It must have been very hard on everyone."

Aggie fixed her with a level gaze. "Bonnie was a nice girl, who was a good enough wife and mother, but she got bored with small-town life and didn't have the character to realize that what she needed was more substance within herself, and not another man. Jave married her because he loved her. She married him because he got her pregnant. She never gave as much as he did, so it didn't work. I don't ever want to see him hurt like that again."

Nancy heard the message there, but replied as though she didn't. "No one should ever be hurt like that. Unfortunately, life isn't as protective as we'd like it to be."

"But *I* am," Aggie said in a distinctly militant tone. "I'd die for my family. I'd even kill for them."

Nancy heard that message, too. Exaggerated or not, she felt lucky she and Jave Nicholas weren't romantically involved. She had no desire to be on the other end of Aggie's weapon of choice, whatever it was. She drew on the acting skills she'd acquired by watching her ex at work. Naturalness was the key.

She nodded gravely and leaned across the table toward Jave's mother. "That's how I feel about my husband," she said, telling herself it wasn't really a lie. She'd often thought of killing and Jerry in the same context. Then she added with genuine sincerity, "And my baby. Nothing had better ever get between me and mine."

THAT'S telling her, Mom.

THE SUSPICION IN Aggie's eyes seemed to waver. Then Pete appeared at the table, requesting a refill on his tea, and Nancy stood to fill his order, leaving Aggie to reevaluate her impressions.

There was more pounding from the roof, and Nancy looked up as she handed Pete his tea. The soggy tiles were looking more and more precarious. Maybe she'd better hire Tom to take care of that as soon as she could manage it.

JAVE BRACED HIMSELF against the gutters that ran around the rim of the roof and studied the seamless patch. Except for the brightness of the new tiles, it would have been impossible to tell that the roof had been repaired.

"Damn, you're good," Jave praised Tom. His brother, braced for balance as he was, gathered tools into his box.

Tom gave him a superior glance. "I hear that all the time," he said with feigned arrogance. Then his eyebrow arched. "Usually from women."

Jave groaned. "Save it, please. I don't believe you for a minute. If you were in such demand, you'd be off in your Jag this weekend with some blonde instead of here with Mom and me and the kids."

Tom gave him an affronted look as he edged carefully toward the ladder, guiding his toolbox along the tiles.

"I'm here because you asked for my help. I'm only doing the brotherly, charitable thing."

Jave laughed as Tom backed down the ladder. "You're doing the geek-without-a-date thing." Then Jave toed his way toward the ladder—only to find it pulled away from the side of the house beyond his reach. Fifteen feet below on the grass, Tom balanced it carelessly with one hand.

"The what thing?" he asked.

"The geek-without-a-date thing!" Jave shouted at Tom fearlessly, turning carefully to crouch down and brace himself on the edge. "The workaholic-small-businessman, spare-time-couch-potato-baseball-freak thing!"

Tom tilted his head sideways. "You know, I like the way you look there," he said, still holding the ladder away. "Sort of like a contemporary gargoyle. The nose and the fangs particularly."

"Daaad!" The front door slammed and Pete's voice preceded the child into the yard. He ignored his uncle and looked around frantically for his father.

"Up here," Jave called. "What's the matter?"

Pete looked up, his eyes wide. "Hurry, Dad. The ceiling fell on Grandma!"

"Oh, God." Tom leaned the ladder back in place and ran inside.

Jave rode the sides of the ladder down with hands and feet and raced to follow.

"I'M *FINE!*" Aggie insisted, though in a faintly pathetic voice that suggested otherwise. "Good heavens, the tiles are only cardboard."

Nancy dabbed at a small cut on Aggie's forehead with a damp cloth, and the boys stood by, one holding a tube of Neosporin, and the other a tin of Band-Aids. Tom examined the tile that had fallen.

Jave leaned down to inspect the injury. "You okay, Mom?" he asked.

"There's hardly any blood," Pete said with obvious disappointment.

Aggie angled him a glare. "I'm fine. But I'm enjoying the attention. Please don't spoil it."

As Nancy folded the cloth and prepared to reapply it, Jave caught her hand and held it away so that he could inspect the cut more closely. "It's hardly more than a scratch, Mom," he diagnosed. "But, by all means, make the most of it. Want me to call for oxygen, or shock pants, or something to make it look more dramatic?"

Then suddenly, without warning, he became sharply aware of Nancy's knuckles in the palm of his hand, of the bite of the topaz in her ring against the pad of his index finger, of the nail on her little finger digging into his.

He turned to her and found her soft, dark eyes on him filled with a message he couldn't interpret.

Nancy knew if she didn't withdraw her hand in a minute, the moment would grow heavy with significance. *Everyone* present would become aware that they were gazing into each other's eyes. But for now, Aggie's eyes were closed and the boys were studying the ceiling with their uncle, so she did a foolish and dangerous thing. She allowed herself to enjoy the sturdy grip, the quiet, fathomless hazel eyes, the fascinating paradox of strength and gentleness that was a kind man's touch.

Then Tom's voice brought her back, and she drew her hand away. "A few of the other damaged tiles are going to be right behind that one," he said. "I'm afraid my hammering worked them loose. I can pull down the bad ones until you have it taken care of. It won't look very good, but at least they won't fall on you."

Nancy nodded, striving for a steady, even tone. "I'd like to hire you to replace them. But first, I insist on paying you for the work you've done today."

Tom shook his head. "No, thank you. This is a sort of 'welcome to Heron Point' gesture. I'll be busy on another job until Friday, but I could work on your tiles the following week. Will that do?"

She nodded agreement. "Whenever you can fit it in would be fine. And thank you for the welcoming gift. That's very generous."

He'd come at Jave's request, she knew. She felt oddly disoriented, thoroughly upset by her reactions to Jave. She was pretending to be married, and here she was playing patty fingers with a man who *must* believe her performance.

She thanked Tom again, then handed Jave the wet cloth and went to microwave Aggie's casserole.

After lunch, Aggie insisted on cleaning up and drafted the boys to help. She grumbled at the spare contents of Nancy's cupboards, and the frozen yogurt that was the only other item in the freezer half of her refrigerator.

"I haven't done any serious food shopping in a week or so," Nancy explained. "I've been busy making the house livable and working on my book."

Aggie lectured her on the importance of nutrition to pregnant women. "Don't be afraid of a little weight gain," she said, taking a last look around the kitchen before closing the dishwasher. "You'll be such a slave to that child forever after that you'll work it off."

Aggie then looked down at her own plump form in a casual black-and-white pants outfit and smiled fondly in Jave's and Tom's direction. Tom stood atop the ladder removing the loose tiles, and Jave stood at the bottom to receive them.

"Until, of course, they begin to take care of *you*. By then, you're entitled to a few extra pounds."

Aggie's manner had changed subtly, Nancy noted, over the course of the past few hours. The woman seemed no longer hostile, but friendly, even warm. She congratulated herself on her convincing portrayal of a married woman.

As Tom carried the ladder back to his truck, the boys trailing him, Aggie gave Nancy her telephone number. "Tom and I live in a house about this vintage on a hill above town. I'm at Jave's house most of the time, so please call me if you need anything. I can imagine how lonely it must be for you way out here with your husband gone. Do you still have your parents?"

"My father passed away," Nancy replied. "My mother is very much alive and living on a yacht in Greece at the moment."

Aggie's eyes widened. "How wonderful that must be. Will she come when the baby arrives?"

Nancy shook her head and walked Aggie to the door. "We don't get along very well. She called to check on me when she heard I was in the hospital, but I asked her not to come. I . . . just don't want to get involved again at this point in time."

Aggie put a sympathetic hand on her arm. "But, Nancy, you are involved. She's your mother. And you're about to have her grandchild."

Nancy shook her head, patting the hand on her arm. "This baby belongs to me alone."

Aggie frowned. "And your husband, of course."

"Yes," Nancy said quickly. "Of course."

Aggie gave her a quick hug. "Well, call me if you find yourself needing motherly advice after all. And you have Tom's business card."

"Yes. Thank you."

As Aggie walked out to the truck, Nancy returned to the kitchen. Jave had carried the old tiles out to the trash and now returned through the back door, pushing it closed and dusting his hands on the thighs of his jeans.

Nancy felt a deep, sharp, alarming awareness of him. She deliberately kept the table between them. She saw his smoky hazel eyes note her careful distance and ponder what it meant.

She assumed her role of married woman. "Thank you so much for bringing Tom by to fix the roof. That was very kind and...neighborly."

It hadn't been neighborly at all, Jave admitted to himself. It had been something else altogether. Something she apparently understood, judging by the panicked look in her eyes every time he came within ten feet of her.

There were confusing messages here, and he was just beginning to get his life straightened out after Bonnie. Confusion was something he didn't need. So they could call it neighborly and let it go at that.

Curiously, it hurt to accept that.

"Take care," he said, picking up Tom's toolbox and keeping to his side of the table as he headed toward the living room.

Nancy found herself wanting to call him back, to grab his arm, to hold him somehow. "Wait!" she called.

Jave turned near the front door, his heart giving an uncomfortable kick. "Yes?"

She took a jar off the countertop and secured the lid as she walked toward him with it. She stopped in front of him and handed it to him. "Your boys liked my Russian tea," she said softly. "Two teaspoons in a mug of hot water." He accepted the tall jar of powdery orange stuff in his free hand. Her fingertips brushed his, lingered for a moment, then she dropped her hand and said firmly, "Goodbye. Thanks for all you've done."

"Sure," he replied. "Good luck."

She waved them off from the porch, feeling a sharp pinch of loneliness when the red-and-silver truck disappeared from view.

She went back into the house, found the kitchen more pristine than she usually kept it, and brewed a cup of black tea. She had to get back to Boeneke and Geneva. The story had been going well before the Nicholases arrived.

She carried the tea to her desk where a midafternoon sun had broken through the clouds and brightened the view of sea grass and ocean from her window. Perfect working conditions, she told herself as she sat down to work.

An hour later, she was still staring at the flashing cursor on the screen. It sat at the end of the last sentence she'd written before Jave and his family had arrived.

Impatient with herself, she went into the kitchen, wondering if Shaman was ready for his evening meal. She refilled his bowl and looked for him on the slope where he always watched and waited. He wasn't there. She called, then chided herself for it. Of course he wouldn't come. He never came when she called.

She looked left and then right, and saw the same view in both directions—miles of empty beach. Even the sea gulls and the sandpipers were somewhere else this afternoon. The sun dipped back behind its tufty pewter screen and everything around her darkened subtly.

Nancy turned her face into the west wind and admitted to herself that she was lonely. She'd valued her solitude until it was invaded by a host of loud and cheerful people who gave her a glimpse of another kind of life, then disappeared—leaving a gray crater in the middle of her day.

MOM. IT'S GONNA BE OKAY. I can feel your grim vibrations. And your spine's a little tight. You're pinching my backside.

Come on. You told me the first time we saw the doctor and he told you I was coming that everything would be all right. That we just had to have faith and believe in each other.

I know that's not easy for you right now because frankly—I wouldn't trust anything that looked like me, either. But I have faith in you. I know we're going to be fine.

Mom? Yo! Are you listening?

"WHOA." NANCY PUT A HAND to the sharp kick on her ribs and rubbed. "Easy, baby. It's all right. Everything's going to be fine. It's just you and me, but we're already a pretty good team. We can do this. Go back to sleep. I have it handled."

Chapter Six

"Do not pick up that magazine while I'm standing here with you," Jave warned his mother. "Or I'm out of here and you can drive yourself home and carry in your own three tons of groceries."

Aggie, standing in front of the shopping cart behind which he waited in the checkout line, gave him a look of complete disdain as she picked up a tabloid magazine and tossed it into her cart.

"Don't be such a stuffed shirt, James Victor Nicholas." She perused the rack filled with other publications of the same type and asked absently, "Where else can you read about things that never happened?"

Jave opened his mouth to answer that and realized the danger. There was no answer. In fact, the question itself was just a little out there.

"You know..." Aggie tossed another magazine into her cart and moved forward with it as the line moved. "Tom missed his last appointment with the therapist."

Jave nodded. "He had a big job that day so he couldn't leave. The principal's new home office, remember? I helped him lay the carpet. He told me he'd make another appointment."

"Well, he hasn't," Aggie said, moving to the back of the cart where he stood and lowering her voice. "And he won't take Judy Taft's phone calls."

Jave nodded again. "I know that, too. And I don't blame him. When he was hurt and there was a chance he might not have use of that leg, she made a token visit to the hospital, left a few messages on the answering machine, and that was it. Now that he's more like himself again, she's willing to give him her time. That stinks, Mom."

Aggie sighed, and for a moment Jave thought she looked like she had that week after the fire when Tom had teetered between life and death. He put an arm around her shoulders and squeezed.

"He's going to be all right—inside as well as out. You've got to stop worrying about every little move he makes—or doesn't make."

"But he never goes out—except with you and the boys." She leaned into him and looked up, her usually wise, dark eyes filled with worry. "I want him to be happy again. I want him to find a nice girl and get married and have babies. When I'm gone, he'll be all alone in that house."

The line moved again and Jave pushed the cart up against the grocery conveyor and began unloading.

"If you want him to be happy," he reasoned, "you have to let him come to that in his own time. What he went through was hard on all of us, but think about how hard it was on him. And we can't make him push it all aside because we're tired of seeing him suffer. He has to get through it his way."

Aggie held a three-roll package of paper towels against her and looked at him over it. "And what about you? When are you going to be ready?"

Jave sighed. He knew she would work her way around to him sooner or later. He had less patience and understanding there. "I'll get to it."

"It's been a year."

"That's not so long."

"It's too long to grieve over a selfish woman who left you and two wonderful little children."

Jave fixed his mother with a warning glance. She didn't comprehend subtlety. "I'm not grieving over her. And I don't want to talk about it."

She considered him another moment while he tried to dispel more conversation by concentrating on pulling the heavy items out of the bottom of the cart.

"I think—" she began again.

Jave interrupted under his breath. "I know what you think. You think you can decide how Tom's and my life should be and make it happen. But you can't. There's a lot of you in us—well, more of you in Tom than in me, but you..."

She smiled, first considering his remark a compliment. Then her expression changed and she asked suspiciously, "What do you mean, there's more of me in Tom?"

He pushed the now-empty cart forward and pulled his checkbook out of his hip pocket. "Well, you know. He's hardheaded, opinionated, quarrelsome, hard to—"

She hit him with the rubber divider bar that separated grocery orders on the conveyor.

"Mrs. Nicholas!" The checker, a tall young woman Jave had gone to school with, pretended shock at Aggie's behavior. "I saw that, Jave," she said. "If you need a witness to parental abuse, I saw the whole thing."

Jave took the bar from Aggie and dropped it into the slot near the register. "Good. I'll send my attorney by tomorrow. And I want to make it clear that the scandal sheets, the praline chocolate drizzle ice cream and the disposable security undergarments are hers and not mine."

"Jave!" This time Aggie hit him with her hand, then dissolved into hearty laughter.

JAVE AND TOM WALKED along the service dock to which the boat described in Tom's newspaper clipping was moored. They stopped at the stern, where a landing net was propped against the rail, and stared quietly.

"Does this look sixty-three feet long to you?" Tom asked in a whisper.

Jave ran his gaze from stem to stern. This was a cabin cruiser from the twenties or thirties, and looked as though it hadn't been scrubbed or painted since it was built. "I think it's an exaggeration," he returned wryly. "By about thirty feet."

Tom frowned as he reread the clipping aloud. "63' Bertram Int'l '72/89. '89 major remodel/update. Charter potential, 3 staterooms, low hours, been loved."

Jave snickered. "Looks more like 'Canoe with two oars, comes with unimpeded view of passing traffic through missing windows. Depth may be sounded through hole in deck.'"

Tom leaned forward to run a hand along the old lapstrake hull. It had been primed in preparation for paint, and the name had been obliterated. "Oak," he whispered reverently. "Jave, this boat has character."

Oh, no. Jave knew that tone. "Tom, if by some miracle this didn't sink and got us out to where the fish are and we caught any, they'd have to swim back beside the boat because no self-respecting fish would want to cruise on this—alive or dead."

Tom gave him a pitying glance. "You medical types are too sophisticated for your own good. This could be a good boat."

Jave humored him. "It probably was when the Vikings used it to raid the English coast, but we need . . ."

Tom patted the hull. The gesture had a more proprietary air than the previous stroke. Jave began to get nervous. "We need something to replace the *River Lady*. I think with a little love and effort, this could do it."

The *River Lady*. Jave thought longingly of the fifty-five-foot fiberglass motor boat he and Tom had bought together before he was married and when Tom had just been promoted to battalion chief. It had been a fisherman's dream. They'd spent all their spare time on it, then Jave had gotten married, and for him that time had been reduced to several weekends a year and one week-long trip every summer.

Tom had tended it like a doting parent, and almost lived on it from June to October. Then Bonnie had left and Jave had needed money for a divorce settlement. And Tom had finally gotten out of the hospital and was anxious to settle growing debts. So they'd sold the *River Lady*.

"Tom," Jave said reasonably, "that was a sleek . . ."

Tom walked up the ramp and stepped aboard. Jave knew he'd lost him.

The galley was small and ancient but efficient. The two staterooms were minuscule but neat. So was the head.

A gruff voice interrupted their perusal. "Interested in the *Mud Hen,* are you?"

"The *Mud Hen,*" Jave repeated flatly. He turned to his brother. "It's called the *Mud Hen,* Tom. Do we really want to own something called the *Mud Hen?*"

A small man, who looked almost as old as the boat, appeared in the doorway of the tiny room into which the men were crowded, heads tucked into their shoulders as protection against the low ceiling.

He offered a hand to Tom, then to Jave. "Captain Wolfe," he said. He wore a baseball cap emblazoned with the insignia of the USS *Kearsarge*. His eyes were sea blue, his skin as leathery as his name would suggest. "Been on the sea for sixty years."

Tom waved the newspaper clipping at him. "Pardon me," he said politely, "but the ad says—"

Wolfe laughed heartily. He had a gold tooth. "That was the *Stormwind*. Sold her yesterday to a lawyer from Portland. This is only…" He named a price that was half that listed in the clipping. Jave thought it could have been cut in half again. "Wasn't gonna sell her, but the missus is in a nursing home and…well…it costs."

Tom turned to Jave. And Jave saw something in his eyes that hadn't been there since he'd gotten out of the hospital. It was enthusiasm.

A love deeper than he even understood won out over financial good sense. And then there was the thought of the captain's lady in a convalescent home.

He smiled at Captain Wolfe. "Would you mind if we look around a few more minutes?"

Wolfe shook his head. "Help yourselves. Price includes the paint job and the repairs already underway. I'll be at the Scupper, tossing down a cold one."

The moment he disappeared, Tom sat down on the bunk—and sank in as though it were a beanbag chair. Jave leaned a shoulder against the doorway and watched his brother laugh. It brought a catch to his throat that he coughed away.

"This is nuts," he said, intending to put on a good show of resistance.

Tom patted the mattress on the bunk that was now even with his underarms. He looked like a man in an inner tube. "I think it's great. Sleekness isn't everything, is it? I mean, I could redecorate this and make it very comfortable." He looked around him with sincere interest. "Think about all the fishing trips this thing has seen, think about the men who've lived on her, and the—"

"Okay," Jave said.

Tom stopped in surprise. "'Scuse me?"

"Okay," Jave repeated. "I'm in. On one condition. Two, actually."

Tom's gaze narrowed and he pushed himself out of the bunk. They moved into the galley, then out onto the deck. The weather had turned, and summer seemed finally to have made its appearance.

The homes of Heron Point were scattered over a hillside that sloped down to the river. In the late-afternoon sunlight, windows gleamed and tall evergreens stood out against the bright blue sky.

Jave and Tom carefully skirted the hole in the deck and leaned elbows on the rail to look away from town and out at the blue river that separated them from Washington State.

"Why do there have to be conditions?" Tom wanted to know.

"To get Mom off my back," Jave admitted.

Tom groaned and put a hand to his face. "Let me guess. I have to start going out."

Jave gave him a congratulatory pat on the back. "Good so far."

"And . . . clean the garage?"

"No."

"Put up her new shower curtains?"

"Nope."

"Install the Casablanca fan in her bedroom?"

Jave shook his head and turned to look him in the eye. "No. You have to reschedule your appointment with the therapist. And you have to promise not to miss any more."

"I was working," Tom said with an indignation that wasn't entirely honest. Jave recognized it immediately. "You were with me. We were supposed to be done by—"

"I know, but *you* were supposed to make another appointment and you didn't. So do it."

Tom pushed up from the railing and turned his back to lean a hip on it. "I'm tired of hearing myself blame myself, and hearing *him* tell me to consider why I want to cause myself that pain."

"Why do you?" Jave asked.

"Because I left Davey!" Tom screamed at him. It was a loud roar that seemed to come out of nowhere. Tom had been the personification of calm since he'd come out of the hospital. But Jave thought he understood. The rage was finally working its way through the pain. That seemed like a good sign. At least he hoped it was. "I..." Tom made a strangled sound that he had to swallow before he could go on. "I left him."

Jave, still facing the hillside, backed up a pace to be able to look into Tom's eyes. They were miserable. They made him miserable. "You thought you heard a woman cry out, and you went to look for her. And the floor gave way on Davey. I know you'd been friends forever. I know he once dug you out from under a wall and saved your life, but that doesn't make you responsible for *this*. Who in the hell do you think would ever blame you for that?"

Tom drew a deep, ragged breath. "I'm sure the Porters do. If I hadn't told him to stay there, it wouldn't have happened. Or if I'd sent him instead, he might—"

"Tom, you can second-guess every move you made, but it'll never make you responsible for Davey's death. And his parents don't blame you. They've asked you to go see them several times. I think you should. It might give you some peace."

Tom turned away from him to frown at the hillside. "I don't want peace."

Jave decided it was time to let that go for the moment. "Well, I do," he said briskly. "So you agree to reschedule your appointment, and you get a date within the next two weeks, or you can buy this rust bucket on your own."

Tom turned back, his expression still tense. It was now also mildly aggressive. "Maybe I *should* buy it alone," he said.

Jave held his glare. "Maybe you should."

The tension hung between them for a moment, then Tom relaxed and pushed away from the rail. He placed an arm around Jave's shoulders and led him toward the ladder. "You own both fishing poles," he said with a feigned whine.

Jave nodded. "Wise of you to remember that."

TOM AND JAVE FACED each other at a small table in a quiet corner of The Scupper Tavern. Between them on the table was the *Mud Hen*'s registration slip and maintenance record.

Tom toasted Jave with his tankard of dark ale. "Thanks. To bringing home the fish."

Jave raised his Guinness. "Just make certain we're well insured."

They drank quietly for a few moments as the waterfront establishment's clientele began to thin out. With dinnertime approaching, the rowdy after-work din began to dissipate, and the bartender busied himself drying glasses and hanging them up on the overhead rack.

"Okay," Tom said, pushing his ale aside and folding his arms on the table. "I'm going to do one for *you.*"

Jave smiled thinly. "Thanks. The *Mud Hen*'s enough to last a lifetime."

Tom pulled the Guinness out of his hand and put it aside. "Will you shut up about that? It's a great boat. Now listen to me."

Jave turned in his chair to lean his back against the wall and took a peanut out of the bowl holding down the *Mud Hen*'s papers. "All right. What?"

Tom grew suddenly serious. But it wasn't the troubled seriousness of earlier. He seemed to be more remote from this particular concern. Jave could only conclude that it was because they were about to discuss one of his, Jave's, problems.

"I've done two jobs for Nancy Malone in the past three weeks," Tom said. Jave's interest was instantly sparked. "A couple of weeks ago I replaced her ceiling tiles." Jave nodded. "Last Wednesday, I replaced a broken window in her bedroom."

"Yeah?"

"Yeah." Tom paused significantly. "It's pink."

Jave raised an eyebrow. "The window?"

"The bedroom!" Tom huffed impatiently. "Will you pay attention? Her bedroom is pink. And you know what's in her closet?"

"What?"

"*Her* clothes."

Jave tried desperately to put the facts together. "Her bedroom is pink," he repeated flatly. "And *her* clothes are in *her* closet. Well, call a cop. She sounds like a threat to national security to me." At Tom's groan, he demanded, "What? What am I missing?"

Tom dropped his forehead onto his folded arms. After a moment, he raised his head again and spoke slowly. "To think that you're entrusted with people's lives. How many men do you know who would be willing to sleep in a pink bedroom? Would you?"

"No," Jave replied, but then he even hated the green one.

"Neither would I," Tom said. "And I mean it's serious pink."

"It was probably that color when she moved in."

"It wasn't. She did it herself. She told me. And there are no men's clothes in the closet. Zip. *Nada.*"

Jave considered what that could mean. "Well . . . her husband's away for three months. . . ."

"I know, but would he take every old tennis shoe he owns? Every tie? Every belt? Every—"

"They just moved in. I mean, a lot of that stuff could still be packed."

Tom rolled his eyes. "All right. Consider this. There is not one family picture on the walls. Nothing. Do you figure she'd wave goodbye to a husband who's going to be gone for three months and not prop up one photo of him on the bedside table? Or on that table she uses for a desk? Wouldn't she even stick one to the refrigerator with a magnet?"

Jave felt a certain vindication of his initial instincts in the matter of Nancy R. Malone. Of course, his brother's suspicions didn't prove anything, but they posed some interesting questions.

Tom watched his carefully controlled expression. "I'm telling you I don't think she's married, Jave," he said finally. "And don't give me that stoic look like it doesn't matter to you."

Jave picked up his Guinness and took a long pull. "I suspected she wasn't married when I did her ultrasound."

Tom frowned. "Then why do you suppose she's pretending? The world's full of single mothers today."

Jave explained about the hospital's grand opening and Amy Brown's extravaganza.

"Amy Brown?" Tom asked.

"PR coordinator. It's a new post with the new administration. She's the administrator's niece. Nice girl, but disgustingly cheerful and with ideas more appropriate to Long Island than Heron Point. I think she's kind of an ugly duckling in a family of swans, trying hard to make good."

Tom grinned. "You probably understand her so well because you relate to her situation—being the Nicholas ugly duckling and all."

Jave rolled his eyes. "Tommy, I don't know how to tell you this, but Mom's been lying to you all these years. You're not the cute one, I am."

Tom sighed with great drama. "How our standards have fallen. So, you mean you think Nancy's doing this for the gifts?"

Jave had given it some thought. "Is that so selfish? If she is single, she doesn't seem to have all that much, and setting up a nursery is a pretty expensive proposition, particularly when there are no friends around for those showers and things women give each other to help prepare. I imagine the prospect of having all that handed to her was very appealing."

Tom drank his ale and leaned back in his chair. "And the hospital wouldn't want to use her for the publicity if they knew she was single?"

Jave shrugged. "The way Amy explained it, the hospital foundation preferred that she find a candidate who fits the conservative American image."

"That of having a husband."

"You got it."

"Hmm. But what made this Amy think she *was* married? Is it on her hospital records?"

Jave inclined his head in perplexity. That was a detail he'd forgotten. "Apparently the records transferred from New York said she *had* a husband." He remembered suddenly her reply to his question about why she'd come to Oregon. "It was a long way from New York," she'd replied. "Maybe," he speculated, "something's changed in the meantime."

"You going to check it out?" Tom asked. "I got the impression you were ... interested."

Jave stared into the corner, his gaze unfocused. She'd haunted his thoughts from the moment he first saw her. And though he'd resisted all emotional tugs in her direction for the past three weeks, telling himself he didn't need the confusion or the aggravation she presented hadn't diminished them. What he felt was something that required action. Where it would lead, he hadn't the vaguest notion. All he knew was that he had to find out.

And he remembered her soft dark eyes looking into his—looking for something she seemed to want desperately. He had the damnedest feeling that whatever it was, he had it somewhere.

He brought himself back to Tom's question. "You doing another job for her some time soon?"

Tom nodded. "Yeah. Next...Friday, I think. I'll check the calendar at home to be sure. I'm cleaning out the gutters and replacing the one on the north side that's hanging."

Jave nodded, his eyes taking on a devious gleam. "That's a two-man job, isn't it?"

"No. I can usually— Oh." Jave's tactic suddenly dawned on him and he halted his denial. "Well, sure. Your day off. You can do the work, and I'll sit in her kitchen and eat dessert. She claims she can't cook, but she loves to bake. Last time, she sent cream horns home for Mom and me."

Jave heaved a long-suffering sigh. "Great. I save the chair and you get the cream horns."

Tom clapped his shoulder. "Builds character."

"I'LL GET STARTED," Tom said quietly as Jave helped him position the ladder. He gave him a conspiratorial grin. "You can tell her we're here."

"Want me to get the gutter out of the truck for you first?" Jave asked.

Tom shook his head. "I don't need it yet. Hey."

Jave had turned away to head for the porch steps and turned back.

"If you get a cream horn," Tom said, "I want my half."

"Oh, right. At what you're paying me an hour, the cream horn's mine."

Jave loped up the steps and knocked on the front door. There was no answer. Tom had parked behind the blue pickup, so he knew she had to be home. And he could hear the sound of the television beyond the door.

Suddenly alarmed that something might have happened, he tried the doorknob. It turned, and he pushed the door open. He peered around it and saw her on a blanket on the floor in front of the television. She lay very still in leggings and a baggy sweater. His heart gave an uncomfortable lurch.

"Nancy?" he called quietly. She did not respond.

From the television came instructions given in a gentle voice by a middle-aged woman in nurse's whites. Jave recognized the routine demonstrated by a young couple as a relaxation exercise in the Lamaze program.

He knelt down beside her and noticed with relief the gentle rise and fall of her breasts. She lay on her side, her head on a pillow, a pillow also between her knees.

Jave smiled as he listened to the instructions from the film she'd apparently borrowed from the hospital. It encouraged complete relaxation. It seemed Nancy had mastered that. She was asleep.

Nancy heard voices, but the images she saw didn't necessarily relate to the words being spoken.

"Take a moment to scan your body," the gentle voice said, "for a part that remains tense."

But the artfully misty pictures she saw were of herself in something long and white and silky in the arms of a man in a white uniform. He stroked her as the soothing voice suggested, but his movements were long and erotic and she moved even more closely into his arms.

He whispered her name. She twined her arm around his neck and pulled him closer.

Jave had no idea what was happening. He knew only that it jangled his nerves enough to scramble thought.

Eyes still closed, dark lashes fanned against cheeks slightly pink with sleep, Nancy curled an arm around the one he'd braced across her to assure himself that she was breathing. With it, she pulled herself up higher and curled her other arm around his neck. She smelled of that floral shampoo and baby powder.

He might have handled that with aplomb, but then she touched her parted lips to his cheek and ran them in a series of little kisses from his ear to the corner of his eye.

He held tightly to his fraying self-control. Did she truly have a husband? Did she think he was him home from sea?

Then she did the one thing that could have snapped his control. She whispered his name.

Nancy felt the firm, smooth cheek under her lips, the strong arms holding her securely, and leaned back to look into his eyes. They were shadowy with the green and gold of all that was precious in nature—all that was becoming precious to her. "Jave!" she whispered.

When she moved her lips to his, Jave was lost. He bent a knee to brace her as he held her firmly in the crook of his arm and helped her have her way with him. Her lips nipped at his then kissed him, angled as she inclined her head and nibbled gently. Then he felt the tip of her tongue dip into his mouth and met it with his own.

They sparred, explored, withdrew, then tangled again to finally draw apart and lean forehead to forehead, gasping for breath.

Nancy knew instantly that something was wrong. It wasn't that it felt wrong—it felt wonderful. But it was a flaw in the pattern she'd grown used to. She felt warm, secure, cosseted. Something was out of tune.

Then she became aware of sinewy arms around her, of a strong shoulder under her head, of flesh against the flesh of her cheek—smooth, suedelike male flesh!

She shoved Jave away with such force that he would have fallen backward if he hadn't been so determined to keep a firm grip on her.

"What are you doing?!" she demanded as she struggled awkwardly to get to her knees. He tried to help her and she shook him off. Her cheeks were crimson now, her eyes blazing. "Don't touch me!"

Jave's instincts told him her response wasn't from the indignation she pretended, but from anger at herself for being caught in such a vulnerable position.

"Easy, Mrs. Malone," Jave said, on his knees a mere foot from her. "It was all your fault."

"*My* fault!" she disputed. "I was asleep. You took advantage—"

"I did no such thing," he denied. "You didn't respond to my knock. I looked in to check and found you on the floor—not moving. I came over, you...must have been dreaming...and the next thing I knew..." He grinned unabashedly. "You kissed me."

"I—did—not!" she insisted in breathy denial.

"I'm afraid you did."

YOU DID, MOM. I heard you. And I shared the dream. It was him. He's got you.

NANCY COULD FEEL the heat in her cheeks. She remembered the dream very clearly, the absolutely vivid reality of it. And little wonder. She'd apparently been living it at the same time. And in her dream she'd been very much the instigator.

She tried desperately to explain herself. "I...I haven't been sleeping well," she said, trying to balance her awkward weight as she pushed herself up. "I must have mistaken you for...for Jerry."

Jave stood lightly and supported her unsteady rise to her feet. The grin vanished and his eyes were deadly serious. "You called me Jave," he said.

She had no idea how to explain that she'd been dreaming of him. Feeling completely off balance, and needing desperately to regain precious ground lost in her "married woman" fiction, Nancy did the only thing she could think of—she made it clear she considered this all his fault.

"You invaded my home!" she accused. "What are you doing here anyway?"

"It's my day off," he replied calmly. "I came to help Tom clean the gutters and put up the new one."

So he did have a good reason. Sort of. She folded her arms over the mound of her stomach and tried to look imperious. She could feel that her hair was atumble and her cheeks warm. "The gutters," she said coolly, "are located *outside*."

Neither her tone nor her manner seemed to impress him. He continued to look amused and somehow pleased. "Tom asked me to tell you we were here."

"Very well," she said. "Thank you. I'll have coffee ready when the two of you take a break."

Jave's eyes swept the living room as he walked to the door. Tom was right, he noted. Not one photograph.

He had an opportunity to check the kitchen an hour and a half later when she invited them inside for coffee. She made a point of chatting cheerfully to Tom and excluding Jave from the conversation. So he let his gaze wander around the room. No pictures. Not a single sign that a man lived here.

The wall of the mudroom was visible from where he sat, and he could see a small pair of grubby sneakers, several non-gender-specific gardening tools and a very large sack of cat food.

No men's sneakers, no baseball cap, no black umbrella.

He caught a glimpse of the pink bedroom when Tom suggested he change a weak light bulb in the hallway before they left. No photos there, either. The closet door was slightly ajar, but the interior remained shadowy, its contents indistinguishable.

He thought, though, that he'd seen enough to give credence to Tom's theory. No man lived here.

Tom was packing up the truck when Jave carried the step stool back into the kitchen, then headed for the front door. He found Nancy on the blanket again, doing the exercises according to the video's instructions. She continued, unaware that he watched.

He approached her and squatted down just behind her. "Excuse me," he said. "But you're not doing that quite right."

Nancy jumped in surprise, then sat up in annoyance. She clearly hadn't forgiven him for that kiss, which pleased him inordinately. "How do you know?" she asked. "Don't tell me radiology also teaches Lamaze classes."

He put a hand to her shoulder and pushed her gently back to the pillow again, repositioning her so that she lay on her side, her knees tucked up so that she was almost in a sitting position.

"Of course not." He touched the base of her spine. She felt heat fill her face and was grateful she was turned away from him. "You're not relaxing completely," he cautioned, "and it's essential to the method. I went through the classes with my ex-wife before Pete was born. Classes are held in a hospitality room at the hospital, you know. I think that would be easier for you than trying to figure it out from a video."

"Participation in classes," she said, "requires a partner. And mine is somewhere down the coast."

"The important thing here," he said, running a fingertip gently from the base of her neck to her waist, "is to learn to relax completely to ease the pain."

Nancy felt that deceptively innocent fingertip touch every vertebra in her spinal column. Feeling rayed in every direction and she fidgeted, thinking it was no wonder it was called the "nervous" system.

"A friend can serve as your coach. Or stand in for your husband so that you at least can get the benefit of the classes."

He spoke casually—too casually, Nancy thought. He knew she didn't have any friends. He was the one who'd brought her home from the hospital, seen that her roof was repaired, saved her desk chair. She didn't know what to make of his suggestion. Actually, she thought she did, but it seemed safer to deny it to herself.

She pushed herself to a sitting position and then had to prop herself there with a hand to the floor. "Thank you, Jave. I'll see about it."

He got to his feet and offered her both his hands. She could struggle up on her own; she did it often. But at almost seven months along, it wouldn't be pretty. And there was something about the simple, solid pleasure of his hand wrapping around hers that she couldn't deny herself.

She placed her fingers in his and felt his tighten around hers as he brought her effortlessly up. The protrusion of her stomach bumped lightly against the waist of his jeans as he steadied her. The baby kicked. She blushed. He grinned.

"Jave Nicholas," she said with a scolding frown. She tried to imbue her voice with displeasure, but its high breathlessness negated the effort. It sounded husky and flustered. His watchfulness had unsettled her from the moment she'd answered Amy's questions about a husband and discovered him standing in the doorway.

But there was something about him today that betrayed more than simple suspicion. He seemed to think he knew something. And he was enjoying taunting her with the possibility.

She had to prove him wrong. Even though he was right.

"Your behavior," she said with a tilt of her chin and what she hoped was frosty, matronly displeasure, "is inappropriate."

The arm he'd cupped around her to steady her remained in place. "You mean your husband would disapprove?" he asked.

"Of course he would," she replied, pushing at his chest. "But what's more important to your physical health at the moment is that *I* disapprove. Now remove your arm."

He smiled amiably. "Can't do that."

She continued to brace his chest away from her with the flat of her hand. "And why is that?"

"Well, it's attached to my body," he replied with bland innocence. "You know, tendons, muscles, messy stuff. I could ampu—"

She closed her eyes, drew a breath for patience, then opened them again. "I mean, remove your arm from around *me*."

He looked into her glare, his suddenly gentle, amusing mood filtering through her determined solitude, reaching inside her. She stiffened, resisting its effect.

"You know," he said quietly, "I'm beginning to think you're attached to me, too, in a very similar way. No muscles or tendons, of course, but stuff that seems to be just as hard to sever. I think I'm going to stop trying."

Excitement and panic grappled with each other in Nancy's chest. Even the baby must have felt the conflict. Nancy felt a kick to her side.

Then she thought desperately of her five-piece Thomasville nursery set, her chocolate, her movies, her clothes...the hospital's reaction should anyone there ever suspect what Jave suspected.

I DON'T KNOW, MOM. Do we really need furniture and chocolate if we could have him instead?

SHE HAD TO TURN the suspicion aside firmly once and for all. "If you don't unhand me this minute," she said, thinking absently that she sounded remarkably like Bette Davis, "I'll call my husband tonight, then I'll call the hospital administrator and report your conduct."

The ruse might have been convincing, Jave thought, if she'd been drawing away from him instead of leaning into the arm she claimed to find so offensive. If the hand at his chest had been pushing him away instead of clutching at his shirt.

"Where is your husband?" Jave asked conversationally.

Her jaw firmed and her eyes flashed. "I told you. He's off the California coast."

"Where?"

"Southern California."

"Long Beach?"

Nancy knew he was trying to lay some kind of trap for her and she found herself less mentally nimble than she wished.

"I'm not sure now," she said, careful to meet his eyes and keep her own level. "He hasn't called me in a few days. They must be some distance from port."

"Well, what if you go into labor? Certainly there's some procedure to follow to get in touch with him."

Before she could dredge up a convincing lie, Tom appeared in the doorway. "All done, Nancy. Ready, Jave?"

Nancy pulled away from Jave and raised a finger at Tom, indicating that he should wait. "I'll send some bread pudding home for you and Aggie."

Tom mouthed a ha-ha in Jave's direction when Nancy disappeared into the kitchen. She returned with two square plastic containers. She handed one to Tom and the other to Jave.

"These are for your boys," she said, a dark glance making it clear she'd included none for him.

He suddenly remembered a last minute request from Pete when he'd left that morning. "The boys wondered if you'd give me the recipe for the Russian tea. They're addicted and we've run out."

She nodded. "Of course. I'll send it to you so you don't have to wait for me to copy it down." She smiled at Tom. "Thank you. That's all the budget will allow for a while, but when that changes, I'll call you about replacing the kitchen floor covering."

"Great. Thanks for the bread pudding."

"Sure. Say hi to your mom."

Jave let the door partially close as Tom headed across the grass toward his truck. Then he turned to face Nancy.

Nancy didn't like the look in his eye. Her threats about her husband and a call to the hospital administration didn't seem to have affected it. He still appeared indulgently superior.

"Is there anything you'd like to tell me, Nancy?" he asked gently. "Last chance."

She smiled sweetly. "Why, yes. Get out."

He gave her a tolerantly scolding look. "I meant anything about yourself. Possibly something that would save us undue embarrassment later."

"There *is* something you should know about me," she said, reaching around him to pull the door wide. She placed a hand on his chest and began to push him backward. Considering her condition, he chose not to resist. "I've read everything Stephen King ever wrote, even the *Bachman Books*. My mother is neurotic, my great grandfather spent time in Taunton—"

"Taunton?"

"It's a state hospital in Massachusetts." They had reached the porch steps and she clutched the front of his shirt in a fist. "And centuries ago, I had an uncle who was an executioner in the Tower of London." She stood on tiptoe until they were nose-to-nose. "In a nutshell, Nicholas, it isn't safe to mess with me. Now, I've been nice about this because you saved my chair and you have a wonderful family. But don't push it. I do not want to see you again, but if our paths should cross, don't you ever touch me again, or when my husband returns, he will make a puree of your arms and legs—and anything else that offends me." She released his shirt and stepped back. "Now, goodbye!"

Jave smiled to himself all the way to the truck. By the time he climbed inside, he was laughing.

Tom, who'd watched the scene from behind the wheel, looked worried. "What in the hell was that all about? It looked as though she was chewing you out royally."

Jave buckled his seat belt, still laughing. "She did."

"What brought that on?"

"She kissed me."

"What?"

"It's a long story."

"I want to hear every word. Did you ask her about her husband?"

"She insists she has one," Jave said, rolling down his window and taking a deep draft of warm, sunny afternoon. "And told me never to darken her door again."

Tom frowned. "So that's it? It's over?"

Jave leaned an elbow on the open window and looked at his brother with a broad grin. "Hell, no, Thomas. It's just beginning."

Chapter Seven

The day after the...episode with Jave—she wouldn't call it a kiss because she'd been asleep when it had begun and infuriated when it was over, and that didn't seem to fit within the parameters of what a kiss should be—Nancy received a call from Amy, another pair of footlets from April and a basket of goodies from her mother.

"I just thought you'd like to know," Amy said, enthusiastically breathless, "that Atkins Auto has donated a top-of-the-line infant seat to our program, and Heron Point Fitness is giving you three months' free use of the facility after the baby's born. Isn't that great?"

Nancy tried to project several months ahead to a time when she would be enthusiastic about exercise. She couldn't quite do it. She was now beginning to feel seriously ungainly and unattractive, and was happy to simply walk slowly up and down the beach, where she wouldn't be seen.

"How nice," she replied, forcing interest into her voice. It was easier when she thought about the infant seat. "How's the work coming on the rooms?"

"Good. The curtains are lost somewhere between here and the warehouse in Buffalo, but we can't put them up for another month and I have faith the freight company will find them by then. How are you feeling?''

"Wonderful," she said. Generally it was true. She attributed a fairly new lethargy to...well, she wasn't sure what, but she was sure she could talk herself out of it as soon as she had the energy.

"Is your husband excited about being married to the Riverview Hospital Model Mommy, so to speak?"

"Oh...he's delighted." Nancy worked harder on the enthusiasm now. She could remember clearly Jave's skeptical face when he'd held her to him the day before and wondered if he'd shared any of his doubts with Amy. It didn't sound as though he had.

"Do you think we'll be able to get a picture of him before he comes home for the birth?"

Nancy winced. "I doubt he'll be able to put in an appearance before the *Courageous* comes back in the middle of September."

"Do you have a snapshot we can use?"

Nancy's heart lurched. She thought fast. "I'll try to find it, Amy, but you know, some of our stuff is in storage, and a lot of things I haven't unpacked yet, and I'm not supposed to move anything too heavy...."

"Of course," Amy said quickly. "Don't do anything to endanger yourself, for heaven's sake. We'll manage just featuring you and *talking* about him."

"That...would probably be best."

The footlets from April had arrived in a manila envelope with a note shaped like a teddy bear. "Hi, Nancy!" it said. "Housekeeping found these under your bed after you left, so I took them home and washed them, thinking you'd like to have an extra pair. Don't forget that I'm a *great* baby-sitter. Love, April. P.S. If your mom and

Willy Brock ever come to visit, please find an excuse to invite me over."

Nancy smiled as she folded the note away and studied the enormous basket from her mother. It was typically overdone—a huge, ornate affair decorated with patterned tissue paper within embossed cellophane with a giant pink bow tied to the handle.

Contained inside was every kind of gourmet treat to nibble on—from smoked oysters to sugar wafers. Attached was a card. "Since you won't let me come and 'mother' you, I'm sending this in my place. Love, Mom."

Nancy felt guilt and aggravation in equal measure, and wished she was enough her own woman that neither would affect her. She dug around in the basket until she found a very large gold-foil-wrapped chocolate truffle. She stood in the middle of the living room, staring at the chair Jave had rescued for her, and ate the sweet. Then she found another one and ate it, too.

ALL RIGHT. *More?*

SHE WAS FEELING PURSUED. Even cornered. How had this happened to her? she wondered. She'd moved thirty-three hundred miles across the country to start over on her own, and somehow, a brief two months into it, she was hearing from her mother more than she had in years, she had acquired an unusual collection of nice but nosy friends, and she'd backed into a place in the spotlight that promised great things for her baby, but might still prove to be her undoing.

And then there was Jave. She didn't know what to do about him except hope that he went away. And that was hardly likely. He was a definite fly in the ointment of her role as the hospital's model mommy. That was bad. But it got even worse.

Nancy had to dig out a package of genuine Scottish shortbread cookies and make a cup of tea before she could even let herself consider this part.

THAT WASN'T BAD, but what happened to the chocolate?

SHE THOUGHT ABOUT Jave Nicholas all the time. He seemed to be everything she'd thought she was getting when she'd married Jerry. Despite a tendency to unsettle her, he was kind and thoughtful, and a man who was apparently willing to go the extra mile for someone else in need. And he made her smile, though she usually didn't give him the satisfaction of doing it in front of him.

She ran a hand over her desk chair and thought about the abuse it had taken in the back of her truck exposed to the rain. Yet he'd practically restored it.

He was kind to his mother, helped his brother, and his children seemed to love him.

But those weren't the qualities that had kept her awake last night and occupied her mind this morning.

She remembered in minute detail what it had been like to awaken in his arms and feel his lips on hers. In fact, with very little effort, she could reconstruct the moment with all its confusion and wonder and sense of deliciously dangerous security.

She understood that thought for the paradox it was. She didn't know how danger could make her feel secure, but it did. His warm, mobile lips on hers had made her feel open and vulnerable, yet the tender competence with which he used them, the gentle strength of the arms that held her, told her with absolute certainty that she could entrust herself to him and be safe—physically, if not emotionally.

And that was at the heart of her anxieties today. She'd come to Oregon to be alone with her baby. To trust herself to bring this baby to life and good health without having to depend on anyone. To raise it alone without the interference or the support everyone else seemed to crave.

She didn't want to be tempted to trust. It never worked out for her.

Well, it was time to do something about it. As a step toward the life she envisioned alone with her baby, she picked up the stack of neatly printed pages on her desk and inspected them one more time. They contained a complete synopsis of her novel, the first three chapters and a cover letter to a Los Angeles agent whose name she'd found in the Northwest Mystery Writers' newsletter at the library.

Confident that this was her best work, that her letter was intelligent and coherent and hopefully witty enough to stand out in the glut of mail the agent probably received, Nancy placed everything in the envelope she'd addressed, placed her palm on it and said a small prayer, then went out to the truck to drive to the post office.

She stopped in her tracks halfway across the yard. Shaman sat on the hood of her truck, dozing lazily in the sunlight. She'd never seen him in the front of the house before; he'd always stayed on the slope in the back. Did this mean he was beginning to feel at home? He was the only one with whom she'd consider sharing her environment besides the baby.

"Shaman?" she called softly, taking small, slow steps.

He sprang tensely to his feet, eyes wide and alarmed.

"Shaman," she chided gently. "Come on. Hasn't this gone on long enough? I've been feeding you for weeks now. Isn't it time... ?"

Apparently he didn't think so. He leaped to the grass in a swift and graceful arch and disappeared around the back of the house.

Nancy sighed and climbed into the truck, shaking her head over the sandy pawprints on her hood.

"CAN I HAVE ANOTHER Frosty?" Eddy asked.

Jave and Eddy sat side by side on the Heron Point Park bleachers, watching the Turner Plumbing Turtles take the field against the Roundhouse Restaurant Rattlers. Jave frowned into the late-afternoon sun, trying to spot number 23 as the tiny athletes ran out to distribute themselves in the fragrant, manicured grass.

The father who coached the team, a saint in Jave's estimation, placed them all carefully, talking and laughing as he worked his way around the bases, then pep-talked the pitcher and the catcher.

"No," Jave replied. "You've already had two and the game hasn't even started yet."

"There he is." Eddy pointed to his brother, who appeared to be all ball glove and hat.

"Right field," Jave said.

"Yeah," Eddy said with a snicker. "Where nothing ever happens."

Jave remembered that he'd once reacted to Tom with the same older-brother superiority, so he admonished gently, "You know, he could really use your support in this, Ed. You've been on a winning team three years running. He admires you. I think he'd like to know you come to cheer him on and not to criticize him."

"He's a dweeb, Dad," Eddy said with no particular condemnation, but simply as though it were a fact. "And look at that. How can you cheer for someone who isn't even thinking about the game?"

Jave choked back a laugh at the sight of his youngest, twirling with arms outstretched like a whirling dervish. He seemed to be in his own little world, fielding the ball apparently the last thing on his mind.

Around the field, various itches were being scratched, shoes were being tied, imaginary foes being swung at with imaginary weapons.

Eddy shook his head with a veteran's concern. "I hope the other team's not any good."

At that the first of the Rattlers took the plate, shouldered his bat, then adjusted what appeared to be a very aggressive pair of underwear.

Eddy collapsed in giggles against Jave, who struggled valiantly not to join him.

"THE OTHER GUYS WON," Pete said later, "because they had a better name. Rattlers are tougher than Turtles."

The boys sat at the kitchen table in their pajamas while Jave made the last two servings of Russian tea.

"You better not let Michelangelo and Leonardo hear you say that," Eddy said. "They won because they have more nine-year-olds. You guys are shrimpy."

Pete seemed too depressed to argue. Jave remembered that Eddy had taken his first loss in much the same way. Life was full of hard lessons.

"I'm gonna watch 'The X-Files,' " Eddy said. He took his tea and reached up to kiss Jave good-night.

Jave leaned down to hug him and caught a whiff of the tea the boys had come to like so much. "Can I have a sip of that?" he asked.

"Sure." Eddy offered up the mug. "It's good stuff."

Jave sipped, found it flavorful if a little sweet, and handed back the cup. "I asked Nancy for the recipe. She promised to send it."

"Oh, yeah." Eddy delved into his pocket and produced a crumpled envelope. "We met her at the post office today, and she gave me this instead of mailing it." He handed it to Jave, picked up the package of cookies they'd been sharing, tucked it under his arm, and headed for the stairs. "Night," he said.

Jave grabbed the back of the cookie package and pulled it neatly away. "Good night," he replied.

Eddy gave him a good-natured grin and went on.

Jave turned his attention to Pete, who leaned his chin on one hand and hooked the index finger of the other in the handle of his cup. He looked for all the world like a Wall Street financier faced with a repeat of Black Friday.

"It's bad to lose," Pete said. "Mr. Walker says it doesn't matter, but all the guys say it's bad."

"It's only bad to lose," Jave corrected, sitting in the ladder-back chair beside him, "if you lost because you didn't try. But that's not what happened tonight. You guys tried really hard. But this summer is the first time you've all played together. It takes time to become a team—sometimes a couple of seasons. Everybody knows that."

Pete sighed deeply and loudly. "That ball came right to me and I couldn't catch it, so that other big kid made a point. I didn't do very good."

"That was a pretty big kid," Jave said. "The ball was coming hard. You'll learn to be ready, to stand so that you're loose when you catch a ball and ready to throw it back."

Pete sipped his tea and rubbed his bare feet together. Jave was reminded of a cricket—one in a brightly striped bathrobe.

"Maybe I don't want to play anymore."

Jave hated working out win-and-lose issues with the boys. He had a laid-back attitude about the whole business himself, but though he didn't care if they won or lost, he wanted to raise children who were willing to compete.

"Then you won't lose anymore, but you sure won't win, either."

There was a moment's heavy silence, then Pete took a big sip of tea and changed the subject. "I know what's going to happen when Nancy has her baby."

Interested, Jave asked, "What?"

"If her truck doesn't start, she's going to call a taxi to take her to the hospital."

"She is?"

"Yup. That's what she said. But Grandma said she should call *us*."

Jave waved the envelope he held. "Did you talk about this when you saw her at the post office?"

Pete nodded. "This afternoon. Grandma was sending back her Publisher's Clearing House thing. She's going to buy me a motorcycle if she wins."

Doubting seriously that she *would* win, Jave felt confident in sharing his enthusiasm about the motorcycle. He propped the envelope up against the cat-shaped napkin holder in the middle of the table.

"Want a ride up to bed?" Jave asked. Before Bonnie left, he used to carry Pete up to bed on his shoulders every night. It had been a small but important ritual. But Pete had refused it since then.

Pete thought about it. "When the big kids play," he said gravely, "sometimes the guys who win get carried off the field."

Jave confirmed that with a nod.

Pete stood and carried his cup to the sink. "But nobody carries the losers."

A mild rebellion had been brewing in Jave most of the day. He'd been walking a careful line with many facets of his life. He'd been trying not to push Pete regarding his feelings about his mother; he'd been trying to let him unfold slowly and find his own feet in his adjustment.

And a similar situation had developed with Nancy. He'd found himself attracted to a woman who by all indications was pretending to have a husband, while still reacting to him, Jave, in a decidedly sexual way—and there seemed to be no pretending *there* at all. So he'd been acting like a man in a fog, afraid of losing himself with the wrong move.

Well, he was suddenly tired of it all.

He swept Pete off the floor and dangled him by his feet for a full ten seconds while the child first screamed, then giggled with unbridled hilarity. Then he turned him and swung him up onto his shoulders and walked upstairs with him.

"Anybody who tries is a winner," Jave said as they reached the landing and angled toward the top of the stairs. "And I love you. To me, you'll always be a winner."

Pete leaned over Jave's head as they ducked under the top of the door to his room. "Mom said I was too little to play baseball," he said.

Jave kept his surprise to himself. This was the first time Pete had brought up the subject of his mother.

"Well, that was last year," Jave observed, "when you *were* too little."

"I wish she could watch me play," he said wistfully. "I mean, if I could play better."

Jave tipped him onto the bed, then sat on the edge of it, looking down into the pensive brown eyes. "I'm sure she'd like to see you play. Only she's kind of far away right now."

"With that other guy."

"Yes."

Pete drew a deep breath and reached over to his bedside table for a Matchbox fire truck Tom had given him for his last birthday. He toyed with it while he thought.

"Do you think she'll have other kids?" he asked. "You know, like Nancy? Will she get . . . ?"

"Pregnant?" Jave asked. Curiously, he could find no jealousy in the thought. What he'd had with her seemed to be well and truly gone. "She might. But that doesn't mean she would love you any less."

"But she isn't *with* me," he said with what seemed to Jave to be eminent reasonableness. He found it difficult to argue. So he leaned on what he was sure to be true, though he couldn't really reconcile it to her actions.

"But she still loves you."

Pete put the truck down and gave him that very direct, adult look that told him he wasn't making sense.

"It's a little like you and the ball," Jave said, bracing himself on an arm on the other side of Pete's body. "You want to hit it. In your mind, you know what to do. But it's just hard to make it all come together. So you just do the best you can."

"But she quit, didn't she? You said you only lose if you quit."

This was the true parent trap, Jave thought. Snared by your own rhetoric.

"Well, sort of. She quit living with us. But she didn't quit loving you."

Pete frowned over that logic, then gave a mighty yawn. Jave pulled the covers out from under him then drew them up and tucked him in.

"Next game," he promised, "you'll do a little better. And the next one, you'll be better yet."

Pete turned onto his side, his eyelids growing heavy.

"You think Mom'll do any better?" he asked.

Jave knew it wouldn't be fair to tell him what he wanted to hear. "I don't think so," he said.

Pete settled into his pillow without another word. Jave stayed until he knew he was asleep.

JAVE'S OFFICE DOOR OPENED and Nurse Beacham walked in. She handed him the department's copy of the *Heron Point Herald*. "I know you'll want to read the sports page before I cut out the recipe on the back. Make it snappy. I'm off in ten minutes."

He smiled at her. "Such a gracious offer, Beachie. Thank you."

"No time for graciousness, Doctor," she said with a theatrical tilt of her head. "I have to save lives and stamp out disease."

He nodded gravely. "You're absolutely right. I'll have this back to you in ten minutes."

"That's a good doctor."

Jave covered the files on his desk with the small daily newspaper. National and local news, sports, comics and classifieds were all covered in twelve pages. He subscribed to the newspaper at home, but his mother usually commandeered it, so he enjoyed perusing the department's copy before he went home.

And this evening there was a very interesting item in it. Very interesting indeed. News that made him fold up the paper, reread the item, then pick up the phone while a small, calculating smile played at his lips.

It had been two weeks since he'd seen Nancy and convinced himself Tom was right—she had no husband. Since then, he'd been biding his time, waiting for just the right moment. And this was it.

"MRS. MALONE?"

"Yes." Nancy didn't recognize the voice on the other end of the telephone, but it had a professional telephone-voice sound. She braced herself, certain she was dealing with an operator somewhere who was about to connect her with her mother.

"This is Serena Borders. Your Lamaze classes are scheduled for Monday, August 15, from 7:00 to 8:30. I was asked to remind you."

Nancy frowned at the receiver. "But... I haven't enrolled for Lamaze classes."

The voice sounded puzzled. "Are you Nancy R. Malone?"

"Yes, but I haven't—"

"Of Box 73, Heron Point Road?"

"Yes."

"Your fee's been paid, Mrs. Malone, and you and your coach are scheduled to start next Monday."

Then a niggle of suspicion began to form in Nancy's mind. She remembered the Lamaze tape she'd borrowed from the library and Jave's suggestion that she take the class in person instead.

"What is my coach's name?" Nancy asked.

"What is your...?" the voice began to repeat, as though unable to imagine why Nancy was asking *her*. Then there was the sound of papers rustling and a terse reply. Now the voice really sounded puzzled. "J. V. Nicholas."

"Thank you," Nancy said. "I'll get back to you about this."

Temper, confusion and genuine concern billowed inside Nancy while she changed out of the sweats in which she'd been writing in all day. She glanced at the clock and decided she had time to shower and change and still be on time to give Jave Nicholas a piece of her mind.

WHAT'S HAPPENING, MOM? It feels like we're gearing up for battle. Please calm down. You're pinching my backside again. Why are we rocking? Whoa. Tights? Gasp! What happened to our sweats? Where are we going? Can you send down some Dramamine?

Chapter Eight

Jave was concentrating on his options for the evening as he walked out to the hospital's parking lot. Tom had taken the boys to Portland with him to pick up supplies and didn't expect to be home until late. His mother, free for the day, had gone to visit a friend on the Long Beach peninsula.

He could pick up dinner at the deli and rent a movie—something with sex and violence that he wouldn't want the boys to see, but that would remind him that somewhere deep inside he wasn't as civilized as his mother and his children thought he was.

He could go to the Y where there was usually a pickup basketball game in progress.

He could lie in the hammock in the backyard with a gin and tonic and remember the *River Lady*.

Each idea had something to recommend it, but it was another lady altogether whose plans changed his.

"You, James Victor Nicholas, can go to hell!" Nancy Malone delivered that suggestion quietly but with apparently heartfelt conviction. She was leaning against the driver's-side door of his truck in black tights and a crisp, long black-and-white top, her arms folded over her ample stomach.

She straightened and assumed a sort of battle stance, her arms at her sides, her fists clenched.

He'd never been quite so pleased with a reaction in his life.

"Nancy," he said, walking around her to open his door, toss in his jacket. The evening was breezy and fragrant, and he swore he could feel the life in it. "How nice of you to come to see me."

"I'm not here to *see* you," she corrected stiffly.

He grinned. "Then you'd better close your eyes, because I'm here."

She firmed her stance. "Don't play games with me, Nicholas."

The very words conjured up many fascinating mental images. His grin widened. "I guess we'll have to save those for a few months down the road. But we could still enjoy planning them."

She studied him a long moment, her eyes snapping and troubled, her cheeks pink, her nicely molded chin dimpled in consternation. He saw her struggle to remain calm. She folded her arms again.

"What are you doing?" she demanded.

He indicated the open door of his truck. "I'm going home. What are you doing?"

She closed her eyes impatiently. When she opened them again, she said with exaggerated quiet, "No. I mean what are you trying to do—to *me.*"

He gave her an innocent look. He'd learned it from the masters of the craft—his sons.

"Well, I've done a few things *for* you, but I wasn't aware of having done anything *to* you."

Her mouth slanted to a cynical angle. "Really. And who enrolled me in a Lamaze class?"

"I did," he replied readily.

"And who enrolled himself as my coach?"

He was quick and ingenuous again with his answer. "I did. But I don't understand—"

"Why did you do that?"

"You weren't doing very well with trying to teach yourself at home. So, I thought—"

She jabbed a finger at his chest, patience apparently deserting her. "And what gave *you* the right to think on my behalf?"

Several nurses walked by on the way to their cars. They turned their heads at her raised voice. Recognizing Jave, they smiled and moved on.

"Would you like to discuss this in my truck?" he asked Nancy politely.

"No, I would not," she replied curtly. "Just answer my question."

"All right." He reached into the truck to roll down the window and hooked an arm over it. "Well, there were several things," he said amiably. "First, I knew you'd get more out of the class. I mean, let's face it. You tried to do it with the tape at home and first you fell asleep, and then you had the position wrong. I'm a doctor after all. I'd like to see you do this right."

"Right," she echoed dryly. "Hippocratic oath and all that."

"Yes. That, and I hate the thought of you squishing your baby and getting me called in in the middle of the night."

She shifted her weight, her eyes dark with disbelief. "You listed yourself as my coach."

"That's right."

"Why?"

He gestured broadly with his free hand. "Your husband's somewhere off the California coast, remember?"

She looked into his eyes for any betrayal of duplicity. She couldn't find it. He was good.

"How do you think he'd feel about my lying in such intimate positions with my radiologist?" she demanded candidly, hoping to shake his ingenuousness.

"Probably much the same as your radiologist feels," he said quietly, "about you lying about your husband."

THERE GOES the furniture and the teddy-bear lamp. Don't admit anything, Mom. Maybe we can still save the chocolate.

SO THERE IT WAS. The words were out, right there in the parking lot, between her battered old truck and his shiny new model. She stared at him openmouthed for a moment as control of the conversation, the whole situation, began to slip away from her. But she grabbed for it and held on.

"What are you implying?" she demanded defensively.

Several visitors walking by turned interestedly in their direction.

He looked back at her evenly. "Why don't we talk about this in the truck?" he said. Then he walked around to the passenger side to open it for her without giving her an opportunity to refuse.

Insistently maintaining her pose, she stood her ground.

"I can't step up that high," she resisted. "And there isn't anything to say that can't be said in..."

As she spoke, he reached under the tarp in the back of the truck and removed a plastic kitchen step stool. He placed it on the ground on the passenger side and waited wordlessly for her to walk around.

She did, surprised despite herself by the amenity.

"My mother has difficulty climbing up that high, as well," he explained, "and I take her shopping regularly." He clasped Nancy's hand to help her up. With little alternative but to stand there holding his hand, she climbed inside.

Jave dropped the stool in the back then climbed behind the wheel.

With him beside her, confined in the small space of the truck cab, Nancy felt suddenly surrounded and strangled by the lie. But her baby had so much to gain from it that she would otherwise never have. So she took the offensive.

"What are you suggesting?" she asked, her eyes steady, her jaw set.

"I'm suggesting, Mrs. Malone," Jave replied, turning in his seat to face her, "that you come clean."

She angled her chin. "Whatever do you mean?"

Jave leaned a wrist on the steering wheel and sighed good-naturedly. "Where *is* your husband, Nancy?"

She replied in the same tone. "I've told you. They're off the Southern California coast somewhere."

"And when was the last time he called?"

She shrugged. "A week. They're often out of touch on that kind of a trip."

Jave inclined his head in a gesture of regret. "If that's true, you might want to examine the status of your relationship."

She frowned. "Why?"

"Because tonight's paper says the *Courageous* is at the San Diego shipyards. Been there for four days."

She tried quickly to save herself. "Oh, right. That problem with the engine. Jerry mentioned it."

Jave shook his head, almost apologetically. "No. It was the electrical system. Story was in the *Herald*."

Nancy stared at him for a full ten seconds while she absorbed the untenability of her position. She swore to herself, then simply sat in the corner of the richly uphol-stered seat and steamed.

"You set me up," she said finally, accusingly. "That was calculated entrapment!"

He nodded without apparent remorse. "And if lying about having a husband was the kind of thing that went to trial, this evidence might prove to be inadmissible. But it isn't."

"No," she said morosely, seeing the five-piece nursery set, the infant seat, the chocolate, slipping away. "It's just the kind of thing that'll go to the hospital administration and beat my baby out of her freebies."

Jave put the key in the ignition. "Not necessarily."

Nancy turned to look at him, tension high in her atti-tude and her eyes. "What do you mean?" she asked, warily.

Jave placed an arm on the back of the seat and leaned toward her until only inches separated them. "I mean," he said with theatrical menace, "that I'm willing to be quiet, but you'll have to be my personal slave, to fulfill *all* my desires, both practical and sexual, then agree to be sold at auction on the back streets of Marrakech when I'm finished with you, and promise not to write an exposé about me or discuss me on 'Geraldo.'"

Her eyes widened, first in horror, then in indignation at his audacity as she realized he was putting her on. And that glimpse of humor in him, coupled with the very real threat his knowledge of her deception presented, suc-ceeded in completely confusing her.

She slapped his arm. "This is no time to be funny!"

He pushed himself back behind the wheel and laughed softly at her over his shoulder. "Actually, it's time to have dinner," he said. "Do you have plans?"

She reached for the door handle. "Like I would have dinner with the man who just threatened to sell me on the back streets of Marrakech."

He turned the key and the engine growled smoothly— not at all like her old truck. He grinned boyishly. "I'm sure you know I wouldn't do that."

She pushed open the door.

"Unless you try to get out of the truck," he amended.

She looked back, slanted him a dry glance, and tried to calculate the best way down without the stool.

"But I *would* tell Amy that your husband doesn't exist," he said. "Or at least that you're no longer married to him. And she'll have to tell administration."

Nancy's heart thumped. When she turned to look at him, he was staring through the windshield, then he turned to meet her eyes, and she wondered what had ever made her think she'd seen humor there. He looked deadly serious.

"You wouldn't," she challenged.

He shrugged a shoulder. "You can believe that if you prefer."

She considered a moment, then pulled the door closed. There seemed little sense in tempting fate if there was an alternative.

"Good," he said, reaching around her to pull out her seat belt. "I appreciate a reasonable woman. Do you like pasta?"

"What about your family?" she asked, feeling the graze of his knuckles across her belly as he reached to tuck the belt into its lock.

"Mom's gone," he said, "and the boys are with Tom. It's just you and me."

Jave backed smoothly out of the parking spot, turned the big truck easily in a very narrow area, and turned toward the small road behind the hospital.

Nancy felt as though her life had taken a sudden and dangerous turn. She wanted to run away, and she wanted to run toward it. She settled quietly in her corner, seriously depressed. It wasn't like her to be indecisive.

CHEZ PASTA WAS HOUSED in a converted cannery on the waterfront. Distressed board and batten gave a trendy look to the walls of glass that looked out on the river, and the railed-in patio that was built over it. The decor was green and white, and a tall, barrel-chested man wearing a white apron over a white shirt and tie and black slacks was there to greet them.

"Jave!" The man gave Jave a hearty handshake then looked with undisguised interest at Nancy, obviously noting her condition.

"Nancy," Jave said, "this is my old high school buddy, John Barstow. John, Nancy Malone, a newcomer to Heron Point."

"Well . . ." John hesitated, obviously hoping for more of an explanation. When one wasn't immediately forthcoming, he bowed politely and said, "Welcome to Chez Pasta. Follow me. I saved Jave's favorite table." He took two menus from a rack near the door and led the way inside.

"I can't believe you did that," Nancy said under her breath as they trailed John to a table in the corner on the patio. "I came here looking for unsophisticated, small-town life and what do I find? Dinner reservations made on a car phone."

Jave took her elbow as they walked down three shallow steps. "But you didn't want an unsophisticated, small-town man, too, did you?" he asked.

"I didn't want *any* man," she muttered, then smiled a thank-you to John as he pulled out her chair.

"The usual cabernet?" John asked.

"No." Jave raised a questioning eyebrow at Nancy. "Mineral water?"

She nodded. "Please."

John went off and Jave smiled knowingly across the table. "I realize designer water is also a disappointment to you, but what can I say? Try as we do to keep it out, the modern depravities invade our idyllic—"

"All right, all right." She cut him off with a condemning look over the top of her menu. "I didn't mean that the way it sounded. I suppose a doctor has to have a cellular phone. It just made me forget where I was for a minute."

But not who she was, or the pickle she was in, she thought. She saw his eyes note that change in her expression.

"Relax," he said. "Dinner first, then you can confide in me over dessert."

"I don't want to confide in you," she said, looking back at her menu.

He smiled. "I know. But you probably don't want to lose all that baby stuff, either."

Nancy looked around, found that they were relatively isolated from the rest of the diners, and put her menu down. "You know," she said, anxious, desperate even, to regain the upper hand here. "*That* is blackmail. *I* could tell on *you!*"

He agreed without apparent concern. "If you were willing to give up all that baby stuff."

"You . . ."

John arrived with their water, interrupting her heated response. Jave calmly made suggestions from the long list of entrées that included every kind of pasta imaginable with a wider range of sauces than she had ever seen, even in Manhattan.

She finally ordered the more familiar pasta *Primavera,* while Jave ordered *Chichiglia* in marinara sauce.

She couldn't help her curiosity. "What is that?" she asked. "I didn't notice it on the menu."

"It's a very large shell stuffed with several cheeses," he explained, toasting her with his water. "I'll let you try one."

She did not toast him back. Sharing from another person's plate was an intimacy. She struggled against that recurring feeling of losing her grip on things.

"I'll spare you the need to worry about squealing," she said. "I'll call Amy Brown myself and tell her everything."

Jave looked into her eyes and saw through the heroic, vaguely martyred expression. He said cynically, "Right. And my mother's going to give up bingo."

Nancy's temper began to blow. "Nicholas, what century are you from? You think you can calmly threaten me with blackmail, and I'm going to sit by and—"

This time John interrupted with Caesar salads. He looked in concern from one to the other. "Is everything all right?"

Nancy smiled up at their host. "They would be better if you'd move Mr. Nicholas to another table."

John winced at Jave.

"Isn't she charming?" Jave asked with a forbearing grin. "Everything's fine, John. Thank you."

John walked away with a concerned look at them over his shoulder.

Jave pushed a bowl of freshly grated Parmesan cheese in Nancy's direction. "Considering your position," he said, "you might try to be more courteous."

"Blackmail," she replied, spooning cheese onto her salad, "doesn't inspire courtesy." But he was right. Unless she truly was willing to tell Amy the truth and risk everything, she had to know what he intended to do. She picked up her fork and measured him with a look. "You said you might be willing to be quiet," she reminded him.

He had unsettled her. He could see it in her eyes, and he was pleased about that. He maintained a neutral expression, trying to keep the upper hand.

"I might," he confirmed. "But I would need to be assured of your cooperation."

Nancy studied him another moment, trying to see beyond the courteous distance he maintained between them. She had no idea where this was going, and she was more than a little uneasy. So far, except for a little mild teasing and a kiss she'd precipitated, he'd been the epitome of kindness and gentleness.

But his willingness to be quiet about her single status suggested that all that could change—depending on what he wanted in return. She had to make a few things clear—and risk losing the precious gifts in the process.

She put her fork down and pinned him with grave, dark eyes. "Let me assure you of a few *other* things first," she said quietly. "You're right. I am single. But I was married when I conceived this baby, and even though the baby and I have been thrown over for a role in a sitcom with a thirty share, I still have a high opinion of myself and big plans for this baby." She drew a deep breath as though that had taken courage. She pushed the cheese back toward him. "So, don't think I'd be willing to do anything foolish or . . . stupid, just to keep the gifts. Because I wouldn't."

He knew precisely what she meant by foolish and stupid, and nothing like that had crossed his mind. Well, it had, but not in relation to the issue of Amy's extravaganza.

"I was kidding," he said, "about using you as a personal slave and sending you to Marrakech."

A little pleat formed over the bridge of her nose. "Then what do you want?"

"I want you to eat your salad." Forestalling her with a shake of his head when she would have insisted on an answer, he pointed to her plate. "We'll talk about it over dessert. Eat."

But John joined them for dessert and regaled Nancy with tales of Jave in their high school days.

"He'd gotten a job bussing tables at the Elmore Pier Restaurant in our junior year. In the meantime, he got a date with Ginger Busfield—" he waggled his eyebrows expressively "—so he sent me to work in his place."

"What happened?" Nancy asked, having difficulty imagining Jave as young and irresponsible.

"He was fired," John said, laughing, "and I was introduced to a restaurant kitchen." He waved a hand toward the crowd of diners inside. "And it's become my life. As far as I'm concerned, Jave owns this table personally." John slapped the edge of the table with the flat of his hand and all the crockery shook. He looked at the last few crumbs of Nancy's sour-cream cake. "Another dessert?"

She groaned and shook her head. "Please. The baby's begging for mercy."

WHO, ME? No, I'm not. Send down more, but skip the mineral water.

JAVE PUSHED his chair back. "Well, maybe we'd better take her for a walk." He handed his credit card to John and pulled out Nancy's chair.

Nancy pushed herself up, and Jave reached an arm around her waist to help her the last few inches. She had to lean into him to slip out of the small space between table and chair. Attraction crackled, but she pretended otherwise as she thanked him and excused herself to visit the ladies' room.

The evening was balmy and blue as they crossed Chez Pasta's lawn to the narrow path that ran most of the length of the river from one edge of town to the other.

Jave took her hand and looped it through his arm, then put his hand in his pocket. "Your husband was an actor?" he asked without preamble.

She'd never wanted to talk about him again, but she knew Jave was finally getting down to business about his keeping-quiet offer, and that she *did* want to settle.

"Yes," she replied, letting her eyes rove the wild, weedy grass that bordered the bank of the river. There were no freighters on the water tonight, just the beautiful arch of the bridge that connected Heron Point to the Long Beach peninsula. Its undulating lines were soothing somehow. "I was writing for 'New York Nights.' Have you ever seen it?"

Jave shook his head. "Sorry."

She shrugged a shoulder. "Doesn't matter. It's a late-night television show about celebrities and New York lifestyles. Anyway, I was trying to write for sitcoms on the side, and Jerry was having auditions every other day."

Jave glanced down at her profile and saw its usual softness stiffen with anger—or was it pain? He wasn't sure.

"We both had high hopes and had decided not to have children for a while so that we could devote ourselves to these careers we wanted so much." A glistening cormorant stood on a piling with its wings outspread and Nancy stopped to admire it. "Why do they do that?" she asked, distracted from her memories. "Are they preening or something?"

He laughed softly. "Nobody seems sure, but there are a couple of theories. One is that they're drying their wings, which are not waterproof. Another is that that's a resting pose that helps their digestion after they've gorged on fish."

"They look like something out of a science-fiction story. Like that's really a cape and they're part man, part bird."

"Must be that imagination that makes you a writer. Far as I know, they're all bird. No man involved."

Nancy gave him a wry smile as she started off along the trail again. "Sometimes I feel that way about myself. All dodo, no man involved."

He pinched her fingers punitively. "You put me more in mind of a goose when you talk like that," he said. "And the 'no man involved' element is about to undergo a change. You were telling me about Jerry."

"Change?"

"Jerry," he prompted. "Finish the story."

With a sigh, she continued. "He got the part of Drago in 'Delta Diary' the same day that I learned our birth control failed and I was pregnant. He told me he loved me, but he couldn't love 'it' when it got in the way of his choices."

The wind began to pick up as the sun slipped toward the horizon. Jave moved his arm to put it around her, suspecting she needed support as well as warmth.

"And you?" he asked.

"I," she said, her voice reflecting surprise, "was already sure I was carrying a girl and felt this weird disassociation from everything else I'd ever wanted and suddenly wanted only her...." She splayed her hand over her stomach and rubbed in a circular motion. She shook her head, feeling as though that had all been a century ago. "I'd made a lot of concessions in our marriage because I thought, deep down, we both wanted each other more than we wanted anything else. But, when Jerry couldn't accept this baby, when it was not only part of him but part of me, it occurred to me that maybe he didn't love me as much as he claimed. Anyway, here I am."

WAY TO GO, Mom. Thanks.

NANCY LAUGHED SOFTLY and glanced up at Jave. "She just rubbed against my hand. I wonder if she knows I'm talking about her?"

"I think you should pick out a boy's name, too," Jave warned indulgently. "Just to be on the safe side. Bonnie was sure Pete was a girl and he's definitely not."

She shook her head adamantly. "That would be hedging bets and an indication of weak faith. I'm carrying Malia Rose."

Jave remembered the ultrasound again and smiled. "All right. But don't say I didn't warn you. Pretty name anyway."

She stopped to look up at him. He stopped, too, expression bland.

"Did the baby turn around while you were testing me?" she asked, her eyes bright with that possibility. "Do you know?"

It drew a smile from deep inside him. "Yes," he replied.

"And I'm right, aren't I?"

"You said you didn't want to know."

"That's right. I don't." She hooked her arm in his of her own volition this time and drew him along. "I know. I'm sure."

"Nothing is ever sure," he said. "That's what makes life an adventure."

"That's why you have to believe in *yourself,*" Nancy insisted. "I'm sure. It's a girl."

"Or a boy who's not going to be happy being called Malia." Jave smiled and walked alongside her around the point that had given the town its name, then up the bay. "Getting tired?" he asked.

"No." She was discovering that she rather liked walking arm in arm with him, even when she had no idea what he intended to do about her married-woman deceit. "In New York, I walked this far from the subway to the office. But the view wasn't this spectacular, of course." Then she said brightly, "Oh, look! A marina."

She began walking a little faster.

"You like boats?" he asked.

"I *love* them," she said. "Well, I mean, I love to look at them. The only boat I've ever been on is the Staten Island Ferry. But I've always thought I'd love to lie on the deck in nothing at all and soak up the sun." She looked up into his speculative expression and added quickly, "Unpregnant, of course, and far away from shore."

He smiled. "Tom and I have a boat here."

"You do? Where?"

They approached the docks where several dozen boats bobbed at their moorings. The harbormaster waved from his shack and Jave waved back. "At the other end. We just bought it. A fixer-upper." As they walked the length of the dock he told her about the *River Lady*. "And we've missed her ever since. Now, we're both getting ahead enough to get something economical. Frankly, it was more economical than I had in mind, but Tom forms these attachments to things.... There she is. The *Mud Hen*."

Nancy looked in the direction Jave pointed and spotted the boat—and felt her heart melt. It reminded her somehow of a seagoing version of *The Little Engine That Could*. She'd just bought the book and several others for the baby in the used bookstore. The story of the little engine that struggled valiantly against impossible odds and *won*, seemed important to own.

When she'd been living in New York and competing with the literary world's clever and sophisticated minds, she'd eschewed such philosophy as saccharine. But now that she had a little life inside her, she had a different perspective. She wanted very much to believe that the human spirit could triumph over all obstacles.

She went toward the platform to board the boat, and Jave loped ahead to help her on.

"We can't go below," he said, stopping her as she headed for the stairs. "Tom has it all torn apart and you might trip over something." He pointed out the large tear in the deck's planking. "And watch the hole."

"It's beautiful," she said with a sincerity that surprised and touched him. Then she asked almost apologetically, "But is it seaworthy?"

He made a so-so gesture with his hand. "Valid concern. It will be by the time Tom's finished. You really like it?"

"Yes," she replied, surprised that he seemed surprised. "Don't you?"

He leaned against the rail to look at the hillside and the lights just going on in the homes that dotted it. "Well, sort of. Because Tom loves it, and working on it is starting to bring him back."

She leaned beside him. "Back from where?" Her voice was quiet. She knew there was a story of some kind attached to Tom.

Jave explained about the old hotel fire, about the loss of Tom's friend and about the girlfriend who'd abandoned him and was only now trying to reenter his life.

"There was no woman crying?" Nancy asked quietly.

Jave shook his head. "He didn't find anyone. But I guess a fire can cause a lot of strange noises. Anyway, the floor also gave way under him, but he was able to catch himself. His right leg is badly burned and hard to look at," he said. Then he added with a quick glance at her, "Not because it's ugly, but because it hurts to know he suffered that. He thinks no woman will want to live with a limb like that. And, though he's built another career for himself, he was a fireman at heart. He thinks he's lost a lot of things that make him less than he was."

Nancy responded to his brotherly concern. She'd longed for a sibling throughout her childhood, but only now, as an adult, was she beginning to realize how much comfort and support a brother or sister could be as one faced life with parents gone and lovers fled.

"The right woman will make him see that isn't true," she said encouragingly. "A year isn't very long to recover from something so traumatic."

Jave nodded. "I'll explain to my family. My mother wants him married and his wife pregnant by Christmas."

Nancy giggled. Maternally aggressive Aggie was such a cheerful thought.

Silence fell between them. Dusk began to settle over the harbor, darkening the quiet water and turning the gentle slope of the hillside purple. The antique globed lights that marked the road and rimmed the marina bloomed to life, and a small green-and-white fishing boat turned off the river into the marina, coming home.

"Are you divorced?" Jave asked.

She nodded. "It was final just before I moved here."

He was quiet a moment, then he turned to look down at her. "Are you heartbroken?"

"No," she replied without needing time to consider. "At first I felt abandoned and betrayed and simply hurt." She sighed and gave him a wry look. "But being alone isn't new to me. When I was a child, my mother left to pursue her own life, and my father was kind but busy, so I learned to fend for myself. I became very good at managing on my own. And I'm getting better all the time. No. I am not heartbroken." Then she smiled. "Unless it would gain your sympathy and make you reconsider your threat to tell on me?"

He folded his arms and leaned a hip on the railing. "The hospital's success and good image means my success," he said. "It's too important to take lightly."

She looked into his eyes, trying to gauge just how serious he was about the issue. One moment he was warm and teasing and she was convinced he'd never do anything to deprive her of this boon. Then that no-nonsense look would come over him and she suspected she wouldn't even be able to guess what he was capable of if he was determined about something.

"Then what's the solution?" she asked.

"I'll be quiet about your husband," Jave said finally, looking up as the fishing boat pulled into a slip at the next pier, "if you'll agree to see me."

Nancy, who'd also been watching the boat, turned to look at him in bald surprise. " 'See' you?" she quoted him. "You mean . . . like . . . go out?"

"Yes." Jave returned her stunned gaze, his own eyes steady. "Dinner, theater, picnics." He slapped the *Mud Hen*'s railing. "Boating."

"But, I . . ." She took several agitated steps and stopped, both hands spread in stupefaction. "I'm . . . seven and a half months pregnant!"

He nodded. "I noticed that. I'm the one who enrolled you in the Lamaze classes, remember? But that's not a problem, is it?"

"Well, yes," she said, apparently amazed he didn't see it. "It's several problems. First of all—I'm ugly." She said it with such conviction, he straightened with a frown. "Secondly, in about six weeks, this is going to be a living, breathing, probably screaming baby who won't give me or anyone near me a moment's peace! And thirdly— I'm supposed to be married to someone else. Are you crazy?" She turned in a complete circle, looking just a little wild, then asked again with a broad sweep of both arms, "Are you *crazy?*"

He caught her hands in his and pulled her to a stop. "Easy," he said quietly. "You've got the picture out of focus, Nancy." He tucked a strand of wayward hair behind her ear in a gesture so gentle she even stopped breathing. "You're beautiful," he corrected, "not ugly. And I know all about demanding babies. I had two of my own, remember? And we can be discreet about spending time together until we figure out what to do about your hospital image."

GO FOR IT, MOM. Are we going to find anyone more perfect than this? He knows about demanding babies. Just make sure there's chocolate in the deal.

SHE STARED AT HIM for a moment, mouth open but incapable of forming words. She paced away from him to the rail, then turned back to him, finally pulling her thoughts together.

"Jave," she asked, "what would be the point?"

"What's the point of any relationship?" he countered. "To learn about each other. To see where it leads."

"But where *could* it lead?" she demanded. "I mean, certainly you realize... we can't... I'm not..."

Jave watched her struggle with the issue she seemed to be sure must concern him, and enjoyed it enormously. As she stammered, he waited with interest, making no effort to help.

Nancy decided she could not deal with this delicately. He was obviously going insane from exposure to ultrasound rays or something and it was her responsibility to be brutal—for both their sakes.

"Jave," she said, "you did my ultrasound. You know that I have a... a..."

He nodded. "An incompetent cervix. Yes, I know."

"Then you have to realize that..." She gestured frustratedly. "Even if I *did*... appeal to you in this condition... that we couldn't..."

He was tempted to force her to fuddle through the explanation she seemed to think had eluded him. It would serve her right. But she was growing more pink, more agitated, and the helpless, frustrated waving of her arms and hands was about to create its own weather system.

"We couldn't have sex," he said for her. He noticed the sag of her shoulders in relief.

"Not that that would be an immediate consideration," she said quickly, chattering now that the words
were spoken. "But if it *did* come to that, I'm a month and
a half from delivery and then it'd be six weeks before—"

Jave shook his head and placed a hand over her mouth.
"You know," he said, "I'm beginning to think that other
parts of you are also incompetent." Then he rapped
lightly on her head to indicate the specific area. "Is the
power on in there? What makes you think I choose my
relationships based on how quickly I can get a woman to
bed?"

Her wide brown eyes softened with regret, and her
lashes brushed his thumb as she closed her eyes. He lowered his hand to allow her to answer.

"I'm sorry," she said, putting a hand to his arm. "I
know that wasn't fair. But I only... mentioned it because..." She hesitated, parted her lips as though to
speak, then shook her head and dropped her hand.

Jave took hold of her arm and pulled her back to him.
He'd seen a glimpse of something in her eyes, a flash of
honesty that reached right inside him and set his whole
world on edge—and he wanted to hear it in words.

He applied the slightest pressure to her arm. "Because
of what?" he asked.

Nancy knew there was little point in swallowing the
words. She was sure he'd read them in her eyes. And she
wanted very much to say them.

"I mentioned it," she whispered as the fragrant river
breeze wound around them and stirred her hair, "because *I've* thought of making love with *you.*" She smiled
thinly in self-deprecation. "It must have been guilt trans-
ference or something."

"Maybe," he suggested very softly, "it was the desire
to make a wish come true." His mouth inched slowly

down to hers while his eyes seemed to chart every milli-
meter of the way.

The hand that held her arm pulled her closer still, and
the other wound itself in her hair and tipped her head
back. He leaned down and, over the interfering protrusion of her baby, kissed her.

Nancy felt herself dissolve into his tenderness like so
much butter on warm bread. His arms were strong but
tender, his lips gentle in their exploration of hers. He
nibbled and caressed, moving from her mouth to follow
the line of her nose, her eyebrows, her cheekbones. Then
he nipped at her earlobe and traced kisses along her jaw
until he found her mouth again.

Jave was keenly aware of her substantial roundness in
his arms, and felt her resist the inclination of her weight
against him. He tipped her a little farther to the side, until she was slightly off balance and had no choice.

"I'm too heav—" Her attempt to protest about her
weight was lost as he held her easily and opened his mouth
over hers.

She clung to his shoulders, the strong muscles there
giving her confidence and allowing her to forget her precarious suspension and concentrate on him.

Her tongue met his, teased it languorously, then explored his lips and the line of his teeth as he touched hers.

She felt his hand moving on her, tracing the line of her
spine, shaping her hip, then using it to pull her closer. Her
belly was wedged against him and the sensation startled
her. Since the day she'd discovered she was pregnant,
there'd been no one with whom to share the wonder, no
one to hold and enfold her and her baby.

*WOW. TIGHT SPOT, MOM. But I like it. I like him. And I
can tell you do. It's hot in here.*

J AVE FELT HER SLIGHT START and straightened, pulling her securely up and into his arms. "What?" he asked in concern. "Are you all right? Does something hurt?"

"I'm fine," she assured him breathlessly. But she continued to cling to him as she struggled for composure. "It was just . . . the baby moved."

He splayed his large hand over the mound of her belly, drawing the breath from her like a gust of wind.

Jave felt strong movement against his palm, then at the tips of his fingers as the baby probably flailed an arm or kicked. He felt Nancy's tension, too, and liked the notion that his touch energized her.

"Feels busy," he said. "You might have to rock her to sleep tonight."

He removed his hand and she was able to draw breath again. A little giddy with relief, she mimicked him teasingly, "'Rock *her* to sleep'? So you admit it's a girl?"

He rested his hands on his hips. "So you admit you'd really be more comfortable with a supporting opinion?"

She vacillated for one moment. He waited it out, realizing her decision would probably set the tone for the months ahead.

She finally shook her head. "No. It's a girl. I know it's a girl."

He placed an arm around her shoulders and drew her with him toward the ladder and the ramp, accepting within himself that he'd already known she was not going to make this relationship easy.

"Well, more power to you," he said, climbing the steps and reaching back to pull her up behind him. "Most of us are more comfortable with a confirming opinion."

"Some of us," she said, balanced precariously at the top of the ramp, "have found that you can't trust support. You can only trust yourself."

Jave, halfway down the ramp, turned toward her. She reached out her hand, certain he intended to help her down the rest of the way. But, she realized, she'd just denigrated the very thing he was ready to offer. Accepting it now would mean a compromise on her part.

His hazel eyes challenged her, his hand, loosely resting on his hip, beyond her reach.

Nancy studied the expanse of unsteady board with its crossbars intended to provide footing that only seemed to confuse hers.

It was on the tip of her tongue to ask for his hand; she knew that was what he was waiting for. But it went against deeply ingrained personal training, and the fact that she even considered it proposed a new possibility that held its own terrors. She decided to go it alone.

She took several sure steps and Jave had just turned to walk the rest of the way down, when the sole of her sandal caught on the next crossbar. Without the bulk of her pregnancy, she would have easily recovered, but the weight pitched her forward and she shouted Jave's name at the same moment that he heard her misstep and turned to help.

He caught her against him. He looked into her eyes and let her feel for a moment that his muscle supported her. Then he lifted her in his arms and carried her the rest of the way down. He set her on her feet at the bottom.

Without a word, he took her hand and started back up the trail. Of course, there was no need for an I-told-you-so, Nancy realized wryly. That look had said it all.

"Okay," she conceded voluntarily. "There are times when it's good to have support. Even for me."

He didn't seem impressed with her admission.

"There are times," she added, "when I can trust you."

"You could *always* trust me," he corrected, "if there were times when you could let yourself believe it."

"That's the hard part," she said candidly. "If you want to see where this relationship goes as you said, that's something you should understand about me. It's hard for me to put my faith in someone else."

That, he guessed, he'd have to allow her.

"You screamed for me when you slipped," he reminded her.

She remembered that clearly. His name had been on her lips before she'd even formed the thought. "That was instinct," she explained lightly—mostly because she didn't feel light about it at all.

"That was trust," he corrected. "And to be sure your baby doesn't come into this world with the same skewed suspicions you have, you're going to agree to see me."

"I didn't say that."

"I know. You can say it now."

She wanted to. It would be dangerous to her peace of mind, foolish and irresponsible in her condition, and generally ill-advised. But she wanted to.

He fell into line behind her to let a pair of lovers coming from the other direction pass by. They appeared to be in their teens and oblivious to everything but each other until they were right upon Jave and Nancy. They laughed as Jave and Nancy stepped out of their way. They continued down the trail, gazing into each other's eyes in the encroaching darkness.

Nancy smiled after them. "Summer romance, do you suppose?" she asked Jave as he moved beside her again. "Or the real thing?"

"Hard to tell," he said. "They usually look the same. You'd have to overhear a discussion of life-and-death issues to know for sure. And don't try to change the subject."

Nancy grinned. "I thought I was pretty slick."

Jave shook his head. "Pete and Eddy make you look like a rank amateur. So what's it to be? You keep company with me? Or you lose your status as Amy's model mommy?"

"Jave," she said reasonably, "there are a few pitfalls here you haven't thought out. What will your mother think? And your children? The afternoon you fixed my roof, Pete spent a little time telling me about his mother. How will he react to his father dating a pregnant woman? Seems to me he'll feel threatened on all sides. And what about our being seen together? How can you be my Lamaze coach at the class held at the hospital when everyone there is supposed to think I'm married?"

Jave nodded. He'd already thought that through. "I'll explain to my family. My mother loves to offer her opinion, but she knows I do what I want to do. And she's always after me to reactivate my social life. Truth is, she'd be thrilled to know I was interested in a woman."

Nancy could guess that might be true. Aggie seemed ever watchful of her boys and her grandchildren.

"Eddy's pretty well adjusted," Jave went on, "and generally accepting of everyone. Pete is another story, but he has to come to terms with his life the way it is, not the way he wishes it still were."

She gave him a softly scolding look. "That's a lot to expect of a little boy."

He admitted that with a nod. "It's a lot to expect of anyone. But it's required if you're going to live a normal life."

"And what about appearances? It'll really kill my chances of being Amy's candidate for the gifts if I'm seen with another man while my husband's supposed to be away."

They'd reached Chez Pasta and turned across the broad expanse of lawn toward the truck.

"We'll establish at Lamaze class that I've become a friend, helping to coach you until your husband gets back. Beyond that, we'll be discreet." He grinned at her as he unlocked the door, then reached into the back for the step stool. "Or you could admit the truth in the interest of being able to conduct our relationship in the open."

She looked at him as though he were crazy. "And lose everything?"

He took her hand to help her up. "Maybe there's another way to acquire all that stuff."

She didn't see it. She even shook her head against the possibility.

There'd be no advantage, he realized, in explaining that to her at this point in time. He locked and closed her door, tossed the stool in the back and walked around to the driver's side.

Nancy looked doubtful. "It all sounds dangerous."

"The whole deceit," he said frankly, "is dangerous. But you started it."

She buckled her seat belt and suggested quietly, "You could just forget what you know and let me carry on as I've been doing."

"Then what'll you do at delivery time when you can't produce a husband?"

"Dating you," she said, pointing a finger at him, "isn't going to help me there, either."

He met her eyes, the hazel of his darkening in the dim interior of the truck to some turbulent and mysterious shade of gold. "You're sure about that?" he asked.

"Well...I...um..." His look debilitated her. She couldn't think, couldn't form a coherent sentence. Her mind was too busy wondering what that question meant, what that look would mean if it could be formed into words. "Jave...I..."

He turned the key in the ignition. "I'm going to be working most of the weekend, but I'll pick you up Sunday afternoon for the arts festival down the coast."

Protest would be useless. He was determined, and her resistance was halfhearted at best. There was trouble here, she knew, but it was all very complex, very convoluted, and she wasn't sharp enough to think about it. She was just a little intoxicated on the fresh, early August air and the look in Jave's eyes.

She nodded and settled back in her seat. The baby seemed to do the same, only she swore she could feel tiny toes wriggling in between her ribs. Was she needing more room? Was she thinking about making a break for it?

ROUGH EVENING, MOM. How're we doing? You know, the walls are shrinking in here.

NANCY WRIGGLED to get comfortable. Six more weeks and the life inside her would become the life in her arms. Excitement warred with terror. Was she ready? She wasn't sure.

As Jave turned the truck out of the parking lot and onto the road, she shifted again as the baby continued to squirm.

Jave glanced away from the road. "You okay?"

"The baby's stretching," she explained, sitting up to relieve sudden pressure against her back. "I feel as though she's redecorating in there, moving my spinal column to make more room."

He kept an eye on the road while reaching behind the seat for a pillow. "Here," he said, glancing away from the road again to hand it to her. "Try that in the small of your back."

She did and felt a little relief—in her back, and in her thoughts.

"I THOUGHT THIS was supposed to be art stuff," Pete announced querulously at high volume as Nancy stopped at a quilt display. The Coast Arts Festival took up all the grounds of a high school, including a standard-size football field. And so far they'd encountered everything from crocheted doilies masterfully created by a ladies' church club, to fine oil, acrylic and watercolor paintings done by some of the West Coast's most renowned artists.

"These are just old blankets," Pete went on.

"Art isn't just pictures," Nancy explained patiently. "Art can be anything that someone works hard to make pretty. Like these blankets."

"They're patched," Pete disputed scornfully.

Nancy glanced up at Jave, whom she suspected was listening while pretending not to. He studied a leather vest at a booth behind them while keeping an eye on Eddy, who was watching an artist hand tool a belt.

"They aren't patches," she said, taking Pete's hand and drawing him to a particularly pretty quilt in shades of pink and blue that was displayed at his eye level. "Quilting is an old art," she said, leaning over as much as her bulk would allow to point out the pattern, "but pioneer women used it because in those days they didn't have big pieces of fabric, so they put together all their little pieces to make what they needed." She pulled the quilt close so that he could see all the tiny stitches. "And for a long time they didn't have sewing machines, so they made all these little stitches by hand."

Nancy traced a fingertip across the width of the quilt, then into every repeated pattern to call his attention to the work involved.

"Wow!" he said, his dark eyes widening as they followed the path she traced. "There must be a million of 'em!"

She smiled. It was a gross exaggeration, but she had his interest.

"Sometimes ten ladies would all work on a quilt at the same time to make the work go faster. They would talk about what was going on in town and tell stories while they sewed."

Pete looked up at her, his eyes brightening. "I like stories."

Nancy nodded. "Me, too. Sometimes a quilt tells a story." She led him to a friendship quilt hanging on a special rack beside the other. Her finger traced the names and dates embroidered on the panels. "This one was given to a lady who moved away from friends she'd had for a long time. And they wanted her to remember them, so they all quilted a square for her and signed it with embroidery. Then they sewed all the squares together."

Pete studied all the names, then he looked up at Nancy. "My mom moved away from us," he said, his big eyes troubled at the thought. "David Fuller's mom *died,* so she *had* to go away, but mine didn't even die. She just moved. Now she can't see me play baseball."

Nancy experienced a mild sense of panic. She felt her own baby tumble around inside her and wondered if she didn't like what she was hearing, was afraid, perhaps, that it could happen to her. She wanted desperately to comfort both of them.

"I'd like to watch you play," Nancy said, wishing she hadn't started this, wishing she'd simply let him dislike the "old blankets" and not brought up an obviously painful subject.

Pete shook his head. "I'm not very good."

Nancy caught his hand and walked farther up the display to quilted clothing, hoping to find something to distract him. "I'll bet you will be," she said. "It just takes time to learn everything."

"Eddy plays really good."

"He's bigger."

Pete sighed, obviously considering the plight of being little. Then he pointed to a display of quilted bags and backpacks. "That's cool," he said, reaching on tiptoe to touch one that was made from denim squares and tied with a bandanna cord. "Do you think a bunch of ladies made that?"

Nancy studied the perfect, even stitches. She knew there were museum-quality quilters who could produce such stitches by hand, but the seams had been shop sewn, she felt sure, and a manufacturer's label was tucked inside the flap.

"Well, I think it was a bunch of ladies in a shop. Would you like to have it?" She began to delve in her purse for her wallet.

"Yeah!" Pete said excitedly, then he quickly shook his head. "But I'm not supposed to ask for stuff."

Nancy gestured for the owner of the display. "You didn't ask, I offered. And if your father complains, we'll just tell him that."

Dave appeared suddenly from behind the rack of bags. "Tell me what?" he asked.

Pete already clutched the bag possessively. "Nancy wants to buy me this," he said, then assured him quickly, "and I didn't even ask her."

Jave reached into his hip pocket for his wallet, and Nancy gave him a look that threatened mayhem if he tried to prevent her from buying the bag herself. He thought it might be interesting to try it just to see what developed, but the clerk was waiting patiently.

"That's great," he said instead. "Let's see." He squatted down before the boy to examine the purchase.

Pete related in detail everything Nancy had told him about quilting. "But this one was made by a bunch of ladies in a shop."

Eddy came to peer over his father's shoulder at the bag. "Cool," he said.

"Would you like one?" Nancy asked.

The clerk, in the act of ringing up the sale, stopped as she raised a halting finger at him.

Eddy shook his head. "No, thanks. I have a Harley one. Black leather. It's *really* cool."

Sure it wasn't politic to buy for one child and not the other, Nancy spotted a baseball cap, also quilted out of denim. She snatched it off its rack and placed it on his head. The clerk raised a mirror behind the counter and they all went to it, Nancy, Pete and Jave peering down behind Eddy to see his reflection.

"I like it," Eddy said with a broad grin.

Nancy smiled at the clerk, who rang up both items while Pete regaled Eddy with his newly acquired quilting information.

They settled down with sausage dogs on a grassy area, where a country and western band played familiar tunes. Jave helped Nancy sit with her back against a mountain ash full of plump red berries, and he and the boys formed a semicircle around her.

Eddy rolled his eyes over the music. "They need some drums or some electronic stuff," he said.

Jave pulled the bill of Eddy's cap over his eyes. "Just listen to the sound. This is good music—written before you could plug in an instrument and mess electronically with the sound it made. This is *real* music."

Eddy blinked at him. "Don't stroke out on us, Dad. I just thought they could do with a little...metal."

"This is sound that's unenhanced," Jave said patiently. "When the ladies were quilting in the old days like Nancy explained, their husbands were probably on the front porch, making just this kind of music."

"Un-en-hanced," Eddy repeated, obviously trying to make sense of the word.

"Nothing fancy added to it," Nancy contributed. "Pure stuff."

"And that's good?"

She considered that, remembering that today's child was accustomed to things that were electronically, medically or psychologically augmented or reduced. It distracted her for a moment with thoughts about the world into which her child was about to be born. Then she looked at Eddy and Pete and decided she'd be in good company.

"Sure it is," she said. "They're making beautiful music without the help of anything but a little wood and string. There has to be more satisfaction in that. And it's an easier sound to listen to."

Eddy listened as though evaluating that remark, then tilted his head from side to side in a so-so gesture that reminded her sharply of his father. "I guess. But I'm more into Guns 'n' Roses."

He picked up his soft drink and took a long swig, apparently considering the discussion over. He took a huge bite of sausage dog, his sneakered foot tapping unconsciously to the music.

Nancy looked up at Jave over the boy's head to commiserate over failing to reinforce his point. Humor was alight in his eyes as he rolled them to express his frustration. She laughed softly.

Pete struggled with a plastic packet of mustard. She took it from him, tore the end off with her fingernails, and handed it back. "Mmm," she said, studying her sausage dog. "I forgot mustard."

Jave began to get to his feet to go back to the stand for another packet. But Pete walked to her on his knees and handed back the packet. "You can have half," he said, sitting with his knees curled to the side so that he could lean against her, "and I'll have half."

Jave sat down again, marveling at the little victory. No one else would have recognized it as such, but he did. For the first time in a year, Pete was offering to share, making an effort to enjoy something. Though he suspected the boy felt as he did—sharing with Nancy didn't require much of an effort.

Nancy ruffled his hair to thank him. Jave saw the boy glance at her, his dark eyes soft with adoration. Jave smiled to himself, liking the turn things were taking.

They attended an art auction in the evening, and drove home with a three-by-four-foot oil painting of a cubist face sharing the back seat of Jave's second vehicle, a blue LeBaron. Pete was belted in between Jave and Nancy, fast asleep against Nancy's bosom. Eddy shared space with the painting.

"How come his face is so weird?" Eddy asked lazily. He leaned far into the corner, studying the painting in consternation. "It's like a profile, only you can see his other eye and his other ear."

"It's a style of painting called cubist," Jave explained. "It allows you to see things in a way you wouldn't ordinarily."

"But why would you want to?"

Jave slanted Nancy a grinning glance. "'Cause it gives you a different perspective. It makes you think."

"But it's . . . like . . . wrong."

"It's not wrong," Jave corrected. "It's just different."

"Why'd we buy it anyway?"

"Because Nancy liked it. It reminds her of Boeneke."

They'd argued over the purchase for fifteen minutes. Well, Nancy had argued that she didn't want him to buy it for her, that it was too expensive, and that her carelessly spoken "I wish I had that for my office" had been simply wishful thinking. Jave had listened patiently, then bought it anyway. Nancy had protested but was secretly delighted. Because Boeneke reminded her of Jave.

"That's her police guy," Eddy said. They'd discussed him on the ride down the coast and planned several solutions to her current plot problems.

"Right."

There were a few moments of silence, then Eddy said sleepily, "Policemen shouldn't be cubist."

Jave smiled into the rearview mirror. "Why not?"

"'Cause you shouldn't be able to see all of them at once like that. Shouldn't they have secrets? You know, things that are hidden, so that the bad guys can't figure them out? Otherwise, they'll know how to get away.''

Jave glanced at Nancy, an eyebrow raised in amazement. ''Is my kid brilliant or what?'' he asked.

Eddy had fallen asleep and missed the compliment.

JAVE WALKED NANCY into her house and hung the painting over her desk while the boys slept in the car. Then he took a cellular phone out of a bag he'd also brought in and placed it on her coffee table. He plugged the battery into a charger.

''What . . . where did you get that?'' she asked.

''Through one of the hospital's suppliers.'' He gave her a few rudimentary instructions, then showed her how to install the battery in the morning. ''This is already programmed,'' he said, ''and the battery has to charge for twelve hours. I want you to take the phone to bed and in the truck with you. You'll have help at the tip of your fingers.''

She opened her mouth, a protest forming out of habit. But he caught her upper arms and pulled her close. He kissed her slowly and soundly.

Though she had no idea how this relationship had come about or where it was going, she understood clearly at that moment what it was like to be cared about—and cared for. Tears stung her eyes as she parted her lips to respond with the heartfelt adoration of a woman who felt cherished.

Jave studied her one protracted moment, then blew a frustrated breath and left, locking the door as he closed it.

She went to the window and watched him pull out of her front yard, his headlights arching through the darkness. It was getting more and more difficult, she thought, her nose and her belly pressed against the window, to watch him drive away.

WASN'T that sweet, Mom?

"NANCY'S GOING TO COME and . . . watch me play," Pete told his father, the news interrupted by a big yawn as Jave tucked him into bed.

"You'd like that?"

Pete opened heavy eyelids and nodded. "I like *her.*"

"I know," Jave said. "So do I." He kissed the boy good-night and turned out the light, thinking as he closed the bedroom door how much he missed her.

THE PHONE WAS RINGING as he walked down the stairs to breakfast. He picked up the cordless in the kitchen, opening the refrigerator as he pushed the On button with his thumb.

"Hello," he said, reaching for a peach.

"Hi. It's Nancy."

The soft voice brought him upright even before she identified herself. He kicked the door closed and put the fruit on the counter, his heart beating fast.

"Nancy," he said. His voice sounded breathless. "Anything wrong?"

"No, I'm fine." He felt relief, but his heart continued to pound. "I wanted to test the phone. The best way seemed to be to call and thank you for it."

"You're welcome," he said. The bones in his legs seemed to turn to butter. He leaned back against the counter for support. "Did you get any sleep last night? Your baby ate sauerkraut."

She laughed. The soft sound over the telephone wire turned the bones in his upper body to liquid. "We slept beautifully. She's going to be an eccentric gourmand with widely varied ethnic preferences. She loves chili, Szechuan, moussaka and anything that reeks of garlic and onions." He was drinking in the sound of her voice, the fact that *she'd* called *him,* when she added with quiet gravity, "And thank you for the painting. Did I ever tell you about Boeneke?"

"You explained him on the way down yesterday afternoon," he replied. "Remember?"

"I mean about him and you," she said.

He had a connection to this character with whom she spent part of every day? And the nights when she couldn't sleep? He tried to sound nonchalant. "Me?"

"You look just like my image of him," she explained.

He heard a disarming vulnerability in her voice. What he wouldn't have given to have the freedom to jump into his truck and cover the miles that separated them.

"Same hair, same eyes. I saw it that first day, when you were doing my ultrasound. The room was dark and you stepped into the light...." She paused. The silence was heavy. "You're him."

He waited as he heard her hesitate again, possibly wondering whether or not to say more. He wanted to hear that that was why she'd liked the painting. That she'd called to tell him she was staring at it now and pretending he was there. But he knew what he was up against. The lady couldn't bring herself to believe in anyone.

"Well...thank you again," she said. "For the phone, for the painting, and for the wonderful time. You have great kids."

"Yes, I do," he said. "Thank you for noticing. I'll pick you up for Pete's game on Thursday night."

"Wonderful," she said.

Had he heard a vague edge of disappointment? Had she hoped she'd see him today? He wasn't one for games of intrigue, but this seemed like an important one. She had to see for herself that she was coming to care for him, coming to need him, coming to want to believe in him. And nothing would underline that like a little absence.

"Have a good day, Jave," she said finally.

He fought down the urge to forget his scheduled appointments at the hospital and drive over to her.

"You, too, Nancy," he replied. "Don't forget to take the phone with you in the truck."

He heard her sigh. "Right," she said, the sound heavy and wistful. "Bye."

Jave punched the Off button on the phone and slapped the antenna down. All *right*. Points were stacking up on his side.

Chapter Nine

Jave ran into his office for a quick sip of coffee between patients and found Tom turning idly from side to side in his desk chair, sipping from the hot cup he'd left on the desktop.

"Moocher," Jave accused mildly. "Now you have to go to the cafeteria and get me another one."

Tom remained in the chair but handed back the cup with a grimace. "Actually, I saved you from a fate worse than motor oil. Who makes that stuff?"

Jave took an appreciative swig. "Patients get the good stuff. The cafeteria saves the bad food for the staff."

"It tastes like a stagnant pond."

"That's where we grow the penicillin. The coffee's a by-product." Jave perched on the edge of the desk and put the cup aside. He studied Tom's rather natty attire of beige Dockers and a blue-and-beige silk shirt. "What are you doing here?"

Tom picked up a marking pen, removed the cap with studied casualness, then recapped it. "Keeping my appointment with my therapist."

"Are you coming or going?" Jave asked.

Tom grinned at him. "I don't know. That's why I'm seeing a therapist."

Jave kicked at the chair, sending it backward a few inches until it collided with the wall. "Very funny. I meant, have you had your appointment, or are you headed there now?"

Tom used his feet to walk the chair back to the desk. "I've had it. Came to see if you wanted to go to the Scupper for lunch and see how the boat's coming."

Jave nodded. "Got one more patient scheduled in five minutes. Then I'm free until three."

"Good. I'll be out in the—"

"Jave! Here's the guest list for the birthing-room dinner. We're—" Amy Brown walked into his office, waving a sheet of paper and clutching her ever-present clipboard to her. She stopped dead three steps inside as her gaze fell on his brother, leaning back in his chair.

Jave looked on in surprise as Amy's eyes widened and darkened, and a quickly indrawn breath fluttered a lacy ruffle that ran across the front of her dress.

A blush, instant and thorough, rose from her throat to her hairline.

Tom got to his feet with an uncertain glance at Jave.

"I'm sorry," Amy said, her voice high and broken. She cleared her throat and nervously shifted her weight. "I didn't realize you had a patient." She backed toward the door. "This can—"

"No, it's all right," Jave said, straightening off the desk. "This isn't a patient. Although one has to be patient to deal with him. Amy, this is my brother, Tom Nicholas. Tom, meet Amy Brown, Riverview Hospital's publicity and PR coordinator."

Amy offered her hand and dropped her clipboard. The guest list she'd intended to hand Jake fluttered to the floor.

With an apologetic exclamation, she bent down for it at the same moment that Tom made a grab for the sheet. He hit her glasses and knocked them off. She reeled backward and her head collided with the corner of the office door. She sagged against it, bleeding profusely.

"Oh, God! I'm sorry." Tom pulled her toward the chair as Jave, unable to believe that he'd seen what he'd seen, called the ER to see if they could handle another patient.

"It might be a good idea," Jave said to Tom two hours later over his bottle of Guinness at the Scupper, "if you didn't date for another year. Or at least get the women you meet to sign their insurance over to you first."

Tom leaned back in his chair, a baseball hat pulled down low over his eyes. "She looked so nervous, she made me nervous. Thank God I didn't break her nose."

Jave nodded dryly. "Yeah. Ten stitches in her scalp isn't half that bad."

Tom drew a deep breath. "All right. It wasn't my finest hour. I don't ever have to see her again."

The merest outline of a notion had formed in Jave's mind several hours ago when Amy had walked into his office and blushed after one glimpse of his brother. It had been even too small to consider a thought, but it had been growing ever since and was now a full-fledged idea.

"Yeah, you do," he said. "Remember the rest of our boat deal?"

Tom frowned, thought, then shook his head. "Oh, no. No, no."

Jave shrugged. "Well, do you have another candidate for a date? You don't want to see Judy Taft and I don't blame you. Who else do you know? As far as I can tell, the only women you're acquainted with are clients—mostly married ones—except for Nancy, and she's mine."

"No."

"The two-week deadline we made is long past. I think you should ask Amy for a date."

Tom shook his head adamantly. "Not a chance. I'll buy out your share of the boat first."

Jave downed the last of his ale. "I don't want to sell."

"Then you can buy *me* out."

"You're the one who knows how to find the fish."

Tom was looking desperate. He pushed his hat farther back on his head. "Like she's going to want to go out with the guy who socked her in the nose, broke her glasses, and sent her to the emergency room."

Jave shrugged as though that was all of no consequence. "She knows everybody there. It was no big deal. Why don't you ask her?"

"Jave," Tom said, leaning toward him on his forearms. "She seemed nice enough. I mean she didn't even shout at me or anything, but she's . . . you know . . . she's not really my type."

"She's a fine, good-hearted woman," Jave said firmly. "With a cheerful nature and a kind word for everyone."

Tom fell moodily against the back of his chair. "Yeah, well, I'm not exactly Pollyanna myself. We have nothing in common. I won't do it."

"I'll do it for you."

"I'll remove your spleen with my crowbar."

"YOUR COACH WILL PROVIDE emotional support and companionship at a time when you'll need him or her more than you've ever needed anyone in your life."

Serena Borders, the American Society for Psychoprophylaxis in Obstetrics-Lamaze-certified trainer, stood in the center of the carpeted room and smiled at the half-dozen couples distributed around her on the floor with their pillows.

Nancy leaned a little self-consciously against Jave, who bracketed her with his knees and quietly awaited instructions.

She shouldn't be nervous, she reasoned, as the instructor gave a brief history of the Lamaze program, and explained that its purpose was to teach relaxation, breathing and expulsion. Nancy, who'd borrowed several books from the library on the subject and watched the film several times, let her mind wander.

Though it refused to wander too far. It seemed to be concentrated, along with every sensory receptor in her body, on the man who supported her weight.

That wasn't so surprising, though, she figured. They'd spent a lot of time together in the past week and she was feeling a closeness to him that was really very strange. She'd been to one of Pete's games and one of Eddy's, she'd helped Aggie make Sunday dinner, and she'd spent yesterday evening on the *Mud Hen* with Jave and Tom deciding on fabric and paint colors for the galley, the head, the small salon and the staterooms.

His family liked her. She liked them. She found herself beginning to want something that couldn't possibly happen here. How *had* she gotten into this? Greed, she reminded herself. Simple, unvarnished greed.

"Effective relaxation," Serena was saying, "will diminish fatigue and pain. Now the first step is to get comfortable. Lie down on your sides."

Serena demonstrated with a handsome couple who appeared either to have never seen each other before, or come to class straight from a sizzling argument. Since the former possibility seemed highly unlikely, Nancy found herself wondering what they had argued about. The man, broad-shouldered and dark-haired, looked vaguely familiar.

Jave told her he managed the Heron Point branch of the First Coastal Bank, that they'd worked on several community projects, and he'd helped him and Tom with a loan for the boat.

The woman was tall, slender and very blond. She had masses of tightly curled hair that fell forward when she lay down. He smoothed it gently back for her, despite his tight-lipped frown. Serena had him lie down beside his partner, close but not touching.

She made shooing motions toward the other couples. "You do the same. Coaches, I want you close, but not touching. It's important for you to learn to relax, too, because when the time comes, our mothers won't respond to tension and fear. At least, they won't respond in a positive way."

Nancy felt Jave's hands on her as he helped her tip onto her side. Then she felt his presence behind her, though she could no longer feel his touch. The skin prickled on her neck, while sensation rayed out from her spinal column like the day she'd tried these exercises by watching the videotape and he'd run a finger down her vertebrae to make her straighten.

To distract herself, she watched the other couples. Beside the demonstrating pair, there was a plump couple who couldn't stop laughing, a very young couple who gazed adoringly into each other's eyes, an older man and woman who had confided they were expecting their first child after fifteen years of trying, and a very pretty young woman whose coach was her best friend—another woman. She was very serious, Nancy noted, and followed every instruction to the letter and with grave intensity. Nancy guessed she was an accountant or an IRS auditor.

"Now, I want you to listen to the rhythm of your own breathing." Serena walked among them, peering down at them as though they were under glass. "Relax your hands, relax your face, relax your shoulders, relax your knees."

She waited a brief amount of time between instructions. Nancy tried desperately to relax, but guessed the effort involved was negating the outcome.

Serena leaned over her and opened the fist into which her hand had clenched. "Relax, Nancy. Relax. Having this baby is going to be a wonderful experience. You're going to enjoy it. Relax."

As Serena walked on to the next couple, Nancy felt Jave's breath against the back of her neck, then his hand. He kneaded gently. "What's the matter?" he asked in a whisper. "You're tight as a drum."

"In case you hadn't noticed," she turned to whisper irascibly, "I am *carrying* a drum. It's big and round enough and it's always beating on me."

That wasn't the problem, of course, but it was the best she could do in front of eleven other people.

She wished he wouldn't touch her, and breathed a sigh of relief when Serena went to the front of the room to deliver more instructions and Jave dropped his hand.

"All right, coaches. I want you to change the level of your awareness now. Notice your 'mother' as she begins to become aware of her surroundings."

For Nancy, who hadn't relaxed in the first place, her awareness of her surroundings was doubly sharp. And it was comprised entirely of Jave.

She'd never been a particularly sensual woman. She'd made love with Jerry, of course, and, before her pregnancy, it had been nice. But it certainly hadn't been everything literature and Hollywood purported it to be.

But, suddenly, it was always on her mind. She wanted to make love with Jave. She fantasized about it. Alone in her bed at night, she swore she could even imagine it happening. His hands on her sensitive flesh, his breath against her breasts, pearling their tips. His fingers and his breath moving down her body, forming a molten pool of sensation that finally forced her to get up and make a cup of tea.

"Now, coaches, I want you to touch your mothers. Touch is a very effective technique in releasing tension. It has to be gentle, of course, but firm. When her mind is occupied during the birth process, your touch will have to be firm to get through. Now touch her head."

Nancy felt Jave's large hand cup her scalp, palm against her crown, fingertips against her temples and her forehead. She felt his energy jolt into her, his calmness imbue her with peace.

She let herself drift along as the technique began to make headway against her tension.

Serena went on. "Touch her side and press lightly inward."

Nancy felt Jave's hand on her ribs on her left side. It stroked lightly forward over the mound of her baby, then back again. His touch was confident, even possessive. She let herself float off on her favorite little fantasy and pretended that they were like most couples here—that he was her husband and this was his baby.

But that was a mistake. As she let reality slip away, she lost her frail grasp on the relaxation technique and tension came back into play. It was rife with awareness of every one of Jave's fingertips moving over her swollen belly in gentle, proprietary circles.

AHHH. TOTAL BODY MASSAGE. I like it. Can we do it again? Watch the ribs, though. And the soles of my feet. Hee! Hee!

SHE BARELY RESISTED a moan. Her body didn't seem to know it was required to be celibate. It did all the things she imagined at night in her lonely bed. It squirmed and pooled with warmth and filled with a desperate longing. Only now she was in a room filled with people, and she was supposed to be concentrating on the little life inside her.

She was suddenly swamped by selfishness. She was going to be a terrible mother. She'd suspected it all along. Here she was supposedly concentrating on her baby and all she could think of was herself and how she wanted this man.

She survived Jave's execution of the rest of Serena's instructions, though she didn't know how. Resolved to endure it, she lived through his massage of her shoulders, the circles he made with his thumbs and fingertips down her spinal column. But she almost lost it during the whole hand press and the scalp massage. "Use a rotating motion on the scalp, as though you're washing hair."

As they all filed out of class with Serena's beam of approval, Nancy noted that the handsome couple looked as tense as she felt. The woman caught her eye, and for just an instant, she felt a curious and inexplicable kinship.

"Bye," she said quietly. "See you next time."

Nancy nodded. "Bye."

She remembered when they'd all introduced themselves at the beginning of class that the pretty blonde's name had been different from her coach's. Had she just chosen to retain her maiden name, or were they not married? Was it one of those designer relationships where couples had a baby but chose not to marry? She knew many couples did that successfully; it just seemed to her like such an uncertain way to run a family. She found herself worrying about them as well as herself.

"Are they married?" she asked Jave.

He shook his head, frowning. "No. She was acting as surrogate for her sister, Ryan's—the banker's—wife. But Cassie died, and now they're working together to get this baby born."

"It doesn't look," Nancy said, watching them walk away, "as though they're happy in their work."

Jave placed a hand at her back and pushed her gently toward the car.

"You don't look very happy, either," he noted as he drove away from the hospital and toward the coast road. "Something you want to tell me?"

Nancy was primed for just that question. After that interminable evening of torture following on the heels of the weeks of anxiety laced with lust and burgeoning dreams that could be nothing but trouble, she forgot the beautiful blonde's problems and rounded on him, eyes turbulent with her own difficulties.

"No, there's nothing I want to tell you!" she said, her voice breaking. "That's what got me into this in the first place."

He pulled over to the side of the road and into the sheltering branches of a row of shaggy cedars. He removed his seat belt and turned to her. His eyes went over her in quiet analysis. He'd had his hands all over her body for more than an hour. He seemed completely unaffected, while she was one raw, raging nerve. That annoyed her beyond description.

"No," he reminded gently. "Claiming to have a husband is what got you into this. You feeling blue?"

"Blue? Blue?" She slapped his hand away when he tried to touch her. "No, I feel Red! Red with a capital *R!* Wildfire, fire engine, gushing blood Red! And don't *touch* me. I've *had* it with your tender pat and stroke, as though you have every...as though..."

She heard herself sounding like a deranged fishwife dealing with issues of id confusion, and stopped. She stared at him while emotion mounted and all her options for backing out of the conversation with dignity intact seemed to disintegrate. She couldn't walk home. Heron Point had no bus system. She didn't have cash for a cab.

She leaned the side of her head against the back of the seat and dissolved into tears. Emotion rolled over and over her, confusing how things were with how she would like them to be, and leaving her feeling jealous and short-changed.

She couldn't understand herself. She'd never been into self-pity. Of course, she'd never wanted Jave Nicholas and been sure she couldn't have him before.

Jave felt severely battered by physical and emotional frustration and repression. Despite all his noble claims to the contrary, he wanted to make love to her every time he saw her, and was forced to remind himself that her condition dictated it would probably be Thanksgiving before that could ever come about. And it was only mid-August now. Three months. God. He expected to implode before Labor Day.

It was going to be hell to hold her, but she needed him.

Nancy felt Jave's arms come around her, and she allowed herself the luxury of leaning into him, of wrapping her arms around his middle and holding on, forgetting that she'd just insisted he not touch her.

He stroked her hair, her back, the mound of her baby cradled between them. "As though what?" he asked.

She shouldn't say it aloud. It would reveal her vulnerability. It would show him what she wanted. And it had always been her policy to keep what was in her heart to herself.

But not only did she have new life in her, that life seemed to be changing her own. Sometimes she didn't recognize herself anymore. She *wanted* him to know what she felt.

"As though this were your baby," she whispered, tipping her head back to look into his eyes. "You touch me as though . . . this were your baby. And I wish she were. I wish she were."

Jave felt every frustration within him melt into insignificance. She could not have said anything that would have firmed his resolve to withstand the physical and emotional tyrannies of this relationship more than those few words— "I wish she were."

"The solution to that," he said calmly, combing his fingers through the sides of her hair, "is very simple."

She sighed softly against him. "Nothing in this entire situation is simple," she denied.

He kissed her pessimism away. "When you become mine," he insisted, "the baby becomes mine." She blinked at him, obviously needing that clarified. He did it readily. "Marry me."

She reacted precisely as he'd known she would. She pushed herself upright and pressed her hands against his chest to force a distance between them. "That would never work," she said, her voice soft despite the firmness in her hands. But that defined her, he knew. A heart and a body always at odds.

But understanding her didn't make it easier to deal with her. "Why not?" he asked pointedly. "It's what you want. I can see it in your eyes. It's there now."

Nancy abruptly turned her face and focused on the world beyond the windshield, as though that gesture alone could deprive him of what he knew. It was dusk turning to darkness, a single pair of headlights coming from the west.

"I know nothing about families," she said, rummaging in her purse for a tissue with one hand, eyes still focused on the windshield. "I could no more take on two little boys than I could..." She turned impatiently toward her purse, further frustrated by her inability to find a tissue. She pulled out her wallet, her makeup bag, her keys, her calendar.

Jave reached over the back of the seat into a fabric organizer attached to it by a loop around the headrest and produced a small travel pack of tissues.

Nancy accepted it with a sodden glance. "Thank you," she said, then dabbed at her eyes and finished her statement. "I could no more do that than I could win the Edgar," she said.

He frowned. They were mere inches apart in the front seat and he fought parallel eruptions of lust and temper.

"Do you approach everything with such lack of resolve?" he asked quietly.

She finally focused on him, obviously offended. Her eyelashes were spiked with tears, her lips still vaguely atremble. "I know my limitations."

He nodded, leaning back slightly to put a little distance between them. It was difficult to be merciless with a woman when he could smell her fragrance and feel the warmth radiating from her body.

"I'm sure that's a good thing," he said, "if you're a tightrope walker or a sky diver. But if you're going to be a parent, you'd damn well better understand that your limits are going to be stretched beyond anything you thought you could handle. Most of the time you're working without a net or a chute, and it's all too important for you to fail to come through."

She angled her chin. "That's precisely what I mean. No one ever came through for me. I'm not sure I could come through for you."

"You're looking forward to your baby," he remonstrated. "How do you expect to come through for her? Why is that different?"

"Because it'll just be her and me," she retorted, her voice rising a decibel. "One-to-one. I can do that. She'll be part of *me.*"

He shook his head and grimaced. "So this impressionable little baby is going to learn all her lessons from a woman who can't trust anyone?"

Nancy opened her mouth to protest his assessment of the situation, then hesitated, unable to produce a convincing response.

While she thought it over, Jave swept a hand gently down her cheek, then pinned her chin between his thumb and forefinger. He felt her stiffen, knew she concentrated on his touch with her entire being.

"And do you really think," he asked softly, "that I don't belong to you every bit as much as she does? I'm not living in your belly, but I know I'm in here." He moved that hand down to the inside of her left breast, right over her heart.

Nancy felt its delicious weight there and closed her eyes against it, swallowing.

"If you walked away from me now, you'd spend the rest of your life wondering what lovemaking between us would have been like. You'd dream about falling asleep in my arms and waking up there. And you'd remember all the things we've done together, and imagine everything that remains undone.''

He leaned down and kissed her lightly, just to remind her what they had shared—and all the promises it held.

"Most lovers," he said, "are tied by the memories of nights of tenderness and passion. You and I..." His hand moved back to her chin and he ran his thumb lightly over her bottom lip. It was trembling again. "You and I are connected by all we know we can have when there's finally time for us. That moment is out there like a light, waiting for us in the distance."

Nancy felt herself being pulled toward him as if she were magnetized. Everything he said was true. She felt as close to him as though they'd been lovers for years, and yet, when she indulged her fantasies, she felt excitement in the dream that somewhere, someday, there would be their first time.

Then her cellular phone rang.

Jave and Nancy stared at each other, unable to surface from that shared thought. Then the telephone rang again, and Nancy delved into her purse for the phone. She raised the antenna, pushed the button, and cleared her throat, groping for a normal tone.

"Hello?" Even as she answered, she wondered who could be calling her. Jave was usually the only one who used the number, and he was sitting beside her.

"Nancy? It's Mother. Where are you?"

Nancy frowned in surprise. "I'm on the road on my way home from Lamaze class. How did you get this number?"

There was a sigh of impatience on the other end of the line. "Just once I'd like to talk to you without having to answer research questions on how I've located you. Jave gave me the number."

Nancy gaped at Jave for a full ten seconds while all the ramifications of the situation came home to her.

"Jave" gave it to her? Not J.V. or Dr. Nicholas, but Jave?

"Mother, how do you know Jave?" she asked, her voice deadly quiet.

Jave thought a definitive, four-letter word and abandoned all hope of Nancy falling into his arms tonight with admissions of trust—however frail—and undying love. He returned her glare with a look of defensive unrepentance.

Another sigh from the other end of the connection. "The aide who answered your phone the day I called you at the hospital mentioned that someone named Jave was taking you home. When I wanted to know how you were, I simply called the hospital, asked for Jave and was connected with the doctor in Radiology."

"And when was this?" Nancy asked.

"Oh, let's see. Three or four weeks ago."

The O shape of Nancy's mouth rounded further and Jave rolled his eyes at her and moved back behind the steering wheel. He should have told her. But Denise had asked him not to. Deceptions weren't safe, but his relationship with Nancy was built on them. He was growing more and more comfortable with them.

Suddenly the most critical question of the moment occurred to Nancy.

"Mom, where are you?" she asked.

"On your front porch," her mother replied, "talking to you on *Willy's* cellular phone. And we're being stared at by a very malevolent-looking black cat. When are you coming home?"

Nancy felt panic begin to close her throat. No. Oh, no. Her mother was here. She fixed Jave with her deadliest look, but he was staring out the windshield, the wrist of his right hand resting on the steering wheel.

"I'll be right there, Mother. Goodbye."

Nancy hit the Power button, pushed down the antenna, and slammed the phone back in her purse.

"What *right* do you have to talk to my mother behind my back?" she demanded.

Jave turned to her with a look of weary forbearance. "Every right in the world. This is a free country. Or don't you *trust* that notion?"

Nancy ignored his sarcasm, too incensed by the thought that her mother and Jave had been in touch without her knowledge.

"She said you gave her this number three weeks ago," she accused.

"That's right," he said, nodding. "She was concerned about you and asked me about your condition. I told her you were doing fine, that your obstetrician and I were keeping a close eye on you, and I gave her your cellular phone number. She got upset when she couldn't reach you at home."

Nancy huffed in indignation. "If I'd wanted her to have the number," she said loudly, "I'd have given it to her."

"She's your mother, Nancy," he said reasonably. "She was worried. You wouldn't let her come to you and you wouldn't go to her, so it made her feel better to have another way to keep in touch."

Her tears were dry now, her vulnerability of a few moments ago well and truly hardened. She donned her wronged-daughter persona like a suit of armor.

"Years ago," she said stiffly, "when I wanted her, she went off to become a star. Well, now I don't need her. Only she's here, thanks to you." She put a hand to her forehead and groaned, the thought of having to cope with her mother more than she could bear. Then she pulled herself together and turned to narrow her eyes at Jave. "This is all your fault. So you're going to get me out of it."

He tried to imagine what she had in mind. He couldn't. "Really," he said. "And why would I do that?"

"Because *it's all your fault!*" she said again at full voice. Then she drew a deep breath and seemed to be counting. When she'd finished, she said in even tones, "And she and Willy Brock are sitting on my front porch."

Jave turned the key in the ignition.

"You're going to do what I tell you," she said, her tone threatening.

He gave her a lazy-lidded look over his shoulder as he pulled onto the quiet road. It was flat and clear for a distance, so he floored it. All the love he'd felt for her moments ago was still there, but was temporarily sealed off by exasperation. "You have a lot to learn about negotiating with a man," he said.

"This is not negotiable," she said firmly and a little desperately. He'd never seen her this frightened, even the day he'd done her ultrasound. He wondered if she was concerned as much with seeing her mother as she was with how she would *feel* when she saw her. "You owe me this," she declared. Then she said quickly, crisply, "I'm going to tell her that you're living with me."

He neither agreed, nor disagreed. "Do you ever handle a problem," he asked, "without lying about it?"

It was a valid question, she realized. That was all she'd done since she'd met him. "I write fiction," she said with a helpless wave of both hands. "Making something up is what comes to mind."

"I think it's becoming a crutch you should take time to deal with."

"I will. As soon as she's gone. Will you do it?"

He considered it. He'd go to the bowels of hell for her, but it didn't seem prudent at this moment for her to know that. "What's in it for me?" he asked.

She let her head fall back against the headrest. "I'll let you live. Only because I'm fond of your children."

The road began to wind and he slowed the car, glancing in the rearview mirror. They were alone on the road.

"And I'll do it," he said, "because your baby needs someone to think of it. And if you get any more distressed, you're going to induce labor."

"It is a *she*."

"If you say so."

YOU TELL HIM, MOM. I'm with you. But I'm excited about meeting my grandmother.

Chapter Ten

Denise DiBenedetto did not look fifty. Jave watched her unfold gracefully from the porch steps as he pulled up to Nancy's front lawn. She wore jeans and a sweatshirt with the St. Tropez logo emblazened on it, and simple white tennis shoes. Hair a little lighter than Nancy's was caught back with a broad silver clip.

She had Nancy's brown eyes, a warm smile and a solid handshake. Jave knew he was bucking the tide, but he liked her.

She embraced Nancy the brief two seconds that was all Nancy would allow, then smiled at Jave. "Thank you for looking out for her," she said. "I wasn't a very good mother and it seems I'm not going to get a second chance, so I appreciate all you've done."

"My pleasure," Jave said. He read something in her eyes that he often saw in the faces of terminal patients. It was a brave acceptance mingled with wild recklessness, a sort of nothing-left-to-lose attitude.

She turned with a smile to the tall, loose-limbed man beside her who appeared to be about her own age. He wore jeans, a well-worn chambray shirt and a gray Western hat. Jave had seen his face on CD covers and on videos. He was nice-looking in a Marlboro Man kind of way, but his gentle voice and manner belied the chiseled features.

"Willy Brock," he introduced himself. "Friend of Denise's. How are ya?"

Nancy shook hands politely with him and led the way inside. She disappeared to make coffee and left Jave to entertain them. Instead, they entertained him.

He understood that Nancy's mother had walked away from her family, and that that had had a lasting and traumatic effect on Nancy. He could relate. Bonnie had done the same to him and their children, yet he couldn't find it in him to hate either of them.

Bonnie was on a search for something he doubted she would find in a new man and a new relationship. He pitied her. But Denise seemed to have such vivacious energy, and he remembered what Nancy had said about her father being there but never available. He imagined it must have been difficult for a personality like hers to live unnoticed, unacknowledged.

Nancy fussed with filters and coffee and heard the sound of her mother's girlish laughter. She wanted to feel annoyed. She didn't. She felt nostalgic instead.

She remembered lying in bed and hearing the sound of it carrying up the stairs and into her bedroom. She remembered that it had soothed her and made her feel safe. But she remembered also how bereft she had been when it was gone.

Nancy pushed the thought from her mind and slammed the lid on the coffee carafe. She placed it on the coffeemaker and turned it on.

She went into the living room to find Jave and her mother laughing together on the sofa, and Willy carrying in two large bags.

Nancy smiled casually, taking the chair opposite the sofa. "Mom, I'm afraid you can't stay here," she said, thinking as she heard the sound of her own voice that that was probably as far from courteous as one could get. "You see..." She indicated Jave with a wave of her hand and fixed him with a look that warned him not to contradict her. "He's living here with me and... well, there just isn't enough room. There's only one real bedroom. The other one's full of all the things I couldn't unpack in my condition."

Denise nodded as though she understood, then patted the sofa on which she sat. "This'll do fine for Willy and me. We're used to hotel rooms and the back of a tour bus. We'll be fine."

"No...you see..." Nancy thought fast. "Jave has two little boys, and that's where *they* sleep."

Denise nodded again. "Pete and Eddy. He was just telling me about them."

Nancy turned up her glare over the forcedly sweet smile she sent Jave. "They're wonderful, but they're pretty rambunctious and I don't think..."

Jave propped his elbow on the back of the sofa and smiled into Nancy's glare. "I think we could stay at my mother's for a few weeks so your mother can be with you when the baby's born."

"No!" Nancy said, inching forward in her chair, her face going pale. She had expected his cooperation. She felt panicky without it. "Jave," she said, an underlying plea in the words she spoke, "I need you here. Mom can't help me if anything goes wrong."

Denise sat up a little stiffly, looking from Nancy to Jave. "I thought you said you were doing fine. That everything was all right."

"Well, it is," Nancy said quickly, "but...you know how these things are...it could change at any moment." She focused narrowly on Jave. "Darling, please," she said, accentuating the endearment, lending it a lethal quality, "I need you with me."

The thought of facing her mother alone was debilitating, even though the alternative was facing her with the man who could ruin her life—in more ways than one.

Jave raised an eyebrow at her little scene, then went to sit on the arm of her chair and put a comforting hand on her shoulder. "All right. All right." She sagged in relief. Then he added, "The boys will stay with Mom, and your mother and Willy can have the sofa." He squeezed her to him as she looked up at him, her eyes ready to ignite. "I'll stay right here. Don't worry."

Denise looked a little troubled. "I hate to part you from your children, Jave."

"It's all right," he assured her. "My mother's about to take them with her to Bend for a week to visit my uncle, then it'll be just about time for them to go back to school. They spend a lot of time with my mother while I'm working anyway."

Nancy thought the evening would never end. Her mother and Willy regaled them with stories about their life on the road. She told herself that there was nothing she could do about this now. Her mother had insinuated herself into her life until the baby was born, and the best thing for all concerned was for her to cope with it graciously.

I LIKE HER, MOM. I have a grandmother!

BUT SHE DIDN'T feel gracious. She felt resentful and angry...and as though she might erupt emotionally at any moment like an egg in a microwave. She hadn't quite recovered from her Lamaze class and her discussion with Jave about their relationship. He'd asked her to marry him. And she'd been about to *consider* it. Then he'd admitted moments later that he'd been in collusion with her mother for weeks.

Jave excused himself just before ten to "check with the hospital," but Nancy guessed he was calling home and explaining the situation to Aggie.

She wanted to run away. But she was getting to the point where all she could manage was a sloppily navigated waddle. No. She had to stay.

Jave helped Willy bring in some more of their bags while Denise helped Nancy make up the sofa bed.

"I'll make you cinnamon French toast for breakfast," Denise said, smoothing the sheets in place. "You used to love that."

"I don't have any cinnamon bread," Nancy said, hoping to dampen her maternal enthusiasm.

Her mother smiled brightly. "That's what supermarkets are for."

Nancy knew there was little point in arguing. Her mother would do what she wanted to do. Then a critical detail in all this occurred to her. "Mom," she said, straightening to put a hand to her back. It was beginning to ache. "I have to explain something to you."

Her mother shook a blanket. "Of course. I'm listening."

Nancy drew a deep breath. "No one knows you're my mother, so... please don't mention it to anyone."

Hurt flashed briefly across Denise's eyes, but she nodded and continued to smile. "I know you're not proud of the fact. I promise not to bring it up."

"It isn't that." Nancy explained about the hospital's birthing-rooms extravaganza, about Amy Brown's enthusiasm and all the gifts involved, about her pretense that Jerry was still around and in the Coast Guard.

Her mother listened quietly, though her eyes widened as the story progressed. "What are you going to do when it's time to have the baby and it's Jave holding your hand instead of the phantom husband? And the hospital staff knows Jave. Won't they be... surprised?"

Nancy nodded, afraid to think about that too closely at the moment. She could deal with only one crisis at a time. "I don't know. But I'll think of something."

"Nancy," Denise said, walking around the sofa bed to place an arm around her shoulders, "when the time comes, your mind will be on anything but explaining yourself. All you'll want to think about is getting the bowling ball out of your stomach. If you're going to come up with a good story, you'd better think about it now. You know..." she said, her tone deliberately casual. Nancy suspected what was coming. "I'd be thrilled to buy all those baby things for you."

"No," Nancy said firmly, moving out from under her arm on the pretext of rearranging pillows. "I'll do it myself."

"Nancy..."

Nancy smiled stiffly. "Good night, Mother." She called a good-night to Willy as he and Jave walked in with the last of the luggage—two guitars.

Nancy stood in the middle of her bedroom in her long cotton nightgown and waited for Jave. He walked into the room a moment later with the brisk confidence of a man who had every right to join her.

"Sorry," he said quietly after the door was closed. "I'd have knocked, but I didn't think it would fit in with your scenario."

She squared her shoulders, trying to look in control of the situation. But all the action did was make her stomach protrude farther and accentuate her vulnerability. Still, she played the role.

"Thank you for your assistance and support," she whispered harshly. "You promised to help me!"

"I did," he said. Hands loosely on his hips, he leaned over her until they were nose-to-nose, he, too, whispering. "That's your mother, and she came a long way to be with you. I know you have grievances against her, but maybe some things have changed since those days. She seems like a sweet and giving lady. Maybe you could learn something from her."

Nancy was too angry and frustrated for speech. She pointed to the old four-poster. "We have to share the bed," she said. "I know that. I wouldn't ask you to sit up all night. But you keep to your side, Nicholas. We may have to sleep together, but we're no longer 'seeing' each other, so don't you *touch* me!"

Nancy went to the far side of the bed. Jave disappeared into the bathroom. Nancy climbed under the covers and listened to the rushing sound of the shower. Jave was out in a few minutes wearing a white T-shirt and a pair of white cotton briefs.

Nancy watched him walk to the light switch, shoulders broad under the thin cotton, back straight and narrowing to tight, muscular hips neatly contoured in the briefs. His legs were long and moved with easy grace. Lust raged in her like a hungry black bear.

She pulled the sheet up over her head and turned to the window. "Good night," she muttered, in the tone one might use to say "Drop dead."

She felt the mattress take Jave's weight and tried to relax, telling herself she could get through this if she just remained calm.

Then he made that impossible by reaching around her, dipping a hand under the bulk of her baby and pulling her back against him. She gasped a startled little cry, but his enveloping arms were too comfortable and comforting to encourage protest.

"We agreed . . ." she began to grumble because she felt she had to.

"No, we didn't," he corrected quietly in her ear. "You dictated. Now you know how I react to that."

"This is all your fault," she said lazily. This bed had never seemed so cozy. With his solid warmth to lean against, she felt all the gnarly concerns of the day smooth out into inconveniences she'd probably be able to handle when she had time to think clearly. She snuffled sleepily, unable to completely abandon the need to be quarrelsome. After all, it *was* really his fault. "I'll never be able to sleep. And you probably won't, either. I toss and turn a lot. . . ."

From the living room, the sound of a country tune blossomed. It floated on the quiet night, her mother's husky, vaguely anguished voice joined by Willy's deep, lighthearted sound. The strum of a guitar provided soothing accompaniment, and Nancy found herself nuzzling into the shoulder Jave had eased under her and drifting off to sleep.

MMM. THIS IS NICE. Cozier than usual tonight, huh, Mom? Nice to lean on somebody who isn't always moving me around.

SHAMAN WAS SITTING on the slope when Nancy went out the following morning with white turkey meat from a can. This was bribery, she knew, but she was beginning to worry about him. It was almost fall. She hated the thought of him stubbornly living out in the wind and rain and eventually even snow.

"He doesn't like me," Denise said from behind her. Nancy turned to find her mother standing in the open doorway.

"He's suspicious of everyone," she said. She tossed out the water in his dish and refilled it from the hose. While she worked, she told her mother about her history with Shaman. "He stays around because he knows I'll feed him. And he comes a little closer than he used to. But he still won't let me touch him."

"Maybe he was abused," Denise suggested. "Or has lived on his own for so long, he's forgotten how to relate to other creatures. You just have to let him work it out in his own time."

Nancy nodded reluctantly, watching the cat refuse to move until she went back inside. "I know. I won't push. I just worry about him, stuck outside the circle of warmth and security because he's afraid to believe I won't hurt him."

Nancy missed her mother's wry perusal of the back of her head. When she turned, Denise had gone inside.

BY MIDMORNING, Nancy had Boeneke and Geneva tied up together on the second floor of a warehouse in which the antagonist had placed a bomb. They had eleven minutes to free themselves and run to safety.

But she couldn't for the life of her come up with a plan that didn't sound like everything she'd ever seen on prime-time cop shows.

She contemplated the monitor and listened to the quiet. Jave had left early for the hospital, and her mother and Willy had gone to town to get groceries.

"Cantaloupe and kielbasa and..." Her mother, doing an inventory of supplies had leaned into the refrigerator for a closer look. Then her head had appeared above the refrigerator door, her eyes wide with surprise. "Napoleons? You still love to bake?"

Nancy, pouring tea, had nodded. "Yes. But I still don't cook very well."

Her mother had fluttered her fingers greedily. "Can I have it?"

"What?"

"The napoleon."

"Yes. Of course."

She'd reached into the refrigerator, pulled out the sweet, and offered a bite to Willy, who stood behind her with a pad and pencil, taking down the grocery list.

He chewed and swallowed. "Delicious."

Her mother took a bite, chewed, and made a sound one would usually associate with the arms of a lover.

"Is this the last one?" she asked.

Nancy nodded. "Jave's mother loves them, too, so I sent some to her."

"Well, tell Willy what goes into them so you can make some more!" And nibbling on the napoleon, she'd moved on to an inspection of the cupboards.

Nancy smiled as she remembered her mother's ingenuous greed. Then she shook off the thought and tried to concentrate on her work.

HER MOTHER AND WILLY returned at lunchtime with a dozen bags of groceries and takeout from the deli.

By then, Boeneke and Geneva had made a daring escape from a second story window before the explosion, thanks to a Swiss army knife in Geneva's purse and the fortuitous arrival of a sanitation truck.

TOM AND AGGIE and the boys arrived at about the same time with several casseroles and a watermelon. Aggie greeted everyone politely but slid suspicious glances toward Denise.

"Jave said he'd pick up some things on the way home from the hospital tonight," Aggie said, stopping in the middle of the kitchen and studying the ample stores that surrounded her. "Maybe," she added, "you should call and tell him not to bother." She went to the refrigerator as though she had every right to. "In any case, I know how you love my pasta *bolognese,* so I've brought enough that you won't have to cook tonight."

"Pasta *bolognese?*" Denise was beside Aggie at the refrigerator. "May I taste?"

Aggie looked from Denise to Nancy, then back again, obviously unsure whether or not the request was for purposes of criticism.

Denise produced a fork, and after a moment's consideration, Aggie elbowed a grocery bag aside, placed the casserole on the counter, and removed the lid. "By all means," she said, her tone aggressive.

Nancy waited a little nervously. She didn't know what she'd do if her mother suggested the dish needed more of something or other and the women began feuding in her kitchen.

But her mother tasted and made that orgasmic sound again. Then she dipped her fork in a second time, cupped one hand protectively under the dangling noodles, and offered the bite to Willy.

He took it and quickly agreed that it was delicious. "That's better than Abrogazzi's in Milan," he said.

Aggie beamed.

"Can you join us for lunch?" Denise asked. "We have cold cuts, cheeses and salads from the deli."

The boys, staring at Willy in his snakeskin boots and his hand-tooled belt with its buckle fashioned out of gold nuggets, followed him eagerly when he suggested they create an assembly line to put the groceries away.

Denise and Aggie worked companionably, pulling down plates and setting out lunch, shooing Nancy back to her computer until it was ready.

Aggie and the boys were still there when Jave came back that evening. Aggie called Tom at home and told him dinner was being served at Jave and Nancy's. Nancy overheard that comment and caught Aggie's wink. She seemed perfectly willing to play her part in their little scenario and had apparently coached the boys to do the same. Both children took the opportunity to hug her, laughingly straining around her bulk and telling her they missed her.

They ate pasta and salad and watermelon until everyone groaned, then they moved out onto the porch, and Denise and Willy played their guitars and sang while the sun set and dusk turned to velvety darkness.

Nancy sat with Jave on the glider, crowded close to him as the children joined them. Pete leaned his weight on the mound of her stomach, leaving her little choice but to lean against the support Jave provided. He placed an arm behind them on the back of the glider and kept it moving lazily with the toe of his Nike on the porch floor.

Eddy leaned over the other corner, mesmerized by the movement of Willy's fingers on the guitar.

Aggie took the wicker chair at an angle to the glider, and Tom sat on the floor, his back against the balusters on the railing. Mo was stretched out beside him on his back, his rear legs pointed, his forelegs curled in a hedonistic display of contentment.

Nancy, gazing into the darkness and concentrating on the music, saw a shadow move in the vicinity of her truck. She sat up, startled.

Jave eased her back against him, his hand soothing her hair. "It's all right" he said quietly. "It's only Shaman."

He was drawn by the warmth, Nancy knew, just as she was. She relaxed, and for the first time that she could remember since her mother left home, she tried to look at her with unbiased eyes.

There was a bittersweetness about her, Nancy noted, and for all the loving glances she sent Willy's way, she often looked away after the contact, effectively shutting him out of whatever lay behind her thoughts. Nancy saw Willy's disappointment, then the loving gaze he invariably returned, followed by a smiling persistence that said more effectively than any words that he was there for the duration.

Denise sat in the crook created by the banister and the porch column, and Nancy had to admire how slender she'd remained. In jeans and a simple pink camp shirt, she looked feminine and supple and somehow eternal. Nancy felt like a walrus on a rock, large and braying, and unable to do anything but occasionally slide off her perch to her next duty.

She wondered idly if she'd ever look like her old self again. This pregnancy seemed to be going on forever, probably because suddenly so much in her life had developed around it—the gifts from the birthing-room extravaganza, her mother's insistence on visiting, her relationship with Jave and her resultant connection with his family.

But the connections grew as she grew, and she couldn't dispel the feeling that the impending birth of her baby girl would just be the beginning of an enormous disruption with far-reaching consequences.

And all at once everything frightened her—childbirth, children, love, reestablishing a relationship with her mother. She considered running and hiding, but at eight months along she could barely waddle, much less run, and she doubted that anything short of the pyramids could hide her.

Nothing was going according to plan. Claiming to have a husband was supposed to secure her position as the hospital's model mommy, but Jave had discovered that it was all a lie and blackmailed her into a relationship to secure his secrecy. So—she'd taken on a boyfriend to convince the hospital that she had a husband. Or something like that.

She finally excused herself, pleading a backache. She kissed the boys—a sincere gesture, not one for the benefit of her deception—and waved a smiling good-night to everyone else, insisting that they stay and enjoy the evening. Then she pecked Jave on the cheek for the sake of appearances and went inside.

In the dark bedroom, she stood at the foot of the bed, listening to the strains of the guitar and wishing things were different. Wishing *she* could be different.

"I can help with that backache." Jave's voice preceded the soft click of the closing bedroom door.

Tension inched up her back to the base of her neck. She put a hand to it, rubbing unconsciously.

"I'm fine, really. You should be entertaining..."

He wasn't listening. He took a small straight-backed chair from the corner and placed it directly in front of her, advising her to straddle it. Then he took two pillows from the bed and placed them between her and the back of the chair.

"Lean into the pillows," he said, pushing her gently with a hand between her shoulders.

Nancy opened her mouth to insist once again that she was fine, but her protest was muffled by the pillow.

"Concentrate," he said, placing his hands on her shoulders, "on putting all your worries out of your mind. Pretend you've just handed them all to me, and you don't have to be responsible for them anymore."

She leaned into the pillows and closed her eyes. "For how long?"

His thumbs began stroking circles down her spinal column, his long fingers working down her shoulder blades and her ribs. "You have to pretend it's forever, or you won't relax."

"Mmm." She was succumbing already to the strength in his hands. She remembered that moment during her ultrasound when she'd moved and he'd come back to the gurney to reposition her. His grip had felt as though it could keep her safe forever. "So you're going to have to raise this baby?" she asked, suddenly relaxed enough to feel playful.

He laughed softly. "That's right. Don't examine the details. Just operate on faith."

Her sigh went a little deeper, her relaxation becoming a little more complete. "I know you're a good parent."

"Thank you."

"Where are you going to send her to college?"

"Oregon State."

"Good school?"

"Great. Produced me."

She smiled into the pillow as his hands repeated their down-and-up journey. "You won't let her date too early?"

"Not until she's twenty."

Her sigh was deep now—all the way to the heart of her real concerns. She exhaled and sloughed them off. "She should have a fussy wedding."

"Of course."

"Since you're dispensing with all my problems," she said lazily, "I can just assume I've gotten my figure back, right?"

Jave rubbed at her shoulders and the base of her neck. "Every delicious curve."

She turned her head. It now felt as though it rested on a springy stem. "Actually, when I'm not pregnant, I'm kind of...flat."

"Since we're operating on faith," he said, "consider that you retained a certain...ripeness just where you want it."

"Mmm," she murmured again. She hadn't the energy for words.

"There." He peeled her gently from the pillows. "Now, let's get you to bed while you're still relaxed enough to sleep."

Nancy accepted his hand up, then turned to lean on him as far as the bed, but found that once she got there, she didn't want to let go of his solidity and all it represented at that moment. She'd shed concerns and responsibilities and he represented everything she longed for with all her heart.

Jave's first instinct was to resist her tug onto the bed. He'd lain there all last night, able only to hold her while his body rioted for closer contact. He didn't know how he was going to deal with that night after night until her baby was born and her mother left.

But her lips were already on his, her hands under his shirt, and he simply hadn't the character to pull away.

They strained together over the obstruction of the baby, and finally pulled apart laughing when the baby's kicks and rolls protested their strong embrace.

Jave pushed himself up, knowing this could safely go no farther.

"The baby objects to being sandwiched between us," Nancy said as Jave lifted her to her side of the bed and pulled the light blanket over her.

No. YOU'VE got it wrong, Mom. I'm happy. That was applause. I like the way things are going!

"I'M GOING BACK OUTSIDE," Jave said, leaning over her to plant a light kiss on her lips. She tried to prolong it, but he drew away. "Do me a favor," he said firmly, "and be asleep before I come back."

Nancy was drifting off when the door closed behind him. She was deep-down mellow, and slipped into a dream of back rubs and babies and strumming guitars.

JAVE SLAMMED THE HANDBALL back with a vicious swipe. Tom barely dodged its ninety-mile-per-hour return and sank to the court floor as it hit the back wall and ricocheted with almost the same ferocity. He covered his head with his hands as it whistled past him. It finally slowed on the next rebound and settled harmlessly in a far corner.

Jave, dripping sweat, leaned forward on his knees and gasped for breath. He angled his head sideways as Tom unfolded carefully from his crouch.

"Had enough?" he laughed.

Tom rolled his eyes as he got to his feet. "I quit three games ago, but you haven't even noticed." Tom grabbed their towels off the bench and tossed one to Jave. "So who is this phantom opponent you're playing tonight? Shall I guess?"

Jave wiped his face. "Don't start with me, Tom," he said as he wrapped the towel around his neck and headed for the showers.

Jave washed under a hot spray. He did not feel better, he thought. Exhausted, maybe, but not better.

Sleeping with Nancy in his arms for a week had his frustration level at crisis point. She was warm and affectionate, but carefully distant whenever the conversation turned to the future. And he'd *had* it. He was determined to have it out with her tonight. He just wanted to defuse his temper by ridding himself of pent-up frustration and exasperation.

He wasn't sure it was working.

"Turn off the hot water," Tom advised from the neighboring stall. "Cold showers really do work. I've done it a lot myself in the past year."

Chapter Eleven

She was trying on clothes when he got home. There was no aroma of dinner underway, no television blaring the evening news, no soothing guitar as a background to everything.

The house was empty, except for Nancy, who stood in front of the mirror on the closet door, studying the simple blue dress with white buttons.

"Where is everyone?" he asked.

"With your mother and the boys gone," she replied, smoothing the line of the dress, "and you going to the gym with Tom after work, Mom and Willy decided to go exploring. You hungry?"

"I'll fix something. You going somewhere?" He leaned a shoulder against the doorway.

"No." She turned toward him with a casual smile before peering over her shoulder into the mirror. "I'm trying to decide what to wear for the photo session tomorrow."

All the hopes he'd carefully cherished deflated and died. The photo session. Amy had mentioned it over lunch in the hospital cafeteria several days before. The newspaper was coming to do a special foldout section on the remodeled O.B. department, and would feature Nancy's tour of the facility. Riverview Hospital was beginning to gear up for the opening of the birthing rooms.

"You're going to go through with it?" he asked, his voice tight.

She raised an eyebrow as she held on to the closet door and toed off the sandals she wore. "Of course I am. Isn't that the point of all this?"

He studied her for one long disappointed moment, and wondered if it was worth a confrontation after all. The time they'd spent together that made him fall in love had apparently had little effect on her.

Careful not to touch her, he tossed his athletic bag into the bottom of the closet.

Nancy fluffed her hair, pretending not to notice his temper. She could guess what prompted his mood, but she didn't want to deal with it now. She'd been fighting tooth and nail for the past week to stay with the plan.

She was beginning to feel a desperate but dangerous need to come clean with everyone, but it was all too entangled now and she no longer knew how to sort it out. Instead of securing her position, the lies had trapped her.

And she had to think of the baby. She was the reason she'd done all this in the first place.

Jave left the room and went to the kitchen in search of something tall and cold. He found iced tea in a pitcher and poured a glass.

He walked out the back door with it, letting the screen door slam. Shaman, about to approach thinking he was Nancy with his food, ran away up the slope. Jave called him back to no avail.

He finally raised his glass to the cat. "Congratulations," he said. "You hold the number two place for emotional holdout, Nancy, of course, being the champ. I imagine you just haven't been at it as long. But don't think you'll ever take the crown. Her technique is too skillful.''

Jave heard the squeak of the screen door behind him and turned to see Nancy standing there, holding a can of tuna and a spoon. He judged by the glower on her face that she'd heard his little self-satisfying lecture to the cat.

He was tired of pussyfooting around the issue, he thought, then berated himself for the pun. Gallows humor, he told himself, was the only humor he had left.

"I'd apologize," he said, watching the cat stiffen alertly at the sight of Nancy and his food, "but it was all from the heart. It would be a lie."

"It's quite all right," Nancy said coolly, trying to lean over the bowl. She'd done it the day before, but she didn't seem to be able to today. That confirmed it. She knew she'd gained fifty pounds overnight. She gave Jave another glower then looked down at the dish again, wondering if she could hit it from this height. She'd also lost all eye-hand coordination in the past few weeks. "Just because you've been calling the shots all this time, you think you actually understand what's going on. But you didn't get it when you intruded into my life, and you don't get it now. Still, that's no reason to pick on the cat."

Jave took the can from her, yanked the spoon impatiently from her other hand, and squatted down to scrape the tuna into Shaman's bowl. Then he straightened and handed the can and the spoon back to her.

"I wasn't picking on the cat," he said, temper rising despite his efforts to tamp it down. "I was just telling him how it is—that he was the king of panhandled love until you came along."

He stalked back into the house, letting the door slam again.

With a growl of anger, Nancy followed him. She tossed the can and the spoon into the sink. She grabbed Jave by the arm as he walked away.

He faced her, hands going impatiently to his hips.

"Panhandled...love?" she asked, separating the words distinctly. She didn't know what he meant by that remark, but she didn't like the sound of it.

"Love that's begged from people so that you get a handout," he explained. "You don't want to give anything to get it, so you just hold your hand out. You did it to me. You do it to your mother."

Nancy's anger swelled to rage. "I never did any such thing!" she denied, her cheeks crimson. "In fact, I didn't want any part of this relationship. You're the one who insisted—"

"Nancy," he said, tipping his head back in exasperation as he interrupted her, "that's so much crap and you know it. You were lonely and frightened before I came along. You responded to me and accepted what I was willing to give—as long as you didn't have to do anything for it."

"That's not—"

"Yes, it is. But I didn't care, because I thought you were a normal and intelligent woman. I thought you would see the advantages of love in your life and that would turn you around."

"I told you," she said, her hands clenching in the folds of her dress, "I don't trust easily."

He shook his head, unmoved by her quietly spoken reminder. "That's just more bull. You trust me. That's not the issue here."

She raised an eyebrow imperiously. "The issue is that you found out I hadn't been entirely honest about my husband and confused a situation that could have—"

He shifted his weight and made an exasperated sound. "Not entirely honest? Don't dress it up, my love. You're a liar! You lie about everything. But what's most important—you're lying, even to yourself, about how you feel about me! And about how you feel about your mother. You love us both. But you've figured out that if you hold yourself apart, if you never admit to anything, you don't have to give anything in return. So you figure you can just sail through life without being beholden to anyone, and that you can have this baby and not *share* it with anyone—and that'll protect this rarefied atmosphere you've created in your own little beachfront kingdom."

The verbal onslaught paralyzed Nancy where she stood, and the incisive accuracy of at least some of it punched her below the belt—and that had become a very large target.

"I don't *have* to share," she said defensively, tears burning behind her eyes. "I'm not married to you, and my mother walked away from me. I don't owe either of you anything."

"Oh, come on." He turned away from her impatiently, then turned back. "So the baby you're carrying is going to have no one in its little life but you, who tells lies all over the place, claims not to trust anyone, and carries grudges for a lifetime? What's that going to do for her development?"

"I don't—" Nancy began a heated reply, full of anger and indignation. Then a sharp pain ripped across her lower abdomen, and she stopped, reaching down with a gasp to cradle the weight of the baby in both hands.

Jave caught her arm. "What?" he demanded.

She ignored him, wondering for a moment if she was imagining pain. This argument did have all the qualities of torture. But the pain continued, holding strong—strong enough to frighten a cry out of her.

MOM! WHAT IS THAT? Is it time? I'm not ready. I mean, it's not like I have a lot to pack, but—ah!

"A...CONTRACTION, I think," she said, fear for her baby crowding everything from her mind. "Jave, I don't understand. I've been taking my medication...."

He placed a kitchen chair behind her and eased her into it. "Relax," he said calmly. "It could just be Braxton-Hicks contractions, but with your history we'd better be sure. And they shouldn't be breaking through your medication anyway. Where's your cellular phone?"

She pointed to her purse on the table as the pain seemed to work its way down and begin to fade.

Jave went for her sweater, dropped it over her shoulders, and led her out to the car, calling the ER on the phone as he helped her in.

"Jave was right," Dr. McNamara told Nancy half an hour later. "It was just Braxton-Hicks contractions."

Nancy nodded, feeling everything inside her relax, including the baby. She'd read about the false labor pains in her mother-to-be book. They were sort of a muscle flexing, a warm-up for the real contractions at delivery time.

FELT LIKE THE REAL THING to me. You know, I was excited about doing this, but after that, I'm beginning to wonder. You're sure there's not another way out?

"EVERYTHING'S STILL all right?"

McNamara nodded. "Everything's fine. I'll just up your Tributilene dose a little bit. You let me know right away if this happens again. We don't want you delivering this baby until that wandering husband of yours is home to help.''

Her relief was slightly deflated by the intrusion of reality—and the many falsehoods she'd created in it.

If her obstetrician was curious about why it was Jave who brought her in, and what the circumstances were that resulted in their being together when the contractions had begun, he didn't let on. He simply handed Jave the new prescription and teased that cellular phones should be required for all pregnant women.

"Jave has become a...a good friend...." she felt compelled to explain. It sounded lame and unconvincing.

Again, McNamara did not let on. "Everyone needs friends," he said. "Take care. I'll see you next Friday. Unless you have another problem, then call me right away."

Jave drove straight to the drugstore and had her wait in the car while the prescription was filled.

Denise and Willy were back when they arrived. Jave explained what had happened, and Denise immediately put Nancy on the sofa, covered her with an afghan, and positioned Willy nearby to play something relaxing. Then she left to make a pot of tea.

Jave went to take a shower.

After a few moments, Denise brought the pot and a Garfield mug to the coffee table and set them within Nancy's reach. Then she insisted on pouring for her.

"You're sure everything's all right?" she asked.

Nancy nodded. "The obstetrician seems to think so. And I feel fine now."

Denise sat on the edge of the table and put a hand to Nancy's forehead as though her daughter had a fever rather than a very ripe pregnancy. "I feel so responsible," she said with such genuine guilt that Nancy frowned at her over the rim of her cup. She could think of a few things her mother should feel guilty about, but the baby wasn't one of them.

"Why?" she asked.

"Well . . ." She gestured toward Nancy's swollen stomach, her movement nervous. "It's my fault that *you* were born with a defective reproductive system."

"Oh, Mother." Nancy didn't like her mother's big-eyed concern. It made *her* feel guilty. "That's hardly your fault. DES was given to lots of women. No one knew what it would do. And my case isn't that extreme anyway. It's just a little troublesome right now."

Denise shook her head. "I don't want the baby to grow up hating me for having caused both of you problems."

Nancy caught her eye. Her mother had meant the immediate problems of preterm labor, Nancy knew. But as the words hung between them, they suggested all the other problems to which Nancy assigned blame to her mother.

Denise held her gaze, apparently willing to discuss it if she wanted to. But she didn't. She lowered her eyes and drank her tea. Denise went off to make coffee for Willy and herself.

JAVE PRETENDED TO BE asleep when Nancy came to bed, and was up and dressed by the time she stirred awake the following morning. He saw Nancy's gaze go to the small bag he'd packed and placed by the door. It contained most of the clothes he'd moved over unobtrusively since her mother had arrived.

She sat up slowly, her eyes regretful but resigned. He didn't know whether to be pleased or angry that she, too, understood there was no other alternative.

He came to sit on the edge of the bed. It hurt abominably to be that close and know it would be foolish to touch her, that nothing would come of what had seemed to hold such promise. But she couldn't let him in, and he couldn't live on the outside, looking in. There was no other way.

"I know you hate the prospect of being alone with your mom," he said softly. Sun shone through the long bedroom window, but the rest of the house was very quiet, as though no one was up. "But we can't do this anymore. It's too hard on both of us. There's no way to know if our argument brought on your contractions, but I don't want to take the chance that the tension between us is going to compound your problems."

She opened her mouth to deny that that was the problem, but felt sure it was—only not for the reasons he thought. She'd been fighting herself over her feelings for him for weeks. And the internal struggles grew as strong as the baby's kicks.

And she couldn't deny a sense of relief. The prospect of opening up to him had been scary. Seeing how much she'd needed him the night before had been just as scary. Feeling the abysmal loneliness that stretched ahead of her without him and his children and his family was terrifying. It was so much easier not to have to deal with it.

So she ignored the tears that slid down her cheeks and nodded.

"You can tell your mom I'm working long hours at the hospital," he said, turning his gaze away from her tearful face to the window, "and that it's easier for me to stay there as long as someone's here with you. Then maybe you can think up some...fiction...to explain why I don't come back." He looked up at her then, his eyes that could have been condemning, teasing instead. "Maybe...an alien abduction, or the girls from 'American Gladiators' kidnapped me for their mascot. I kind of favor that one."

She tried to laugh, but it came out as a sob. She swallowed it and smiled. "Then we'll go with that."

"If you do have any trouble," he said, "and you need me for whatever reason, call. I'm just twenty minutes away."

She nodded. Her throat was too tight, too painful to permit sound.

"Bye, Nancy." He kissed her cheek, then he was gone.

MOM? SHOULDN'T WE be doing something? Like going after him? We don't want to lose him, do we?

NANCY SAT PERFECTLY STILL, ignoring the baby's kicks as she heard the front door close quietly, then the sound of Jave's car pulling out of the driveway. He could go back to using the truck now, she thought irrelevantly. Now that he no longer had to accommodate her graceless bulk.

As the sound of his car engine drifted away, the relief she'd felt at not having to deal with their relationship dissolved completely. In its place, a cold loneliness planted itself and took firm root. She wrapped her arms around her baby and told her in a strangled whisper that it would be all right.

Food, she thought. Food would make her and the baby feel better. She slipped on a robe and padded out to the refrigerator. She opened the freezer in search of the Nutri-Grain waffles she used to pop in the toaster before her mother arrived and started making frittata for breakfast—and her eyes fell on a half pint of Columbo frozen yogurt—Chocolate Cappuccino Twist. It hadn't been there yesterday. Jave must have bought it last night when he filled her prescription.

She burst into helpless sobs, unaware of her mother's concerned voice as she raced out of the living room toward her.

NANCY THOUGHT SHE LOOKED a little like a *T-rex* who'd just had her hair done. She caught her reflection in the glass that surrounded the nursery, and saw the unfamiliar swoosh and spiking of her bangs, the elegant upsweep of her hair. The topknot, she felt, made her head look like a grape with frightened hair, placed atop a watermelon.

"Are you feeling all right?" Nurse Beacham barked out as though it were an order rather than an expression of concern. "I heard you came into the ER the other night with contractions."

Nancy drew a breath and forced a smile. She knew she had to have one somewhere, even though she felt empty of anything remotely resembling cheer. It didn't have to be spontaneous. She could do it.

"False labor," Amy said before Nancy had to. She rolled her eyes dramatically and pretended to wipe her brow. "Don't think she didn't terrify the entire committee." She placed an arm around Nancy's shoulders and squeezed. "Our model mommy having her baby three weeks early in ER would have ruined *everything*. But here she is, safe and sound and ready to be the spokeswoman for Riverview's new birthing rooms. And in just two weeks, Jerry Malone will be back with the crew of the *Courageous* and at Nancy's side as the countdown begins."

The photographer raised his camera and framed the two heads close together. Amy grinned broadly, and Nancy dug deep for a similar expression. He snapped the shutter.

The tour continued, and Nancy made more of an effort to appear enthused and excited. And she *was* enthused and excited about the baby, but another part of her was barely able to function because she missed Jave so desperately.

Now she couldn't even recall all her arguments about why they couldn't stay together. They'd seemed so logical once and now paled in importance beside the emptiness his absence created in her life. And he'd been out of it only three days.

She found herself wondering how he was doing, if Aggie and the boys were having a good time at her brother's, how Tom was.

The tour ended in a conference room where Amy had collected and artfully arranged all the gifts the merchants had donated to Riverview's model mommy. As her entourage looked on, Nancy walked slowly into the room and into the midst of all the riches any new mother and baby could ever imagine. The gifts sparkled like a mound of treasure in some Ali Baba nursery.

Everything was there—the furniture, the silver cup and spoon, baby shoes, lingerie, chocolate cigars, elegantly monogrammed envelopes that probably contained gift certificates.

She went straight to the crib. It was made of oak with painted white details and baby animal decals decorating the flat surfaces. It matched the dresser beside it, the chifforobe, the toy trunk. Attached to it was a mobile in patterns of black and white, the only colors a baby could see for the first few months.

And Nancy felt nothing. She couldn't quite believe it. She picked up the colorful baby quilt folded at the foot of the crib and brought it to her cheek, trying to inspire feeling, to renew the maternal avarice that had once raced through her at the thought of all these treasures. Nothing.

She felt herself go pale with panic. She touched the shade on the teddy-bear lamp, the state-of-the-art infant seat, the hand-embroidered infant carrier from a local craft shop. Nothing.

Her heart began to beat faster. She put a hand to her forehead, suddenly feeling unsteady.

"Okay, that's it." Nurse Beacham pushed her way through the group, took Nancy firmly by the arm, and pushed her into the Boston rocker placed near the crib. She shooed everyone toward the door, including Amy, who tried to stay, pleading friendly concern. Beacham was firm. "You've had this poor woman on her feet for two hours. Give her a few minutes to herself, then I'm going to see that she has lunch and a nap."

"But..."

"Out!"

"NANCY, YOU SHOULD TALK about this." Denise placed a cup of tea on Nancy's bedside table and sat on the edge of her bed. Beacham herself had driven her home at the end of her shift, and had April follow with the truck. Then they insisted on walking her to her door.

Nancy had tried to persuade them that she was fine, certain disaster would result if Beacham saw and recognized her mother or Willy Brock. She was already looking askance at the black Lincoln in the driveway.

"Second car," Nancy said.

Beacham opened her mouth, probably to ask her why she hadn't driven it to the hospital instead of the truck that now required three men and a crane to place her behind the steering wheel, but Nancy stepped into the house and immediately placed the screen door between herself and her Good Samaritans.

"Thank you," she said, her tone more perfunctory than grateful, but she was desperate to be alone and give in to a primal scream.

Beacham and April disappeared in Beacham's car, just as Denise and Willy walked in from the back porch. Denise was dirty from head to toe, and Willy seemed to be acting as her beast of burden, carrying odds and ends of wood, a bag of potting soil, a trowel and a toolbox. "We put in a window box outside your bedroom win—" Denise began.

Nancy excused herself, claiming a long, tiring session at the hospital.

She now repeated the excuse to her mother, who was perched on the edge of the bed.

Denise shook her head and folded her arms, looking very much as though she had settled in. "Nancy, please," she said quietly, "I've been there. You don't have what you need to get from day to day—I can see it in your eyes. Tell me why Jave is suddenly gone."

"I told you." Nancy took a sip of tea and scraped up a small quantity of patience. "He's working long hours this week at the—"

Denise cut her off with a nod. "But that's the result of your problem, not the reason for it. Why did he leave? What did you do?"

"What makes you think it was *my* fault?" Nancy grumped.

Denise seemed to consider her for a moment, then she took a breath, as one would before jumping off a cliff. "Because there's a lot of your father in you—the good and the not so good."

Nancy turned accusing dark eyes on her. "Daddy was there when you weren't," she reminded brutally. "Whatever my problems are, they're probably more from what *you* didn't give me than from what *he* did."

Denise faced her attack with a steady gaze. "Your father *was* tenacious," she said. Nancy couldn't decide if it was an admission or an accusation. Then her mother leaned toward her, her blue eyes urgent. "For you, the child, that…that…permanence…was a good thing. For me, the woman, his inability to let go of antiquated notions and personal prejudices was like being imprisoned. He didn't want me to sing, even in church. He wouldn't hear of my joining a band when the opportunity came because he was convinced everyone who worked on the road lived lives of depravity. He didn't want me doing anything he couldn't control. So I left."

"You left *me!*" Nancy shouted, the sound ringing with resentment and a child's anguish. She put one hand to her baby and the other to her mouth, unable to trust what else might emerge if she made no attempt to hold it back.

Denise closed her eyes, then heaved a deep sigh. When she finally opened them again, a tear spilled over and she said huskily, "So you *do* care."

Nancy saw the same vulnerability she'd seen in her the other night when she'd blamed herself for her problems with the pregnancy. It wasn't that easy to ignore this time because she understood what it was to want what you couldn't have and to feel the need to run away.

"I loved you," she accused weakly.

Denise brushed away the tear, her voice still a little high. "You still do, darling. That's why you think you hate me."

"Mother, don't be cute."

"I'm not. I'm trying to be honest." Denise placed a hand over the one on Nancy's stomach and smiled grimly. "I did a purely selfish thing that I can't explain away, except to tell you that I felt I would die if I couldn't sing. Your father wouldn't hear of it, so I did what I had to do to save myself, knowing I'd be no good to you otherwise."

Nancy heard that calm explanation and tried to understand. But remembered pain got in the way. "You ruined my life, Mom."

Denise shook her head, rubbing a hand gently over Nancy's. "No. I may have ruined your childhood, but your *life* has a potential bigger than even you realize. And so does everyone's. I didn't know that until I got away from your father and had a chance to live mine."

Nancy thought back to the empty routine of her father's life. Work, home, golf, work, home, golf. Year after year.

"He wasn't a bad person," Nancy defended stiffly.

"No, he wasn't," Denise said. "I couldn't have left you with him if he had been. And you needed all the things at that age that I couldn't guarantee when I started out on the road—good food, health insurance, school and a comfortable routine. Your father *wasn't* bad. The trouble was, he wasn't anything. He wasn't good. He wasn't wicked. He wasn't kind. He wasn't hurtful. He *wasn't*. And life shouldn't be made up of negatives. It should be filled with positives." She sighed wearily and brought her hands back to her lap.

"It took me two more marriages to figure that out. I married my second husband because when I was with him, I wasn't lonely. But I wasn't happy, either. I married my third one because he owned a club, and when I was with him, I wasn't without work. But I wasn't happy, either."

She sighed again, and this time it had a restorative sound. She smiled. It was the smile of someone who'd been very unhappy and knew a smile didn't have to be wide to be genuine. "So I was alone again when Willy walked into that recording studio in Nashville. He listened to me sing, then came and asked me who had broken my heart."

Tears began to flow as she went on. "I told him I'd broken my own heart because I'd left you so I could find myself. And I couldn't get you back." She swiped at her tears and recounted grimly, "This wasn't long after that week you came to stay with me and husband number three. It was like Dante's Inferno on fast forward, remember?"

Nancy smiled thinly at her mother's description of events. It was pretty accurate.

"Anyway, Willy reminded me that every day is a chance to turn your life around, to try to set things right, to make amends, to do good instead of nothing."

Nancy shook her head, her emotions in a turmoil, her world revolving in a faulty orbit. "Mom, I've tried to just forget, but..."

"I don't expect you to forget," Denise corrected gently, "just to try to understand. To imagine, if you can, how I felt, and see if you can forgive me. But mostly..." She caught one of her daughter's hands and held it between her two. "Your father believed only in himself. And what he had, he didn't want to share. Do you remember him as a happy man?"

Nancy remembered a man who provided all of life's physical necessities, but none of its magic.

"No," she admitted, "I don't."

Denise squeezed her hand. "Then love his memory, please, but don't be like him. Don't be afraid to share what you are and what you have, and don't be afraid to trust, even if you find that it's misplaced."

Denise lowered her gaze to their hands and held Nancy's so tightly that she barely resisted crying out.

"I know you trusted me, and I failed you," she whispered, looking up. Her eyes were profoundly sad. "And you trusted Jerry Malone, and he failed you. Well, I don't know where he is, but I want to make that up to you. I like to think that I'm different from him. He chose his career over the baby because he didn't want to have to consider what was best for it over his career. I did what I did because I was weak, not because I was selfish. And I knew if I didn't get my own life together, I could never be anything to you."

Her voice was tight and breathy. She swallowed and smiled tentatively. "A woman is never too old to have a mother, is she? Let me be your mother now. Let me be the baby's grandmother. Let me be nosy and call you with advice, and send you cartoons out of the newspaper and gaudy souvenirs from our travels. Let me buy T-shirts from everywhere for the baby."

She dropped Nancy's hand and wrapped her arms around herself, as though she'd suddenly grown cold—or prepared herself for a rejection.

"But, if you can't trust me again," she said, "don't let what Jerry and I did stop you from trusting Jave. I know Aggie isn't exactly impartial, but she makes him sound like something pretty special. And you can just tell that his boys adore him." She smiled grimly. "Children are tough critics." She stood abruptly. "Well . . . I guess I've lectured you long enough."

Nancy caught her wrist before she could move away. Denise stood immobile. Nancy tugged her back onto the edge of the bed.

"He doesn't live here," Nancy admitted on a broken sigh. "I asked him to say he did so that you wouldn't want to move in with me." She made a self-deprecating grimace.

Denise's eyes widened. She turned the wrist Nancy held and caught her hand. "What is your relationship? I'd have sworn you were lovers."

Nancy groaned and explained about the early relationship that had never been simply professional—about him saving her chair and bringing Tom over to fix her roof. She told her about Jave guessing she had no husband, that she was lying for the sake of the gifts. "He literally blackmailed me into a relationship."

Denise said interestedly, "Define 'relationship.'"

Nancy shrugged, embarrassed. "Well, my condition doesn't allow anything physical." She gave her mother a blushing side-glance. "Though he does kiss very well and gives the most delicious body massage." She grew serious suddenly and laced her fingers nervously. "And he asked me to marry him."

Denise blinked. "You mean you've never made love and he proposed? I can't believe you let him walk away!"

Nancy shook her head, her eyes wide and wounded. "I didn't. He decided to go. And now nothing means anything. I sent a book proposal to an agent, and I got a letter from her yesterday saying she thought it was very good and she was sure she could sell it for me."

"Nancy." Denise squeezed her hand. "That's wonderful!"

Nancy shrugged, her gaze unfocused. "It should be, but it isn't. And you know what else?"

"What else?"

The pain she'd been suppressing all day to keep smiling for the camera suddenly overcame her attempts to hold it at bay any longer. It pummeled her.

"Today they took me into the room where all the baby furniture is being held for us, where they're keeping all the wonderful things that I thought Malia needed...." Her eyes brimmed as she concentrated on that moment and the reaction she simply couldn't understand. "And I didn't feel anything. I mean, that was why I did all this—lied and pretended, and lied again." She sighed and narrowed her gaze on her mother as though she held the answer. "I didn't even care." She leaned toward Denise's shoulder as tears began to fall. "I'm going crazy, Mom," she wept.

Denise wrapped her arms around her and squeezed, relishing the feeling for a moment before laughing softly and answering, "I don't think so, darling. I think you're going sane."

Chapter Twelve

"Jave! Have you heard the news?"

Jave looked up from paperwork to see Amy Brown standing just inside his office, clutching her clipboard. Her eyes behind her glasses fairly gleamed, and she smiled from ear-to-ear.

He hadn't heard anything in the past few days that warranted that kind of excitement. In fact, most of the news in his life this week had been bad. He wondered idly if Tom had asked her out.

"Unless you're talking about the new frozen yogurt machine in the cafeteria," he said, beckoning her to the chair beside his desk, "I haven't." He glanced at his watch. "But you've got to make it quick. My mother and the boys are coming to pick me up. We're taking Tom to dinner for his birthday."

"Tom." She folded into the chair, her cheeks growing pink. "How is he?"

Well, that answered his question. If Tom had asked her out, she needn't have asked after his health.

"He's fine," he replied, putting his pen aside and turning toward her. "What's up?"

She gave a toss of her head and tapped her pen against the clipboard on her knees. "The *Courageous* is back!"

Uh-oh. Nancy. The problem in the San Diego shipyard must have changed the ship's plans. What would she do now?

That question was answered for him the next moment when Amy leaned closer and said excitedly, "I called Nancy and she said she's bringing her husband in to meet me."

Jave maintained a studiously neutral expression. "Bringing him in...to meet you."

"Right. Isn't that great? Just in time for our big publicity push. We can even reshoot the special-section pictures we took the other day to include him, and still have everything out in plenty of time. I can't believe I got this lucky!"

Jave stared at her a moment, trying to decide what this could mean. Then it occurred to him. Nancy must have found someone else to plump out the lie. How she'd done it didn't concern him. He just hoped it all worked out for her.

Then an even more distressful thought struck him. Had the *real* Jerry Malone come back, deciding he'd been a fool to leave Nancy and their baby? That, unfortunately, didn't concern him, either.

He smiled at Amy. "Great. I hope it all goes beautifully and that you get a bonus."

Amy sprang to her feet. "I only hope I get to keep this job. My sister Jane's a lawyer, Peggy's a model, and I'm kind of plain and really not genius material. I'm sort of the family..." She bobbed her head from side to side, then shook it briefly, apparently deciding against a description. "Well, I need to do well."

Jave nodded. "Don't we all."

"If you wander by my office in about fifteen minutes," she said conspiratorially, "you can see Jerry Malone."

Something that had been tightening inside Jave for almost a week now yanked painfully. "No, thanks," he said. "I've got a lot of work here."

She frowned. "But I thought he was your friend. I mean, you went to her first Lamaze class in his place."

No, he didn't, he thought. He went to that Lamaze class for himself. But Amy wouldn't understand that.

He smiled offhandedly. "I'll see him later. Right now, the three of you have a lot of plans to make."

She accepted that and left his office with a cheerful wave.

Jave stared unseeing at the pile of work on his desk. In his mind's eye, he saw Nancy standing on the back porch steps, trying to lure Shaman toward her. He pictured her walking hand in hand with his younger son through a maze of colorful quilts, talking excitedly as Pete listened with big-eyed adoration. He remembered how she'd lain in his arms, the bulk of her baby between them, obstructing their closeness, yet somehow intensifying it. And he vividly recalled the feel of the baby's movement against his hand, against his stomach, when Nancy curled into his body in sleep.

But that was over. He concentrated for one moment on the sense of profound loss that inhabited and surrounded him, then tried to keep in mind that his family would be here at any second. He had to shake off the dark mood. But he'd been living with it for days, and he suspected it would be with him for a long time to come.

WILLY PULLED the black Lincoln into the hospital parking lot. He glided to a stop near the side entrance, then turned to Nancy, seated beside him.

"This okay?" he asked.

She nodded. She felt remarkably calm. "Fine."

"You're sure you want to do this?" Denise, seated in the back, leaned over the front seat. "There might be another way."

Nancy shook her head firmly. "No. This is the way it has to be. You're sure you don't mind doing this for me?"

Denise shook her head. "Of course we don't. But you're sure it'll work?"

Nancy sighed philosophically. "I'm not sure of anything, but if you two can distract the photographers long enough for me to talk to Amy, this might all end as just a minor disaster rather than a major one."

Willy grinned that calm, gentle grin Nancy was beginning to truly appreciate. "Disasters are our specialty, minor or major. Let's go."

He came around to help Nancy out of the car, then followed behind with Denise as she walked into the hospital.

The corridors were quiet, Nancy noted. Dinnertime. She just prayed she wasn't too late.

She rounded a corner, calm slipping away. Her heart began to beat a little fast as she picked up her pace. She turned into the radiology department, not surprised to find the reception area dark, the office staff gone for the day.

But there would be a technician on duty during the night. And Jave would still be here, finishing up the day's paperwork. In the brief time they'd "lived" together, he'd seldom been home before seven.

But there was no one in Jave's office. Nancy stood in the doorway, staring with a sense of disappointment that felt fatal. The little cubbyhole seemed suddenly cavernous in its emptiness. An emptiness even larger opened up inside her. Tears burned her eyes and she made a small sound of distress. Jave was gone.

BREATHE, MOM! I'm not getting any air. Where is he? I don't hear him. We haven't lost him, have we?

SHE JUMPED AT THE SOUND of a loud squeal behind her and turned to see that a crowd of nurses, volunteers and candy stripers had clustered around her mother and Willy, cutting her off from them.

It was ironic, she thought, that that part of the plan was working, when its major element had just fallen apart.

With a little sigh of despair, she turned back toward the office, thinking she would sit in Jave's chair and try to plan containment of the disaster—when she saw him coming in her direction from an open door across the room. He was pulling on a summer-weight mossy green sports jacket over a shirt with a thin stripe, open at the neck. As he stopped several feet from her, she noticed that it affected the color of his hazel eyes.

Air seemed to be trapped in her lungs. She stared at him for a moment, unable to say anything.

Jave had hoped he'd be spared this. In fact, he'd dressed quickly, planning to be out of the building before she arrived. If his family wasn't here yet, he'd have waited for them in his truck.

But now that she was standing there, he was glad he hadn't escaped. It was good to see her again. She wore a soft shade of pink and reminded him of a very plump bouquet of rhododendrons. Her longing eyes reminded him how much they'd enjoyed together, even though all he felt now was sadness.

He drew a deep breath and tried to be bigger than his grief. "Hi," he said. "It's good to see you."

"Yeah," she whispered after a moment. "You, too."

They stared into each other's eyes, then, unable to stand it another moment, he said conversationally, "I hear your...*husband*'s home." He emphasized the word, hoping she would explain it—hoping he could take it.

She nodded. "I'm going to Amy's office right now. Will you come with me?"

He thought that was a lot to ask. "It's Tom's birthday tonight, and the family's coming to pick me up for a party at Chez Pasta."

Chez Pasta. Nancy had such sweet memories of that night.

She studied Jave's eyes for some sign that she wasn't crazy to do this, that her instincts were on target. But except for a flare of emotion in his eyes when she'd first seen him standing there, his expression was carefully remote.

She rubbed a hand over her baby, looking for comfort and support, and felt a firm kick. That was it, she decided. Confirmation. There was nothing to do but do it.

She smiled, took Jave's hand, and drew him out of the office. "I promise not to keep you very long. Come on."

Jave had little choice but to follow. There was a squealing crowd around Denise and Willy. They skirted them skillfully and headed for Amy's office. The *Heron Point Herald*'s photographer was taking pictures of the celebrities, and a reporter was shouting questions from the back of the crowd.

"How come," he asked as he was tugged along, "you brought your mother here? I thought—"

"To distract the photographer," she said over her shoulder.

"Why? Isn't that why you're here? To be photographed with your 'husband'? Where is he, by the way?"

Amy's office was three times the size of Jave's and contained an oval-shaped conference table. Amy stood at the head of it when they walked in, and gathered around it were the hospital administrator and his assistant, Nurse Beacham, and several other members of Amy's committee.

Nancy stopped just inside the room. She hadn't counted on anyone being here but Amy. Whatever confidence she'd had that this might work abandoned her completely. She was certainly in for a very public humiliation if it didn't. Not that she didn't deserve it after all she'd done.

All the men around the table stood, and Amy smiled as she approached her, though she seemed obviously confused.

"You look wonderful," she said to Nancy, then her eyes passed over Jave and peered behind him. "Where's your husband?"

Nancy drew a deep breath and decided some things were more important than pride—or safety. She lifted the hand she still had linked with Jave's. "Ladies and gentlemen," she said, "I'd like to present my *future* husband, Dr. Jave Nicholas."

There was a long, pulsing silence. Then there were frowns of confusion, wary glances exchanged. Nancy looked up at Jave.

Jave, accustomed now to her dramatic schemes, remained calm. Not that he could have done anything anyway. He had no idea what the hell was happening.

Then he looked into her eyes and saw the pleading there. Only this time it wasn't pleading for his compliance with her scheme. She was pleading for his love.

He stared down at her, unable for a moment to believe what he saw.

"Tell me," she whispered, hope naked in her eyes as the committee began to grumble among themselves, "that you haven't withdrawn the proposal."

Before he could answer, Amy asked, "But where's the father of your baby?" Then apparently realizing the indelicate nature of the question, she began to stammer, "I mean . . . well, you know . . ."

Nancy didn't want to bring Jerry into this conversation. This was about truly starting over for herself and the baby, about love and trust and the kind of generosity Jerry had never understood.

But Jave hadn't said anything yet, and there was a good chance she'd been all wrong about the outcome of her brave confrontation with the truth.

She opened her mouth to try to clarify the situation when Jave said clearly, "*I'm* the baby's father."

With those few words, Nancy felt a lifetime of loneliness wash away, a world of love and trust open up. She squeezed Jave's hand, and thought she would have died for him at that moment.

Amy glanced hesitantly at the committee and smiled nervously. Then she turned back to Jave. "I don't get it," she said candidly. "You didn't know each other then. She was in New York. You were here."

Jave nodded, unable to remember one grim moment of his past. All he could see, all he could feel, was sunshine.

"No, I wasn't there at conception. But we all know that's not what fatherhood is about."

Nancy held his arm in her two and faced the committee. "I was married, got pregnant, and was abandoned. I came here with very little money to start over, and when Amy proposed that I be the star of your birthing-rooms event, I pretended Gerald W. Malone was still in the picture so that I could acquire for my baby all the things you were offering, things I could never get otherwise."

Jave leaned down to kiss her upturned face, basking for a moment in the adoration there. Then he picked up the story. "But I suspected the truth, fell in love with her, and a lot of things have changed for both of us in the past couple of months. This woman and this baby are now mine."

"But..." Amy began, hands spread helplessly.

"I know." Nancy reached out to touch her arm. "Of course you'll need a new mother for your project. I relinquish any claim to the gifts. And I apologize sincerely for the trouble I've caused."

Amy made an effort to pull herself together. She tugged on the ruffly sleeves of her mint green dress. "But we promised them to you. And while we like to think that the model family is composed of mother and father and two point three children, that doesn't really apply..."

Nancy shook her head. "Thank you, but I want you to pick another mother. None of the photos you've taken has appeared yet, and our Lamaze class had several couples who'd be perfect candidates."

Then Amy said for her ears alone, "But I know how much you wanted the nursery set and the—"

Nancy gave Amy a hug, her heart feeling suddenly as swollen as her belly. "I think what I really wanted for my baby was a father, and because I knew I couldn't give her that, I wanted to give her everything else." She beamed at Jave. "But I don't need that now."

The administrator came forward, followed by Nurse Beacham. "The decision is yours, Mrs. Malone," he said. "But please don't think we'd reject you because the situation isn't . . . traditional." He smiled at Jave. "We're all, of course, very fond of Jave."

Jave nodded. "Thank you, Frank."

"All those wonderful gifts," Nancy said firmly, "should go to some mother who needs them as much as I thought I did."

"Very well," he said. "Amy?"

Amy squared her shoulders. "Yes, Uncle Frank."

"Back to the drawing board."

She breathed a sigh. "Yes. Right away." Then her attention seemed to be caught by something beyond them. "Isn't that . . . ?"

Everyone turned to look.

Nancy smiled at the woman in the doorway. "Mother," she said.

Beacham gasped in girlish disbelief, "Denise Di-Benedetto and Willy Brock!"

The office was suddenly filled to capacity with the celebrities, followed by Aggie, Tom, Eddy and Pete.

"What's going on?" Aggie asked Jave as the boys ran to Nancy.

"Lots of things," he replied, hugging his mother, and laughing as he held her close. "I'm getting married, you're about to have a third grandchild, and we have to haul all the baby things up from the basement."

She pushed against him to look into his eyes. "You're kidding."

"I'm not."

"Oh, my God." She fell against him again, wrapping him in a stranglehold. "One down. One to go. I can't believe it."

Hugs were distributed with emotional abandon. Jave found himself holding Beacham, who had tears in her eyes. "Good work, Doc," she said with a sniff. "Didn't know you had it in you to make such an intelligent decision."

Tom squeezed the breath out of him. "All *right!* A house in constant need of repair in the family. I like it." Then he grew serious, the rough year they'd weathered together right there in his eyes. "Good going. Be happy."

Then Jave found himself looking down at his boys. Eddy's grin was broad, his eyes bright. "This is cool, Dad. Russian tea anytime we want it!"

But Pete's eyes were incredulous. Jave lifted him into his arms. "Is it true?" his son asked.

Jave nodded. "Nancy and I are getting married."

"Yeah, but I mean about the baby. It's gonna be ours?"

"Right."

Nancy, who'd been passed from hug to hug and now found herself beside them, overheard the question and leaned into father and son with concern. "Is that okay, Pete?" she asked.

His smile was sudden and wide. "Yeah. It's cool. And now you can come to all my games."

ME, TOO. I'll be there.

NANCY LEANED HER HEAD against him and kissed his small hand. "Every single one."

She felt a jab at her elbow and found Nurse Beacham standing beside her. She pointed toward the crowd gathered around her mother and Willy. The group of nurses and candy stripers from the hallway had also spilled into the office. "Could you introduce me?" Beacham asked with uncharacteristic shyness. "I have all her CDs and I've taped all her videos. I stood in line all night when she came to Seattle."

Nancy hugged the nurse, thinking life was full of the most delightful surprises. She'd never have taken Nurse Beacham for a country and western fan.

"Of course." She took Beachie's arm and used her pregnancy as a method of parting the crowd. People moved away as she smiled apologetically. "Mother," she said into Denise's smile of surprise. "This is one of your biggest fans. Nurse...Beachie, what's your first name?"

"Medora." Beachie held out her hand and smiled widely when Denise took it.

"Medora," Nancy said formally, "I'd like you to meet my mother, Denise DiBenedetto and her fiancé, Willy Brock."

"Aren't you lucky, Nancy," Beacham said, her expression clearly star-struck, "to have Denise DiBenedetto for a mother?"

Nancy gave her mother a wink. "Yes," she said firmly. "I am."

Denise smiled, her eyes brimming. "Thank you, darling," she said. "I needed that."

The crowd eventually dispersed and the Nicholases and Nancy and Denise and Willy collected in the hallway, preparing finally to go off in celebration of Tom's birthday.

As everyone else drifted toward the parking lot, Nancy remained in the hallway, frowning in concern at the sight of Amy Brown, sitting alone at her desk, wondering, probably, what had happened to all her brilliant plans for the birthing-room extravaganza.

"I feel so bad about Amy," Nancy whispered to Jave, who'd remained beside her.

"Everything's in place," he said, pulling her into his side. "All she has to do is find another mother. I can't believe it'll be that difficult."

"I know," Nancy said. "But she wanted so much to do this well. And she's so...sort of...vulnerable. I don't know what it is, but she makes you want to take her home and take care of her."

Jave smiled wryly. He'd had that feeling about a woman before, and it had gotten him into no end of trouble.

"Why don't you just invite her to my party?"

Both turned in surprise to find Tom standing behind them.

"Why don't you?" Jave challenged.

Tom studied him for a moment, looked with an uncertain frown at the young woman now leaning back in her chair and fiddling forlornly with her pencil, then drew a breath. "All right," he said, "I will," and disappeared into Amy Brown's office.

Nancy stared up at Jave, wide-eyed with surprise. "Tom and..." She pointed toward Amy.

"Don't even say it aloud," he cautioned. "Or Mom will think she's got two down."

"Two... What?"

He kissed her temple as he walked her to the parking lot. "I'll explain later. We have to have something to talk about on our honeymoon."

JAVE WALKED NANCY DOWN the aisle on Labor Day weekend, then took her for a two-day honeymoon at a bed and breakfast on the river.

He'd been reluctant to take her any distance from the hospital at that late date, and she wanted to be home on Tuesday to see the boys off to school.

"I don't ever want them to think," she explained to Jave, "that they're less important to me than the baby is."

They lay wrapped in each other's arms on their wedding night in an upstairs room decorated in crisp yellow and white. The windows were closed against the change-of-season chill and the gauzy fog blanketing the ship channel.

His hands moved slowly, endlessly, over her, then over the baby, who seemed to rise against his touch in response.

Nancy concentrated on the wonder of their unique threesome—and the utter frustration that that third party imposed on them.

She sighed against Jave's shoulder, her fingertips exploring the strong lines of his chest. "Some way to spend a wedding night," she grumbled.

He kissed her soundly and drew away with a groan of reluctance. "I'll settle for it. I've got you and you're not getting away. I can live with knowing that *one day*, I'll finally be able to make love to you."

"Oh, Jave." She rubbed her cheek against his shoulder and stroked his chest, following the jut of his ribs to the flat plane of his stomach. "There's no reason for you to spend *your* wedding night this way." She stroked lower, planting kisses on his chest. "Let me make love to you."

He caught her hand before it could make his denial any more difficult. "No," he said.

She propped up laboriously on an elbow to look down at him in surprise. "No?"

It had been hard enough to say the first time, but he made himself say it again. "No." Then he cupped the back of her head in his hand and smiled. "Our first time is not going to be without your pleasure."

She kissed his shoulder. "I'll enjoy doing my part, Jave. I promise you."

He shook his head. "No. Six weeks after this baby is born, it'll be you and me and a night that's twelve hours long. Until then—" he pulled her down into his arms "—I'll be happy just to hold you."

"For eight more weeks?"

"For as long as it takes."

Nancy hugged him fiercely and laid her cheek against the steady beating of his heart. Despite her bulk, she felt lighter than air. This is what it is to be cherished, she thought. Every worry halved, every happiness doubled— and everything shared.

They lay quietly, listening to the quiet thrum of a freighter going upriver. Nancy asked in a whisper, "Jave? Are you still awake?"

"Barely," he replied lazily.

"*Is* our baby a girl?"

He hesitated. "Are you sure you want to know? I mean, you've been convinced it's a girl all this time."

She looked up into his face in the darkness. She could see his loving eyes and his indulgent smile.

"You said," she reminded, "that when I trusted you as much as I trust myself, you'd tell me. And I do. So is it?"

He laughed softly and raised his head to kiss her. "Yes," he said. "It is."

Chapter Thirteen

Malia Rose was born at 2:32 a.m. September twenty-third in the back of Willy's Lincoln on the way to Riverview Hospital. She was delivered with terror and great excitement by her father and her maternal grandmother.

Wow. Mom. Hi! Well, here I am.. What do you think? I hope you're not disappointed. I'm not. You're beautiful.

And that's him *touching my hand. Wow. Hi, Dad. I heard it all, you know, and I love you, too. I am so glad to be out. What are those lights up there? Stars? So that's what they look like from this side.*

NANCY WAS ASSIGNED a birthing room, though she'd already accomplished what the room was intended to encourage.

"I'm so glad," she told Amy, who leaned over the bed to admire Malia's thick dark hair, "that circumstances made you choose another couple. It would have been awful if your model birthing-room occupant didn't even arrive at the hospital in time to do what she was supposed to do."

Amy laughed. "That's all right. One day Malia will be able to flaunt her birth in a Lincoln Town Car."

Riverview Hospital's shower of gifts had been bestowed three days before on a young couple from Virginia who'd just moved to Heron Point a month earlier—ironically, with the Coast Guard. It was their first baby and they were thrilled beyond description. Everyone, including the hospital's administration and birthing-room extravaganza committee, was delighted.

Denise spent hours watching Malia. "I helped deliver her," she said over and over. "I can't believe I helped deliver my granddaughter."

Willy sat by strumming lullabies.

Denise presented Nancy with a pile of tissue wrapped in a pink bow. Nancy opened it and discovered a slightly frayed pink blanket appliquéd with kittens and sailboats. Someone had sewn on a new silk binding.

Nancy squealed, old memories bubbling to the surface of herself at a very early age holding it, wrapped in it, dragging it. "My blanket!" she breathed.

Denise emitted a laugh that sounded like a sob. "It was one of the few things I took with me when I left. I made it for you when I was carrying you, and now it's Malia's."

Nancy pulled the hospital blanket from around the baby and wrapped her in the relic from her own childhood. She pulled her mother close so that the three of them shared an embrace. Then she kissed her cheek. "Thank you, Mom."

TOM HELD MALIA with remarkable ease. "She is the prettiest little thing." He turned to Jave and said brutally, "You can tell you had nothing to do with her looks." Then he sighed and brushed the thick hair back with the tip of one long finger. "But I suppose she'll grow up to be honorable and responsible and charming and we'll have to admit your influence after all."

"Speaking of charming," Jave said, "have you thought about asking Amy out again?"

Tom walked across the room with the baby to show her her reflection in the mirror—and to dodge the question, Nancy guessed. She caught Jave's eye across the room.

"You seemed to have such a good time at your party," she said.

Tom nodded. "She's very nice. But...you know. I'm not...I don't want to get serious about anybody at this point. The business takes most of my time and...that's not fair to a woman."

"She asks about you all the time," Jave said.

Tom kissed the baby's cheek and handed her back to Nancy. "Gotta go," he said. "I'm picking up lumber this afternoon to start on your addition to the beach house. When's your Mom leaving?"

"Tomorrow," Nancy replied, feeling genuinely sad at the prospect. "She and Willy have to be in Houston for a concert."

He nodded. "Neat lady," he said, then leaned down to kiss her cheek. "You, too. See you when you get home."

"Do you think," Nancy asked Jave as the door closed behind his brother, "that he didn't enjoy that evening with Amy?"

Jave shook his head. "No. I think he enjoyed it too much." He smiled speculatively. "He's a man with a heart. He'll come to realize he can't live alone forever. We just have to be patient.''

"Speaking of which,'' Nancy said with a frown, "when my mother leaves, there won't be anyone around to feed Shaman regularly. We'll have to bring him home to your house.''

Jave winced at the thought. "And I get to catch him, right?''

She smiled winningly. "My hero.''

MINE, TOO!

AGGIE CROONED PROMISES of extravagant dishes "worthy of such a princess,'' and the boys simply stared in wonder. Eddy held her briefly, then handed her back, obviously uncomfortable, but Pete sat with her in a rocker near the window. Eddy leaned over the back of it to supervise.

"You're going to come to all my games,'' Pete said softly, "and I'll make you Russian tea and read you my favorite books.''

DEAL. CAN I play with your toys?

JAVE, SITTING ON THE BED with an arm around Nancy, watched his sons and daughter in the chair and felt peace settle inside him and take root. He knew the scene wouldn't always be this idyllic, but under the quarrels, big and small, that were bound to come, there would be the bond of a family formed by something even stronger than blood—love that was the result of conscious choice and determination and devotion.

"Did you ever see anything more beautiful?" Nancy asked on a tearful whisper.

He hugged her tightly. "It ties," he said, "with the look in your eyes."

SHAMAN CAME HOME to Jave's house two days later in a live trap Tom had fashioned out of oak and wire mesh. It had been baited with tuna, and he was freed in the kitchen, where a bowl of the same waited for him. Mo was temporarily closed in the backyard.

Jave, Tom, Aggie and the boys watched in disbelief as the trap's door was raised, and the cat walked out and went straight to the dish as though he'd been doing it all his life.

"I thought he'd run and hide," Tom said.

"Yeah," Eddy agreed. "I thought he'd freak!"

Pete knelt beside Shaman and petted him. The cat continued to eat. Pete looked up at his father with a big grin. "He knows he's home."

Nancy, who'd just fed Malia and couldn't seem to make herself put her down, came to observe Shaman while absently patting the sleeping baby.

Jave reached out to pull her into his arm. "He's acting," he said in surprise, "as though he's always lived here."

"Of course." Nancy leaned into him and gave him a teasingly superior look. "Even a streetwise—or a beachwise—cat, knows he can't live on handouts forever. Sooner or later he has to move in somewhere, be willing to do his part as a member of a family."

Jave turned his attention to her, the smile in his eyes acknowledging her conviction. "Is that a fact?"

"It is. I have it on good authority." She kissed his chin and said for his ears alone, "I'll be soooo glad when six weeks are up."

He nodded grimly as he squeezed her close. He put a gentle hand to Malia that almost covered her completely. "That'll be November fifth, but who's counting?"

Chapter Fourteen

November 5

Jave and Nancy climbed aboard the *Mud Hen,* carrying a picnic basket between them. It was the evening of November fifth, and rain fell in torrents. They wore roll-neck sweatshirts Denise and Willy had sent from their Southwest tour.

The marina's lights ringed the darkness like moons, and several boats with live-in owners were brightly lit against the night.

"Let me find the light in the galley," Jave said, leaving Nancy at the top of the ladder with the basket.

A small glow appeared below and Jave reached up to take their overnight fare.

Nancy handed it down then followed, holding on to the overhead, still careful of the almost perpendicular steps.

Jave lifted her off the last few steps and into his arms. She clung to his neck, drunk with the freedom of being alone. with him and of having passed her six-weeks' checkup with flying colors.

Jave held her against him and felt the love and the trust in her embrace. During their four-and-a-half-month relationship, conducted without the distraction of sex, they'd learned more about each other than he guessed most couples learned in the first five years of marriage.

They were now irrevocably connected by thought, emotion and yearning. But he was anxious to finally share the passion.

He tightened his grip on her as he thought about how long and how forcefully he'd capped his desire for her.

She bit his earlobe and dipped the tip of her tongue into his ear.

He groaned and hunched his shoulder. He'd wanted to approach this slowly, to show her that despite the endless longing, he could be patient and tender and remember that this was their first time.

"There's... ah... champagne in the basket," he whispered, moving the few steps toward the table, still holding her.

She planted kisses along his jawline. "I'm not thirsty."

"Pâté and—"

"Not hungry," she said against his mouth. "Except for you." Her eyes smoldered as she looked into his.

His resolve toppled and he carried her through the elegantly renovated salon and the beautiful blue-and-grey stateroom without even noticing Tom's hard work on their behalf.

Jave placed Nancy on the queen-size bed that took up the entire space. She pushed at his sweatshirt and he yanked it off, then drew hers up over her head.

Nancy was delighted to see his impatience. In the two months they'd been married, she'd had evidence over and over of his strong character and personal discipline. Now she was thrilled to know that though he'd made restraint look easy, it hadn't been—and that he was as desperate for her as she was for him.

He reached under her to unhook her bra, freeing her swollen, blue-veined breasts.

She resisted an urge to cover them. The mother in her appreciated their function, but the vain woman in her longed to retain the size they'd become while smoothing them to alabaster.

"They're ugly," she said.

Jave's eyes concentrated on them a moment, then he kissed each one with a tenderness that negated her claim.

"They're like Carrara marble," he said, looking up into her eyes. "Only warm and silken, like Malia's skin."

Vanity restored, Nancy lifted up as he tugged her leggings off. They brought her panties down, too, and he tossed both out into the salon.

He expelled a ragged breath as he stared down at her lean hips, her stomach still slightly, charmingly rounded by the pregnancy, her long, slender limbs.

"I can't believe I can finally make love to you," he said, his eyes reverently perusing every plane and hollow. "Even yesterday, I wouldn't have believed this, but I almost want to just sit and stare and savor the moment."

Nancy braced herself up on an elbow, caught his shoulder, and traded places with him.

"Tell you what," she said, leaning down to kiss his lips. "You savor while I undress you."

He relaxed, willing, at least for the moment, to let her take over.

She unzipped his jeans and inched them down, prepared to tease and tantalize him. But as she uncovered every formidable inch of limb and masculinity, she found herself as awed as he had been.

"You're magnificent," she whispered, clutching the jeans and briefs to her. Then she added on a note of wonder, "And you're *mine!*"

Jave swallowed a lump in his throat, humbled by her expression. He took the clothes from her, tossed them aside, pulled her down to him, and wrapped her in his arms.

They moved against each other, silky skin to suedelike flesh, muscle to soft curve, angular limbs to supple arms and legs.

Nancy felt her heartbeat quicken and her breath fail. Jave felt his mind go—all thought and control lost to sensation too long suppressed.

He tucked Nancy into his arm and braced himself on his forearm to reach down to her knee. She raised it for him and he stroked gently from it to the juncture of thigh and body.

She sighed against him, her small hand exploring his back and over his hip.

Jave's hand covered her femininity. He applied a small amount of pressure, as though making a claim. Mine.

Nancy rose against him, offering an admission. Yes. Yours.

He dipped a finger inside her and every receptor in her body relayed the sensation. It was an affirmation of rightness, an acceptance of truth, life and love just as she knew it was intended to be.

She moved restlessly against him.

"Hurt?" he asked in concern.

"No," she whispered, reaching between them to touch him, enfold him. Inside her, pleasure was already blossoming, expanding, ticking out of control. "Come to me," she pleaded. "It's been *forever.*"

He rose over her, the only coherent thought in his head calling for care. But she banished even that with the nimble artistry of her touch.

He entered her in self-defense, but carefully, intent on withholding his pleasure until he'd prolonged hers. But her body closed around him and the sensation surpassed everything he'd imagined even in the darkest depths of his frustration. Pleasure stormed over him, touching every hidden corner of his being. Yet, at the heart of what he felt, there was something spiritual—a satisfaction so complete it seemed to come from the depths of the universe.

Nancy took Jave deep inside her, startled for an instant by a mildly painful pressure on still-sore stitches.

He made to withdraw, but she held him to her, taking him deeper until the simple perfection of their connection eased her discomfort. She felt as though they were lovers in a fine sculpture, destined to embrace for all eternity.

Then he began to move within her, reminding her that they were not only a work of art, but also one of genuine flesh and blood.

She clung to him, moved with him, and felt herself reborn as they climaxed together. Passion confined for so long reacted like dynamite at the end of a long fuse. Flame burst, sparks flew, and their entire personal terrain was changed forever.

They lay wrapped in each other's arms, legs entangled, comfortably cocooned in the small space of the stateroom. Rain fell rhythmically overhead as the *Mud Hen* rocked gently in its slip. The darkness felt magical.

"What time is it?" Nancy asked.

"Ah . . ." Jave raised the arm with which he held her to him so he could check the illuminated dial of his watch. "Eight twenty-one," he replied.

She snuggled against him, pulled that hand to her lips and kissed its palm, marveling that anyone could feel this wonderful. "At 8:21 on November fifth, Jave and Nancy Nicholas finally made love for the first time. Do you believe it?" She tilted her head back to look into his eyes, her voice suddenly grave. "Did you feel everything I felt? Could you possibly be as happy as I am?"

"Nancy." Her name on his lips said everything. The sound was filled with all the tenderness and the passion with which he'd made love to her. "I've never known what I feel at this moment. I can't imagine what the boys and I did without you and Malia." He kissed her soundly to underline that truth. Then he added wryly, "And had I *known* what it was like to make love to you, I'd have died of the frustration long ago."

She sighed and kissed his throat, very satisfied with his reply. "Eight twenty-one on November fifth," she said. "We'll have to celebrate every year."

He reached under her to lift her atop him. "And 8:59, 9:32, 10:06, 11 . . ."

HARLEQUIN®

AMERICAN ◆ ROMANCE®
®

COMING NEXT MONTH

#605 THE COWBOY HIRES A WIFE by Jenna McKnight
1-800-HUSBAND

Wade Montana rode the orneriest bulls on the rodeo circuit, but he had no idea how to keep his niece from missin' her mommy. Tamin' broncos was sure easier than sharin' his RV with a teary-eyed little filly. When he spied a billboard for 1-800-HUSBAND in his rearview mirror, he hoped to God they had wives, too!

#606 MAKE WAY FOR MOMMY by Muriel Jensen
Mommy & Me

It seemed so simple when Jo Arceneau agreed to be a surrogate mother for her sister. But with her sister out of the picture, Jo was left carrying the baby for her brother-in-law, the enigmatic Ryan Jefferies...a man she'd always wanted but could never have.

#607 DADDY CHRISTMAS by Cathy Gillen Thacker
Accidental Dads

Snowbound in a Colorado ranch two days before Christmas with the gallant and gorgeous Matt Hale brought on a bad case of cabin fever for Gretchen O'Malley. Six weeks later she developed morning sickness, too!

#608 MOMMY HEIRESS by Linda Randall Wisdom
Accidental Dads

Without cash or credit, heiress-on-the-run Cori Peyton was stranded in a backwater Kansas town, with no one to help her—except sexy small-town doc Ben Cooper. And boy, did she need his help, especially when he told her she was pregnant!

AVAILABLE THIS MONTH:

#601 THE LAST BRIDESMAID
Leandra Logan

#602 NANNY JAKE
Lisa Bingham

#603 MOMMY ON BOARD
Muriel Jensen

#604 CLOSE ENCOUNTER
Kim Hansen

Take 4 bestselling love stories FREE

Plus get a FREE surprise gift!

Special Limited-time Offer

Mail to Harlequin Reader Service®

3010 Walden Avenue
P.O. Box 1867
Buffalo, N.Y. 14269-1867

YES! Please send me 4 free Harlequin American Romance® novels and my free surprise gift. Then send me 4 brand-new novels every month, which I will receive months before they appear in bookstores. Bill me at the low price of $2.89 each plus 25¢ delivery and applicable sales tax, if any.* That's the complete price and a savings of over 10% off the cover prices—quite a bargain! I understand that accepting the books and gift places me under no obligation ever to buy any books. I can always return a shipment and cancel at any time. Even if I never buy another book from Harlequin, the 4 free books and the surprise gift are mine to keep forever.

154 BPA ANRL

Name	(PLEASE PRINT)	
Address	Apt. No.	
City	State	Zip

This offer is limited to one order per household and not valid to present Harlequin American Romance® subscribers. *Terms and prices are subject to change without notice. Sales tax applicable in N.Y.

UAM-295

©1990 Harlequin Enterprises Limited

HARLEQUIN®

AMERICAN ◆ ROMANCE®

"Whether you want him for business...or pleasure, for one month or for one night, we have the husband you've been looking for. When circumstances dictate the need for the appearance of a man in your life, call 1-800-HUSBAND for an uncomplicated, uncompromising solution. Call now. Operators are standing by...."

I ❤ 800 HUSBAND

Pick up the phone—along with five desperate singles—and enter the Harrington Agency, where no one lacks a perfect mate. Only thing is, there's no guarantee this will stay a business arrangement....

For five fun-filled frolics with the mate of your dreams, catch all the 1-800-HUSBAND books:

Coming to you only from American Romance!

Their idea of a long night is a sexy woman and a warm bed—not a squalling infant!

To them, a "bottle" means champagne—not formula!

But Matt Hale and Ben Cooper are about to get a rude awakening. They're about to become

Join us next month for a very special duet, as Matt and Ben take the plunge into fatherhood.

Don't miss

#607 DADDY CHRISTMAS by Cathy Gillen Thacker

and

#608 MOMMY HEIRESS by Linda Randall Wisdom
Available November 1995

You've never seen daddies like these before!

Become a
Privileged Woman,
You'll be entitled to all these Free Benefits.
And Free Gifts, too.

To thank you for buying our books, we've designed an exclusive FREE program called *PAGES & PRIVILEGES*™. You can enroll with just one Proof of Purchase, and get the kind of luxuries that, until now, you could only read about.

BIG HOTEL DISCOUNTS

A privileged woman stays in the finest hotels. And so can you—at up to 60% off! Imagine standing in a hotel check-in line and watching as the guest in front of you pays $150 for the same room that's only costing you $60. Your *Pages & Privileges* discounts are good at Sheraton, Marriott, Best Western, Hyatt and thousands of other fine hotels all over the U.S., Canada and Europe.

FREE DISCOUNT TRAVEL SERVICE

A privileged woman is always jetting to romantic places.

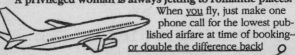

When <u>you</u> fly, just make one phone call for the lowest published airfare at time of booking— <u>or double the difference back!</u>

PLUS—you'll get a $25 voucher to use the first time you book a flight AND <u>5% cash back on every ticket you buy thereafter through the travel service!</u>

PROOF OF PURCHASE

Offer expires October 31, 1996

HAR-P66